HOW TO TRAIN YOUR *Billionaire*

OTHER TITLES BY KENDALL RYAN

A Beginner's Guide to Forever

The Forever Formula

Penthouse Prince

How to Date a Younger Man

Playing for Keeps

Wild for You

The Boyfriend Effect

The Fix Up

Boyfriend for Hire

The House Mate

Only for Tonight

Filthy Beautiful Lies

For a complete list of Kendall Ryan's titles,

visit www.kendallryanbooks.com.

PRAISE FOR KENDALL RYAN

"*Flirting with Forever* is such a sexy, romantic best-friends-to-lovers story. Kendall Ryan's books always make me smile!"

—Devney Perry, *USA Today* bestselling author

"Empowering, emotional, sexy, and gorgeously romantic in all the best ways. *All the Way* is absolute perfection!"

—Helena Hunting, *New York Times* bestselling author

"Sexy, smart, fun, and just a damn good time."

—Avery Flynn, *USA Today* and *Wall Street Journal* bestselling author

"*A Beginner's Guide to Forever* surprised me in the best way possible . . . Simply put, one heck of a good read. As always, Kendall Ryan delivers lovable characters that have relatable journeys and a connection that you can't help but root on."

—*Harlequin Junkie* (Top Pick)

"Seriously sexy friends-to-lovers romance with a ton of heart."

—Frolic

"A total, utter must read."

—The Book Fanatic

"With simply adorable characters and a story that had me laughing out loud as well as sighing with appreciation, this was another great read from Kendall Ryan."

—The Overflowing Bookcase

"A TOP FAVORITE FOR THE YEAR."

—Red Cheeks Reads

HOW TO TRAIN YOUR *Billionaire*

KENDALL RYAN

This is a work of fiction. Names, characters, organizations, places, events, and incidents are either products of the author's imagination or are used fictitiously. Otherwise, any resemblance to actual persons, living or dead, is purely coincidental.

Published by Montlake, Seattle

www.apub.com

EU product safety contact:
Amazon Media EU S. à r.l.
38, avenue John F. Kennedy, L-1855 Luxembourg
amazonpublishing-gpsr@amazon.com

ISBN-13: 9781662530951 (paperback)
ISBN-13: 9781662530968 (digital)

Cover design by Ashley Santoro
Cover image: © Michelle Lancaster PTY LTD

Printed in the United States of America

HOW TO TRAIN YOUR *Billionaire*

Chapter One

Embrace Your Quirks

Frankie

"So, you had no idea this was coming?" Tessa asks through the phone.

I heave my laptop bag onto my shoulder and let out a long breath. "None whatsoever."

Just like any other weekday, I trudged downtown by way of the city bus. But this time, when I got to the office, my boss called me in to say I was being laid off—effective immediately. I'd cleaned out my cubicle in a state of shock and hugged my work bestie goodbye, and now I'm wandering the street with an overflowing cardboard box carrying my personal effects.

I'd promptly called my best friend, Tessa, still feeling numb and confused. She's been my person for the past decade or so and always has fantastic advice. I need it now more than ever.

"You're a terrific accountant, you'll find something in no time."

"Lies, all lies. If I was so terrific, why'd they let me go?" I groan. "I'll sell feet pics to get by if I have to."

"Francesca," Tessa says firmly. She reserves my full name for times such as this—when I'm melting down. And it must have the desired effect, because my mouth snaps shut. *I am a terrific accountant, damn it.* "You'll find something else," she says sternly. "And in the meantime, I'm here for you—anything you need."

"Thanks," I grumble, sinking onto a nearby bench.

Setting the box beside me, I release a long, weary exhale and realize the bus schedule doesn't have any return trips this time of day. It looks like I might be here for a while.

But if there's one thing my thirty years on this planet have taught me, it's to expect the unexpected. Skirt tucked into the back of my underwear on the city bus? No big deal. Smoothie stain down the front of my cream silk blouse? Just your average Tuesday.

Last week, I dropped my phone on the sidewalk, and it exploded into a million pieces. The week before, I had an incident with a tube of superglue and ended up gluing my fingers together for half the day. That was a great look for the client meeting, let me tell you.

In real life, I'm a walking disaster—inexplicable mishaps seem to follow me wherever I go. Maybe that's why I crave the structure of my work. Being an accountant is the one thing I'm good at. Numbers have always made sense.

And not to toot my own horn, but I'm pretty much *amazing* at what I do. During my eight-year tenure with Prime Solutions, I'd like to think I made a positive impact. I automated the monthly reporting, identified a six-figure savings, and found overlooked deductions on this year's corporate tax return. Not to mention, I planned all the office birthday parties. Rosa in marketing is turning sixty next month. Who will be there to make sure she gets more than the standard sheet cake and birthday card? Probably no one, that's who.

I really wish I hadn't spilled my protein shake, because I'm now starving.

Spotting a vending machine, I sandwich my phone between my ear and my shoulder. "I'll call you later, okay?" I say to Tessa.

"Of course. I think we need to put a wine-and-wedge on the calendar."

"Yes, please."

Wine-and-wedge Wednesdays started after college, when we entered the working world and quickly realized how chaotic and exhausting adulthood could be. One particularly brutal week, after we'd both survived another miserable round of meetings, deadlines, and bad dates, we met up for happy hour at a cozy little bar downtown. The kind of place with dim lighting, an extensive wine list, and the perfect ambiance for unwinding. Tessa ordered us both glasses of the cheapest chardonnay they had, along with a wedge salad. The salads were massive, topped with blue cheese, crunchy bacon bits, and that perfect creamy dressing. We indulged in wine and girl talk, and somehow soon, we were laughing. Not because anything was funny, but because it was enough to remind us that life wasn't all bad.

Now, it's like a sacred tradition for us. It sounds simple, but it makes everything seem a little less overwhelming.

"Bye, babe. Chin up," she says.

I make an incomprehensible sound.

A small group of commuters carrying laptop bags shuffle past me on my way to the vending machine. They're in a hurry to get where they're going and seem oblivious to my inner turmoil.

I stop in front of the vending machine, torn between the hot CHEETOS and the sensible protein bar. I swipe my card and punch in the code for the CHEETOS. If there was ever a time for comfort food, it's this one.

The machine makes a whirring sound, but my snack stays put.

Rude!

I swipe my card again and watch, *again*, as the vending machine takes my two dollars but doesn't give me my snack. I repeat this process twice more before pounding my fist against the glass. "Come on, you bastard!"

A man dressed in a suit that probably cost more than my entire wardrobe notices the commotion and pauses. "Everything okay?"

"No, everything is not okay. Are you seriously asking me that right now?"

If I were in a better frame of mind, I'd notice that the guy is very cute and very tall and has really nice eyelashes.

"Do you need any help?" he offers, watching me with a curious expression.

Turning sharply, I glare at him. "Help? No, I don't need help—I need this stupid machine to work! This is the fourth time it's eaten my money!"

He holds up his hands, clearly out of his element. "I'm sure it's just a glitch. Maybe you can try to get a refund or something."

"I don't need a refund," I snap angrily. "I need a snack! And I don't need some guy in a suit telling me how to fix my problems."

A muscle in his jaw twitches as he appraises me. "I'm just trying to be helpful. I didn't mean to—"

I cut him off. "Just forget it. I don't want your help. I just want one thing to go right for me today. Is that really too much to ask?"

Suit guy must realize my question is rhetorical, because he wisely stays quiet. The way he looks at me gives me a weird, wavy feeling in my stomach—which I promptly ignore.

The last thing I expected on my bingo card today was an annoying finance bro on his way to his corner office to witness my public meltdown on a city sidewalk.

Whatever. I can eat my feelings later.

Abandoning the vending machine, I turn to retrieve my box from the bench where I left it, only to realize it's no longer there.

"Are you kidding me?!" I shout at the universe. *"Seriously?"* Gesturing like a lunatic at the bench and then toward the sky, I notice that suit guy is now scurrying away quickly, shaking his head in disbelief.

That box didn't contain anything of real value—just my potted cactus, a few framed photos, various notebooks, and a cardigan from Anthropologie that I loved.

I can't say I'm even surprised. I've always been the poster child for cosmic misfortune.

Case in point—I was bitten by a sloth on the corporate retreat to Costa Rica last year. I once took the wrong suitcase from the airport—it was full of men's clothing. And I accidentally sent the $950 I owed for my portion of the rent to the wrong Venmo—that was more than an annoying blunder. It's not like I have an extra grand lying around. Thankfully my roommate was good to cover me while I spent the next few months scrounging.

Basically, if things *can* go wrong, they will. It's just how my life goes.

~

"Stop pouting and eat your wedge." Tessa takes a sip from her glass of chardonnay.

I dutifully shovel another bite of salad into my mouth. "Happy?" I say around a mouthful of blue cheese.

"Frankie." She gives me a stern look. "You are going to be fine."

Maybe. Eventually. But it's only been two days. While I'm not typically one to wallow, aren't I allowed even a brief pity party? A short layover on the quarter-life-crisis express . . .

I stab a grape tomato with my fork. "I need a job. And a vacation. And to lose ten pounds." I need my roots done, too, if I'm being honest.

"You need a boyfriend," she says, smiling.

"*Not*," I grumble.

We've been through this. Tessa was constantly trying to set me up with her coworker's son, or her eyelash girl's brother. Basically, if he had a functioning penis, Tessa wanted me to ride it.

I giggle to myself. Okay, that's not exactly true—but she does seem to be rather obsessed with the state of my love life. Who am I kidding? I don't have a "love life," and I'm perfectly okay with that. I haven't dated at all in the past two years. After several bad breakups, I put myself on a sabbatical. Nowadays I'm happy to have great friends, a cute apartment, and a career that I love. Except, my brain reminds me, I no longer have one of those.

"I'm serious, babe. You're going to find a great job, but I really think it could lift your spirits to have a little fun in the meantime and end this self-imposed relationship detox."

"I'll consider it."

Tessa has dubbed me "boy sober." As someone who's experimented with dry January and sober October, I understood the assignment. A brief period in which I would abstain from dating. I would emerge at a later time more in control and able to make better choices—at least in theory.

I smile, remembering the guy who witnessed my public meltdown. "There was the cute guy in a suit that I possibly scarred for life yesterday."

"A guy in a suit? That'd be a first for you . . ."

I roll my eyes and order a second glass of wine. "I could date a guy in a suit."

Tessa laughs. "Are you for real? Your normal type is red flags. Tattoos. Bad boys. Ex-cons."

"Not true." I roll my eyes.

"Frankie!"

"Okay," I say, relenting. "So Tanner had an arrest warrant, which he said was *probably* just a technicality."

She stares at me. "And Jesse had full sleeves, tattoos on his neck, and *zero* goals."

Tessa has a mishmash of colorful tattoos adorning her right arm, so why would she care about a couple (dozen) tattoos? A purple hummingbird was her latest addition. Her personality is basically like Halloween—playful, spunky, and a little weird.

"And Brendon . . ." she continues, "don't get me started on Brendon. Don't even mention his name."

"See." I grin sheepishly. "That's exactly why I'm on sabbatical."

If my life were a book, it would be titled *Frankie's Bad Taste in Men*. Chapter 1 would be "Red Flags Are Just Decorative Banners, Right?" Chapter 2 could be "Swipe Right for Chaos."

The bartender delivers our wine and removes the two empty glasses. And I pray for a topic change, since the last thing I want to talk about is my spotty dating history. Because she's right—I wouldn't know how to pick out a decent boyfriend if my life depended on it. It's all the more reason to stay single.

Tessa turns to me. "Anyways, I can always ask around at my work—see if they need anyone in the office. It's a long shot, but maybe?"

"Sure, that'd be great," I say half heartedly. She's the head of events for an art gallery. They only have a small handful of office employees. *Long shot indeed.* But at least I have a friend like Tessa in my corner. Ever since my mom died, I've depended on her even more. It's tough feeling so alone in this world. I think losing my job must have brought my feelings of inadequacy even more up to the surface.

When I get home that night, I do as Tessa instructed and fix up my résumé. After emailing it over to her, I spend two hours applying for jobs before I collapse into bed with a slight headache from the two glasses of wine we had at dinner.

In the morning, I wake to a single email in my inbox. An invite for a job interview the very next day for an accounting position. My prospects are looking up already.

Chapter Two

It's Okay to Not Be Okay

Hayes

It's late on Friday, and I should be deep into the workload waiting for me, but the headache that's been building at the base of my skull threatens to derail my entire afternoon. My laptop is open to a presentation titled "Risk Mitigation," but I'm unfocused, my mind stuck elsewhere.

My work in my family's office isn't brain surgery, but it *is* important to me. Being born into great wealth sometimes feels like living in a gilded bubble—everything is available, but the expectations and scrutiny can be suffocating. I've learned to manage the pressure—but only barely.

A knock on the door snaps me back to reality.

"Come in."

My assistant, Greta, enters, carrying a stack of documents. "Your conference call with the legal team is in two hours. Do you need any last-minute changes?"

I shake my head. "No, no changes. Just . . . Can you make sure everything's set up for the videoconference with the West Coast team?"

"Absolutely. Everything will be ready. And I wanted to let you know that your one o'clock is here early. I've placed her in the sitting room."

"Thanks." For once a potential hire is on time. I've had a hard time filling this role for a junior accountant with someone capable. But given her résumé, Francesca Anderson is more than qualified.

I finish typing the email and click Send before rising from my desk. As I head down the hall toward the front sitting room, I can hear Greta chatting with the candidate. Greta can be a bit socially awkward, but I appreciate her attempts at being cordial.

"My nephew turns ten tonight, and we're going out for arcade games and pizza," Greta says.

"Every birthday should include pizza. It's practically a law," I hear the candidate answer, her voice warm and friendly.

Greta chuckles a little too enthusiastically. "Exactly."

I round the corner and stop dead in my tracks, because apparently the junior accountant candidate, Francesca Anderson, is the *psychopath* I met a few days ago by the vending machine downtown.

She gives me a shaky smile, clearly recognizing me as well.

I decide the only way to get through this is to be all business. That way, I won't notice her full lips . . . or the fact that I'm suddenly paying far too much attention to a junior accountant's button-up top.

Plus, remembering what a disaster she was quells any interest from my misplaced libido.

"Miss Anderson? I'm Hayes Winters." She rises to her feet and gives my outstretched hand a firm, efficient shake.

"You can call me Frankie, everyone does," she says, much calmer and more composed than she was the last time I saw her.

"Great, and I'll leave you two. You're in good hands, Frankie," Greta says. "Hayes is fantastic at making difficult things look easy."

I nod my gratitude to Greta, who's blissfully unaware of the awkward tension stirring between me and the monster in the cream-colored suit.

"You can follow me to my office," I say, turning for the door as soon as Frankie grabs her purple sparkly portfolio covered in a barrage of stickers.

That's a . . . bold choice.

"Thanks for coming in today. Take a seat." I gesture to the chair across from my desk. "Before we dig in, did you have any questions?"

She slides into the chair in front of my desk, placing her hands in her lap. "I have to admit, the whole family-office concept was new for me. This wouldn't be a personal assistant position, would it? Because with my background, I would really prefer to stay in accounting."

"No, we have a team who handles lifestyle management."

"Lifestyle management?" She blinks at me. "What does that entail?"

"Handling personal affairs of the family, like real estate purchases, managing yachts and private jets, arranging logistics for travel, personal security, things like that."

"Wow. I mean, I've seen the show *Succession*, but I guess I didn't think people actually lived like this." She grins nervously, clearly out of her element.

She's acting so normal now, it's almost a shame I have to do this.

"I'm sorry, but can we just cut to the chase and address the elephant in the room?"

"By all means." Her smile softens and then fades, as if she senses where I'm headed.

Maybe she was hoping I wouldn't have the balls to mention it. But it's not in my personality to sidestep things that are uncomfortable—I'm more of a bulldoze-my-way-straight-through kind of guy.

I lean forward, placing my elbows on the desk. "First, what kind of person assaults a vending machine? Truly. I'd like to know."

She frowns. "Is that one of your standard interview questions?"

"It is."

She pauses to straighten her shoulders. "I was having a bad day, in case you didn't notice."

I did notice, which was why I stopped to offer my help. She looked tired, pale. A little sad. And while I don't deal with emotional women well, I wanted to lend a hand. And then she all but bit my head off. We run things very drama-free around here, and based on what I saw, Francesca Anderson is a loose cannon.

"I figured as much, but it still speaks to your character—I can't exactly have an employee who might have a bad day and go off the rails on a potential investor. We all have bad days sometimes."

She makes a noise that I can only describe as an annoyed huff.

She's annoyed at *me*? That's rich.

"I think we can both agree this is going nowhere," I say calmly, folding my hands on the desk in front of me. "I might as well save us both the time. This interview is over."

"You're an ass." Frankie grabs her sparkly portfolio and rises to her feet.

I press my lips together. Most people don't speak to me this way, so her response is a little unexpected.

My great-uncle Charles chooses that moment to peek his head inside my office. "Hazey?" His gaze moves from me to Francesca. "Everything okay?"

"Everything's okay, Uncle Charles," I say, rising to my feet. The last thing I want him to do is worry. His health has been on a steady decline lately. The man is eighty-two. Why he hasn't retired by now is beyond me. "Frankie here was just leaving."

"You bet your butt I'm leaving," Frankie snarks. "Your nephew is a giant *man-baby* who can't look past something I did when I was *hangry*. I could do this job in my sleep, but whatever, it's your loss, dude."

"Huh?" Uncle Charles says, scratching his temple, failing to catch on.

"Exactly," I mutter.

Frankie moves past the desk and toward Uncle Charles. He takes a step closer, blocking her path.

"What position were you interviewing for?" He looks genuinely curious, his gray bushy eyebrows raised.

The sooner I can get her out of my office, the better. I have no idea why my uncle is meddling. *Read the room,* I silently plead.

She blinks at him. "I'm an accountant, and I love it. But I know I wouldn't be happy working for someone like *that.*" She jerks her thumb toward me with disdain.

I release a slow breath and count backward from ten. *You're Hayes Winters, you finished undergrad in three years, you've negotiated eight-figure deals, you climbed Machu Picchu. You can survive one annoyingly attractive junior accountant.*

"I see," he says, sliding his glasses into the front pocket of his cardigan. "I like your spunk, Frankie. I've never seen someone stand up to Hayes the way you did. We should talk."

What the . . .

Uncle Charles hands her his business card, which she annoyingly waves at me with a fake smile before tucking it into her hideous purple portfolio.

Holy plot twist, Batman.

I'm hunched over my desk later when Malachi strolls into my office without so much as a knock, his energy a stark contrast to my somber mood. He's all smiles and mischief, typical Malachi.

"I've got good news. We're going to Palm Springs for a guys' golf weekend. Jet's all set. We depart Friday after lunch," he announces with a grin that I've come to know means trouble.

I lean back, rubbing my temples as I eye him warily. "The last time I agreed to one of your 'harmless' weekends, I ended up in a holding cell with a souvenir armadillo and a very awkward phone call to my lawyer."

He chuckles, the sound echoing in my too-serious office. "Ah, but what's life without a little adventure? Besides, you need this. You've been all work and no play. It's not healthy."

Malachi is one of my closest friends, and he's right; we haven't hung out in ages. Still, I can't help but smirk at his concern, knowing full well that Malachi's idea of fun usually involves some level of debauchery that I'm not sure I have the stamina or the bail money for at the moment.

"Your version of *stress relief* tends to add *more* stress in the aftermath," I remind him. "And besides, I've promised my sister she could stay with me this weekend."

He waves off my concerns with a flick of his wrist. "I'm sure you could reschedule. Besides, it's *golf*." He enunciates the word. "How wild can it get?"

I raise an eyebrow, knowing full well that with him, even a game of golf could turn into an international incident.

He leans one hip against my desk, his expression softening. "Look, I know you've been under a ton of pressure lately. Between running point on the sale of the media division, and . . ."

I hold up one hand, stopping him. "Can we just *not*?"

He releases a slow breath. "Fine. Have fun babysitting all weekend."

Chapter Three

When Life Gives You Lemons, Make a Playlist

Frankie

There's embarrassment, and then there's *this*—interviewing with the man who witnessed your most recent worst moment. Honestly, the interview was over before it even began. The universe must really hate me.

But I guess there was one silver lining to being kicked out of Hayes's office. Curiously, his uncle Charles invited me to meet him for coffee this morning. I wasn't sure what to make of his invitation at first, but I figured why not. These people clearly had money and connections. I'd be stupid not to follow through on a potential lead. Call me old-fashioned, but I don't relish the idea of soon being homeless.

I listened to my best hype-up playlist this morning while getting ready, and since I had no idea what kind of coffee this would be, I dressed in what Tessa would call smart-casual. I didn't want to appear like I was trying too hard, but I wanted to look put together. I wore my nice jeans, with no rips or holes, and a pink silky top. Simple ballet flats and a giant purse, which contains like half my life. What? I like to be prepared for anything life throws my way.

When I enter the café, my eyes scan the room. I spot Charles at a table in the back and head straight there. He's your stereotypical elderly white guy—thinning silver hair, slumped shoulders, and a frown that makes him look like he just bit into a lemon.

"Good morning," I chirp, slipping into the chair in front of him.

"Morning. Charles Winthrop." He extends one age-spotted hand in my direction. We've technically met, but now that I'm facing him across a conference table, the name hits different. Like stepping into a history book.

There's a Wikipedia page about the Winthrop family. They've been featured in *Forbes* magazine and countless news articles. They're like the Vanderbilts. I haven't personally read much about them, but I think their fortune was made in the late 1800s and early 1900s in oil or something. They have donated hospitals to cities and funded public universities. I know enough to know they are a *very* big deal.

I think of Hayes, and things begin to click into place—the finely tailored suit and Rolex on his wrist. Thank God I didn't wear sweatpants to this meeting. I already feel like I'm having an out-of-body experience. I feel like I'm starring in a reality show I'm definitely not qualified for.

I give him a polite smile and try not to do anything embarrassing. I don't think I've ever had coffee with a billionaire before.

"I'll cut to the chase," he says, leaning in. "I've never seen someone speak to Hayes the way you did."

I roll my eyes. "Yeah, well maybe he wouldn't have such a stick up his bum if more people did."

He seems amused by me, more than anything. "I suppose that's a possibility. And you've worked as an accountant . . . ?"

"For the last eight years, and I love it . . . I'm just starting to wonder if it doesn't love me back."

"Were you let go?" Those blue eyes fix on mine, and his bushy gray eyebrows lift.

Shaking my head, I lean closer. "Corporate downsizing. Prior to that, all my employee reviews were outstanding. Believe me, it was a total crock of—" I catch myself and flash him my best *not*-about-to-swear smile.

"You will never find peace if you're fixated on things you cannot control."

I stare hard at him. "Say that again."

He does, more slowly this time.

Nodding, I lean forward. "You'll never find peace if you're fixated on things you can't control. That's good. I like that."

"Well, it's true. How would you like to work for me?"

I blink at him, unspeaking. "Doing what? Because if you think I'm looking for a sugar daddy or something, you have another think coming . . ."

Charles's shocked expression eventually gives way to a look of amusement. "I'm looking for a travel companion."

"What's a travel companion?" I blurt, thoroughly unprepared for where this morning has taken me. "Actually, could you put a pin in that? I saw a giant chocolate chip muffin in the bakery window that was practically calling my name when I came in. I can't focus until I eat. You want one?" I rise from the chair and begin digging through my monstrous purse in search of my wallet.

"A chocolate muffin?" Charles sounds confused.

I nod. "If you don't eat something, your blood sugar could get low. Low blood sugar could lead to hypoglycemia. If left untreated, hypoglycemia can lead to blurred vision, seizures, and even death . . ."

Charles continues blinking at me, like I'm a difficult math equation he's trying to solve.

"Don't tell me you're one of those health nuts," I scoff. My personal belief is that life is too short not to indulge—which I do often.

"Okay," he eventually relents, but I think mostly because he wants me to stop talking.

After a quick trip to the counter, I set a double chocolate muffin in front of Charles on a saucer with a mental *ta-da!*

He stares down at it and pokes it with his fork. "Wow. That's *quite* a breakfast."

"That's a breakfast of champions right there."

I dig into my own muffin, wiping the crumbs from my cheek. "So . . . you were about to tell me what a travel companion is."

"So I was." He pauses to take a bite of his muffin. "Dear God . . ." He groans and looks up at me, bewildered. "Why have I never tried one of these?"

I shrug.

"My cholesterol be damned, this is incredible." He takes another bite, and we eat in silence for a few moments. Chocolatey goodness explodes over my taste buds, and I hum to myself, happy as can be, at least for the moment.

Finally, Charles finishes his muffin, except for a few crumbs, and wipes his hands. "I'm looking to hire someone—a travel companion—to accompany me over the next few months as I visit some of my properties. I have poor eyesight, due to macular degeneration, and I could use help with my luggage from time to time. But mostly I'm looking for someone to socialize with, since globe-trotting alone doesn't appeal to me."

Abandoning my own muffin, I give him a puzzled look. "Why not invite someone you're close to? A family member maybe? Surely they'd enjoy a free vacation, right?"

"Yes and no. I lost my wife very young, and I never remarried. We never got around to having kids ourselves, and while I'm close with my nieces and nephews . . . they're all busy with their own lives."

One of his nephews is Hayes—enough said. I wouldn't want to travel with him either.

"Speaking of family . . . I didn't see a ring, so I assume you're unmarried?"

"Happily single," I chirp.

Charles nods. "Very good. Anyway, I enjoy travel and have a number of homes I'd like to visit. And I hate trying to line up dates that could work for others and just end up feeling like a bother. I'd prefer to go when I want to go."

"I get that," I say, having always been very independent myself. I would hate relying on other people.

"I'd like to get to know you a little better if we're really going to consider this. What would make you a good travel companion?"

I consider his question. I'm a ton of fun and liven up any situation, but I try to imagine myself traveling to new places with this elderly man . . . What would that actually be like? And what role would I play?

Strangely enough, I can actually picture it. I didn't have a father growing up, and my mom has been gone for three years now . . . I've kind of missed having the steady influence of someone older in my life. Someone who's weathered a few trials and come out the other side. I could picture us chatting casually over coffee—or maybe chocolate muffins. It's oddly . . . appealing. Or maybe all this sugar has gone to my head and I'm romanticizing the idea. I decide to play along for now, even if I'm not sure I want the job.

"First, I guess, is my ability to keep my cool when things don't go according to plan. And I'm good at talking to new people, so I tend to make friends wherever I go." Charles is studying me from across the table. "I'm not picky with food, and I have no allergies, so I never order off a special menu and am easygoing about where or what to eat."

"That can be helpful, I agree. What else?"

"I'm a good listener and conversationalist, I have a wide range of interests, so I know the basics about a lot of things and can a least start a conversation. I'm generally a positive person; it takes a lot for me to complain."

"Very good." Charles nods.

"Oh, and I'm small, so I don't mind taking the middle seat on a plane." I grin, pleased with myself that I thought of such a detail.

"We will be flying first class, there are no middle seats."

"Oh. Even better." My smile widens.

"Is your passport current?" Charles asks.

I nod. "Where are you looking to travel to, exactly?"

"I was thinking we should start with Montana. I have a property outside of Big Sky that I haven't been to in ages. I've been advised we should take the first trip as a trial run and that it should last no longer than a week to make sure we don't want to kill each other by the end. I can be a lot to put up with, I've been told."

"That sounds reasonable. I've never been to Montana. But should we talk pay? Expenses?"

"I'll match whatever your last salary was, and the only expenses you'll have are your own souvenirs or personal items."

Wow. It's a generous offer. It's kind of surreal, to be honest, but I'm still totally unsure if it's the right move for me. "Can I think it over?"

"Of course."

~

On my way out of the coffee shop, I call Tessa and fill her in.

"Maybe your luck is turning around, Frankie."

She's kind of right. It seems like it could be. But I want to make a good decision. "On the one hand . . . dream opportunity. But on the other, I've always loved being an accountant. Math is the only thing in my life that's always made sense and never let me down."

"I hear you," Tessa says cautiously. "But I think this job could be good for you."

"Yeah maybe, but if I accept, I feel like I'd be starting over." Facing a new set of challenges.

"Perhaps, in some ways. But accounting is always going to be there. You can always go back to it."

I consider her advice, and the weight of this decision feels heavier than it should be. Could I really explain a six-month gap in my résumé to my next accounting firm? Not to mention I'd be leaving my comfort zone far behind. Was I really okay with that? Then again, Charles's name would be an excellent line on a résumé, even with the term "travel companion."

I've never imagined being wealthy or spoiled—never even wished for that life. While other people chased status, I was happiest in the background. Quietly working. Keeping my head down. Remembering birthdays. That was my comfort zone. I was damn good at what I did.

Whenever I stepped outside that lane . . . things tended to go sideways.

So the idea of a whole new trajectory—even one as exciting as jet-setting with Charles—fills me with uncertainty. Because when the spotlight hits me, something usually breaks. Sometimes literally.

It seemed like most people my age had things figured out. They knew what they wanted next—marriage, kids, a mortgage, maybe a golden retriever.

Taking this job felt like the opposite of settling down. Not that it was a bad thing. The whole marriage-and-kids thing wasn't necessarily on my radar yet.

Sure, I wanted that someday. It just felt . . . a long way off. I've always been a bit of a late bloomer.

And maybe, deep down, I also questioned whether I'd ever meet someone who *fit*. None of the men I met have been worth evolving for.

And based on my spotty track record, it wasn't likely. Which meant it was best not to get my hopes up.

"I feel like my entire life plan fell through."

"So, make a backup plan. I think this detour could be exactly what you need."

She might be right. Traveling the world for a few months was probably a dream come true for some people—a once-in-a-lifetime opportunity. And after being laid off, I promised myself I'd never get emotionally attached to a job ever again. I wouldn't love an organization that didn't love me back.

"It's only a few months, Frankie. After it's done, you can go right back to accounting."

Still processing all of this and more, I think of Charles, who seems every bit like a genuine, grandfatherly type, though I have nothing to base this on. But he seems normal, almost sweet. I wonder if, in some strange way, we'd be good for each other.

"I'm going to do it," I announce.

Tessa gives a little cheer. "That's my girl!"

Chapter Four

Find Balance in the Chaos

Hayes

My younger sister, Madelyn, is absorbed by weaving tiny rubber bands together on her Rainbow Loom. She's made me countless friendship bracelets this way, and even a key ring.

"How do you feel about purple?" she asks, tongue out in concentration.

"I'm good with purple." I nod.

I can't say I ever expected to have Madelyn in my life. I was an only child until I was twenty-two years old. Until my dad had a midlife crisis and fathered a secret love child. But when your family is as prominent as mine, secrets have a way of getting out.

Maddie's now eight, and while my parents have mostly worked things out, I wouldn't say they're happy. It's a story for another time. Madelyn's mom has actually handled the whole thing pretty well and shares custody with my father, who sees Maddie on the weekends. I see her a few times a month—we're each other's only sibling, and even though we're as different as night and day, I think we both look forward to the time we spend together. When I take her to the park, or out shopping, people assume I'm her father. It's unconventional, but I absolutely adore her, and I'm grateful she's in my life.

"Why can't we go to Wiggle World?" Madelyn asks with a pout.

Wiggle World is literally hell on earth. I would rather give my left testicle than endure another minute at that soul-sucking place.

"I wish we could," I say with a frown. "I heard Wiggle World actually closed down."

Madelyn's appraising gaze snaps over to mine. "What? No way. My friend Legacy was there last week."

Legacy? People name their children the strangest things these days.

"Yeah, it's really a shame what happened, but they've closed up for good."

"Hey, Alexa!" she shouts. "Is Wiggle World open today?"

Alexa informs us that Wiggle World is indeed open today, and then cites today's hours in a robotic tone. I want to strangle it with its own cord.

She grins. "See, I told you it's open."

You can't lie to kids anymore. It's really a shame what the world's come to.

"No Wiggle World, Maddie. What else do you want to do today?" I offer.

"We could get a pedicure." She smiles at me.

I glance down at my feet. "I think I'm still good from the last time."

"Ice cream?" She smiles wider.

"It's almost dinnertime," I say, glancing at my watch. "Shouldn't we eat something nutritious first?"

She scrunches her nose. "Ice cream for dinner is fine by me."

What the hell. You only live once. "Sure, let's do it, kid."

The truth is, I need this break. The distraction of a weekend spent catering to the whims of an eight-year-old is exactly what my brain needs. Work has never been busier, my relationship with my parents has never been more toxic.

I need a weekend where the biggest decision I have to make is whether or not to order one scoop or two.

"And then we can watch *Sing 2* later. You'll love the gorilla, Johnny," she informs me with a look of absolute certainty.

I chuckle and grab my keys.

My phone rings, and I expect it to be my friend Malachi calling to rub in all that I'm missing in Palm Springs. But when I see it's my uncle Charles, I decide to answer.

"Hello?"

I hold open the door for Maddie, who happily trots along the stone path leading to the garage.

"Hayes," he says, sounding excited about something. "I'm glad I caught you. I wanted to let you know that I've figured out the fix for my travel schedule."

I'd kind of forgotten he mentioned wanting to take some time to travel this year. I'd sort of blown it off, to be honest.

"Oh yeah?" I ask.

"Yeah. I've decided to hire Frankie to accompany me."

He did what? Frankie, as in that sociopath Francesca? My brain skids to a stop.

"Hayes?" he asks. "Are you still there?"

I'm momentarily speechless, because I'm in absolute shock that he went and did this. He's normally such a responsible and methodical person. *What is he possibly thinking?*

I press a knuckle to my temple. "I'm here. I'm just . . . processing."

"I really think it will be the perfect solution, and in fact she's going to accompany me next week to Big Sky."

My brain sputters as a bewildered look overtakes my face.

Maddie has stopped skipping along the sidewalk to watch me with a curious expression.

"Did you check her references?" I ask, stepping carefully over the sidewalk chalk drawing of a dragon Maddie created earlier.

"I did, yes. They had wonderful things to say about her."

"And has she signed an NDA?"

"Of course," Charles answers.

Well, that's a relief. It still doesn't mean I'm okay with this. Hiring her to complete specific tasks is one thing; employing someone as your personal companion, someone who will accompany you on trips and spend hours, days, *weeks* living alongside you . . . it's a very intimate arrangement. I honestly don't know what my uncle is thinking. Who am I kidding? He clearly isn't. The old man must be losing it. I've heard about this kind of thing. Next thing you know, I'll be taking away his car keys. He can't be trusted anymore.

I release a slow breath, trying to compose my thoughts. "For the record, I think that's a terrible idea, Uncle Charles. We hardly know her. And you know I don't like to meddle, but from what I've seen she's irresponsible at best, certainly careless, and I don't like the idea that she'd be the one in charge of looking after you when she clearly can't even look after herself."

"Hayes"—his tone is scolding—"Frankie is here on speakerphone."

"Hiya, Hazey," she says, sounding chipper.

I groan and run a hand through my hair. "Hello, Francesca," I manage to grit out, somehow sounding professional instead of exasperated, like I feel.

She huffs a breath. "Call me Frankie. Everyone does."

"I'm not everyone."

How this woman has managed to get under my skin so thoroughly in such short order, I have no idea.

I unlock my Maserati and hold open the passenger door for Maddie. "Are we still going for ice cream?" she asks at my sullen expression.

I nod and say into the phone, "I have to go. We'll talk about this later."

I have no idea what voodoo this woman did to lure in my uncle, but this conversation is far from over.

Chapter Five

Take an Unplanned Adventure

Frankie

"Are you game?" I flash a deck of cards at Charles.

"What is it?" he asks, pushing down a pair of reading glasses to the bridge of his nose so he can peer over at the purple-colored card game. He'd been deep into a crinkled issue of *The Wall Street Journal* ever since we boarded.

We're thirty minutes into our flight to Bozeman and are currently seated in row two of the airplane—I've never been in first class before and am trying to play it cool. The flight attendant has already stopped by, confirming our lunch menu, and is delivering drinks row by row to our fellow first-class passengers. I followed Charles's lead, and since he didn't order alcohol, I opted for a ginger ale.

"It's a get-to-know-you type game." I give him a playful wink.

It's also geared toward people who are dating, but whatever. I missed that detail when I ordered it from Amazon, and even though I was packing up to leave when it arrived, I was hoping this would help Charles and I get to know one another a little better.

I still wasn't quite sure how our arrangement would work. Would I even be a good travel companion? What if his standards were impossibly high and he fired me? Or worse, what if he turned out to be a creepy old man and I had to fly back to New Jersey with my tail tucked between my legs. I didn't know if I could handle too many more massive failures this year. It'd be better if he and I got to know each other, to determine if this whole thing would work or not. If not, I could at least cut my losses early and head home.

Charles folds his newspaper in half and deposits his square reading glasses into his jacket pocket, giving me his full attention.

I remove the cards from their packaging. At the airport, we discovered we share the same birthday—May 15—which felt like a small sign from the universe that maybe I was on the right path.

"How do you play?" he asks.

"I guess I read the question, and we both answer?"

"Sure," he says.

"A unique food or special treat you enjoy," I say, reading the top card.

My brain flashes back to the chocolate muffins I bought us in the coffee shop.

"That's easy. Liverwurst and onions."

The vomit emoji flashes through my brain, but I manage to keep that to myself. "Never had it. What's liverwurst?"

"It's a kind of sausage made from liver."

Vomit emoji. Crying emoji.

"Mmm," I say, forcing myself not to gag.

He nods. "You'll have to try it sometime."

I flip over the next card. "Guilty pleasure?"

"I don't understand the concept of a guilty pleasure. If something brings you pleasure, why should you feel guilty about it?"

The man has a valid point.

"Favorite hobbies?" I try next.

"Pass," he says.

Why do I sense that he doesn't have any besides dabbling in the stock market or checking his bank statements? I let it go.

"Pet peeves?" I ask next.

"Card games like this one." He gives me a pointed look.

I flip to the next card, undeterred. "The perfect way to spend a Sunday afternoon?"

"Enough with the cards." He places his hand over mine, lowering the deck of cards to my tray table. I think I've annoyed him with my questions, and I suddenly feel childish that I didn't read his mood, that I couldn't rein myself in.

He's right. This is silly. What, did I think we were going to share our favorite colors? Or bond over our shared love of friendship bracelets?

Maybe he prefers to read quietly on a flight, or maybe he wants to nap. He is pretty darn old. Maybe he does need to nap or he gets cranky like a toddler. I tuck this information away for later.

When I meet his eyes, I realize that Charles is studying me with a soft smile. Maybe I haven't annoyed him, after all.

"Tell me about your life, Frankie. About your family."

And so I do.

I tell him all about Tessa and her lovable quirks, about how she's the one who encouraged me to take this job. How she's always there for me, the kind of family you choose.

I steer clear of my rocky dating history, thankful when he doesn't pry. Old people tend to do that. They want to know why you're still single. But he doesn't pester me about it, which is a relief. I also successfully swerve around the topic of my father, satisfying Charles's curiosity with the fact that I've never met him, so there's not much to tell.

But I do tell him all about my mom, Hannah. She raised me as a single mom in the working-class neighborhood where I was often alone until nearly bedtime because she worked two jobs. I smile, telling him about our tradition of volunteering at the soup kitchen every Thanksgiving and how we used to make gingerbread houses from those little store-bought kits every Christmas. We didn't have much, but Mom always made everything feel exciting and special.

"My best memory of her, though—" I pause as a twinge of sadness settles in my chest. I swallow, proceeding cautiously—the last thing I want to do is cry in front of my new boss on day one. He'll think I'm a basket case. "Is one summer—I think I was in the seventh grade—you know that awkward age where you start to worry about what others think. Well, we didn't have money for a proper summer vacation, we never did. But Mom was determined that year. I had several friends who were all out of town, traveling to faraway places with their families. I tried to tell Mom it didn't bother me, but I think deep down she knew it did. She said if she couldn't afford to take me to Paris, she would bring Paris to me.

"She made each room in our apartment a different theme—a different country. We had warm croissants and played French pop music in the kitchen. She'd taped a huge photo of the Eiffel Tower to the fridge. We ate grocery store sushi and listened to traditional Japanese music on the balcony. And that night we camped out on blankets in the living room, eating New York–style pizza and watching *Breakfast at Tiffany's* on the TV. We painted each other's toenails Tiffany Blue. It was the best day."

When I finish, I realize I didn't do a very good job at keeping my emotions at bay. Tears silently streak down my cheeks, and I sniff and wipe them away.

Charles pats my knee with his warm, wrinkled hand.

"I'm sorry," I manage around a lump in my throat.

"Don't be," he says encouragingly. "Sometimes, it's the simplest things that leave the most lasting impressions. Your mom didn't need a passport to take you around the world—she gave you something far more valuable: the magic of making the best out of what you have. That's a gift not everyone knows how to give."

I sniff again. "I guess I never thought about it that way. I just liked spending the day with her, being silly. She worked so much. It was nice to just be together."

"Thank you for telling me that story. Reminds me that sometimes it's the simple moments that shape us."

I huff and give him my best side-eye. "Yeah, but that's the thing . . . I have no idea who I am."

Charles studies me for a beat. "Maybe not. But I think you're someone who keeps going, even when it's hard. Someone who feels things deeply and doesn't pretend otherwise. That says something."

"Thanks," I murmur, throat tight.

It's more grace than I've given myself in a while. And somehow, coming from someone who barely knows me, it hits even harder.

I'm saved from any further embarrassing emotional displays when the flight attendant appears with two trays. I fumble with my tray table as she delivers our lunches. There's real cutlery and tiny crystal salt and pepper shakers. And the food looks delicious. Those poor suckers in coach . . . How would I ever go back?

I place the white cloth napkin in my nap and watch nervously as Charles inspects his pasta primavera. We got very deep, very quickly. Which is mostly my fault, I realize, but I decide to roll with it.

"What about you?" I ask, carefully forking a cherry tomato. "Life story?"

Charles uses his butter knife to smear softened butter onto his multigrain roll. "You want the condensed version? I am eighty-two, you know?"

I make a show of glancing at my watch. "It's a three-hour flight. I'll take the long version."

He's surprisingly talkative once I get him going. He tells me about his late wife, Betsey, and how they met at a dance hall. She was there with a date, but he stole her away. They were married within eight weeks. I can't even imagine such a thing nowadays. Red flags galore . . . but I can tell that what they had was real. So much so, that when she passed away from ovarian cancer when they were still in their early thirties, that was it for him. He never dated or felt the desire to move on. It's heartbreaking, honestly. To live your whole life alone like that. Although he also had plenty of adventure. He loves his work, and he's traveled extensively. Despite his young heartbreak, he's had a great life.

It's strange, listening to someone who's acutely aware they're on the final leg of their journey. But he doesn't seem sad or depressed about it.

"Did she share your love for liverwurst?" I ask, hoping to keep things upbeat—in light of both of us essentially sharing our greatest losses.

"God no," he laughs. "She couldn't stand the stuff. Even the smell of it would turn her stomach. I had to sneak it when she wasn't around."

It sounds like Betsey and I had at least one thing in common.

When we land, there's a uniformed driver waiting for us, holding one of those signs like you see in the movies, but instead of containing the name "Winthrop," it says "Wincock."

I flash Charles a curious look, raising my eyebrows.

"It's good to be a little inconspicuous." He shrugs.

"And you thought using the word Wincock was the way to do it?" I shake my head.

From the Bozeman airport, it's a forty-minute drive to the house. Charles mentions that he has an SUV parked there, which I'll be free to use during our stay.

We drive through a gated neighborhood, passing by houses and sprawling ranches every few minutes. The landscape is vast and serene, with open spaces that stretch as far as the eye can see.

Charles casually shares a bit of trivia, noting that the name "Montana" comes from the Spanish word *montaña*, meaning mountain—which seems fitting.

When we finally arrive, the house surprises me. It's actually more understated than I expected. Sure, it's probably a multimillion-dollar property, but it has a restrained charm. There's a three-car garage, a lovely flagstone porch, and a huge stone chimney. The real star, though, is the property itself—acres of gently rolling hills with breathtaking views of the Beartooth Mountains in the distance.

Is this really how the other half lives?

Inside, the house is just as impressive. There are four spacious bedrooms, and in mine, a private bathroom that has the prettiest dark-green tiles, and ceilings supported by rustic wood beams. I love it immediately.

May in Montana turns out to be beautiful but chilly. As the sun starts to set, I decide to get to work lighting a fire in the massive stone fireplace that sits at the center of the great room. The warmth quickly fills the space, making it feel like home—if only for a little while.

Charles wanders in with his newspaper. I'm certain he's read the whole thing cover to cover with how crinkled it is and how much time he spent staring at it on the plane. I find myself wondering again about his other hobbies.

"Have you ever played *Wordle*?" I ask when he settles into the armchair beside me.

He gives me a confused look.

"Give me your phone."

He hands it over, and after I do a decent job of masking my shock at how very large the font sizes and icons are, I install one of my favorite apps. When I hand his phone back, I explain the workings of the game. He catches on quickly.

"What's a five-letter word that starts with *O*?" he asks me after some time of staring down at his phone.

"Ocean?"

He shakes his head. "No, there's not an *N* in this one."

I check my phone and text Tessa to let her know I've arrived in my first destination as a travel companion.

How are things going? she asks.

I consider her question.

If I expected things to feel strained or uncomfortable between us, I'm glad to see I was wrong. We alternate easily between comfortable silences and small talk. We just click.

Great, actually, I write back.

"Occur!" Charles says after several minutes of deep concentration.

I don't even scold him for ruining today's puzzle for me, because he looks so pleased with himself.

Look at me, I must be growing.

After dinner Charles and I unwind on opposite sides of the huge plush sectional. The fire has died down to a whimper but still glows and crackles softly as the TV plays in the background.

"For every hour of international news you insist on watching, we'll watch a rom-com," I announce, waving a hand at the TV screen that plays scenes from a German newscast.

"I'm not watching a rom-com with you," he scoffs.

"Come on, old man. Remember the chocolate muffins. You might just like it."

The words are out before I can stop them. Too much? Maybe. But he just rolls his eyes, and something in my chest eases.

Later, when I glance over, I realize he's sound asleep in the recliner, his features softened in the flickering glow of the fire. I remove his reading glasses, and the newspaper from across his chest, then I sink back down onto the sectional, still in some disbelief about this new journey I'm on and the unexpected twists that brought me here. I pull out my phone and snap a selfie of me smiling on the plush couch while the fire glows in the background and send it to Tessa.

Cutie! she replies.

For the first time in a long while, I feel a deep sense of peace, as if everything is exactly where it's meant to be.

~

All of that changes in the morning when I learn that Hayes will be flying into Bozeman today. Any sense of peace I felt last night looking out over the mountains has evaporated. *Poof. Gone!*

I do my best to ignore him for the first several hours. I heard him arrive, heard his and Charles's voices in the living room. The fact that I needed to stay very busy in my bedroom was beside the point. What the hell is he even doing here? He was too busy to travel with his uncle before. Now that I'm in the picture, he suddenly wants the job? Well, I have no plans of heading back home, so he needs to back the hell off.

Sensing that he's only here to check up on me, or torment me, doesn't leave me with any warm fuzzies.

Two hours later, I'm in the kitchen when I hear the deep rumble of his voice.

"Francesca?"

I groan and look for somewhere to hide. But my laptop, charging cord, phone, and notebook are spread out over the kitchen island. I consider shoving myself into a pantry cupboard when I hear him call out again.

"Not today, Satan," I grumble under my breath. I'm searching for a local restaurant with liverwurst, of all things . . .

"There you are," he says, stopping in front of the kitchen island.

"What? What now? What could you possibly need from me that you can't get from someone else? Someone to wipe your butt for you? Or maybe to dislodge the large stick up your rear?"

He stiffens. "As charmed as I am that you seem to be fascinated with my backside, no, my needs have nothing to do with either of those things."

I give him a once-over. He appears to be unamused, his chiseled features stern and a five-o'clock shadow dusting his square jaw. His intense, stormy-gray eyes seem to hold a thousand unspoken secrets. Not that I care.

"My uncle's car appears to be blocking me in."

"Oh." I smile and blink at him coyly, suddenly aware I just verbally assaulted him. "I'll move it."

When I return to the kitchen, I do my best to ignore Hayes, which isn't easy.

He exudes effortless charm, and the way his broad shoulders fill out a shirt is enough to make anyone's pulse race. Anyone but me, that is. I'm boy sober. I want to stick out my tongue and taunt him. Tessa would be so proud.

"Do you have the Wi-Fi password?" he asks.

Chuckling to myself for being so clever, I turn to him. "Sure. The network is NachoWiFi. And the password is PrettyFlyForWiFi—all one word with caps."

Hayes looks dumbfounded, utterly and completely out of his element. "Oh—kay." He draws the word out, clearly missing my attempt at humor.

But he must get onto the network despite me, because he lets it drop. Heading to the pantry, I help myself to a snack. Good thing I stocked up on all my favorites from the gas station on the way into town, because there weren't any good snack foods to be found in this house.

Deciding to take the high road, I gesture to Hayes, who's still seated at the kitchen island. "If you want a snack, feel free to help yourself."

He looks over my assortment of Chili Cheese FRITOS, Easy Mac, FLAMIN' HOT CHEETOS, microwave popcorn (extra butter), and Cool Ranch Doritos, and shakes his head. "Thanks, but I don't eat gluten, GMOs, food dye, or processed meat."

I hand him a Cup Noodles. "Maybe this?"

He reads the ingredients list and shoots me a deadpan look. "I'm traumatized."

Rolling my eyes, I mutter, "More for me."

"Are you . . . counting your chips?" His voice rings out behind me.

I turn toward him. "I get eleven. It's the USDA recommended serving size."

His eyes widen. "Have you always been this honest?"

I nod, selecting another chip.

"What about those two?" he asks, noticing I've taken more than the serving size.

"Everyone knows you get a bonus chip. Two, if the first one you grab is weird."

"Weird?" He squints. One of the chips is brown. "Were you dropped as a baby?" he asks, narrowing his eyes like he's mulling over the possibility.

I take my pile of chips, balanced on a paper towel, to the living room, knowing that I won't be able to enjoy my snack in peace if he's here to watch me eat. I'll probably chew too loud or eat too fast for his liking. Plus, what kind of absolute *monster* doesn't like Cool Ranch Doritos?

Seriously, I'd like to know.

I can't wait to tell Tessa about this.

At best he's a spoiled rich boy without a care or real problem to be found. At worst he's an egomaniac who takes pride in pointing out how he's better than everyone else. *I don't eat processed meat.*

He can stick his meat where the sun don't shine.

I snicker to myself.

Chapter Six

Keep Your Enemies Close

Hayes

After completing my MBA, I dove right in, and now I oversee a team that does portfolio management, estate planning, philanthropy, and tax strategy. I get very little time off—which, I'll be the first to admit, is by choice—and *this* is how I'm choosing to spend it? I need to get my head checked.

I darted off for Big Sky, needing to check on my uncle—to oversee this ill-fated trip—to make sure that Francesca wasn't going to fleece the old man for everything he had. I had no way of knowing if she was a gold digger or a con artist or what. Something was off about her, that was for sure.

Plus my uncle Charles is one of the good guys. He's kind and thoughtful and doesn't have a vindictive bone in his body, unlike most members of my family. I can't help it if I feel protective over him. Plus, I don't know Francesca *at all*. Other than the googling I did. Someone needs to look out for my uncle. He's a literal billionaire at the final stage of his life. I'm not ignorant as to what could happen. There are news specials on this kind of thing.

I round the corner and find them in the dining room just as the sun is setting. Take-out containers are spread out before them, and Francesca is smiling. Her mouth is too big—she has one of those smiles that just refuses to fade—and she seems to always be smiling. It irritates me. What is there to be so happy about?

"Okay, so I ordered takeout from a German restaurant," she says to Charles. "Liverwurst and onions."

My uncle's eyes light up with excitement. Weird, but whatever. Not here to judge.

"Sorry, I didn't know you'd be eating with us," she says to me. I can tell she's lying. She was *hoping* I wouldn't be eating with them. And by not ordering me any food, she was ensuring I wouldn't be.

"It's fine. I made plans with a friend in town." I press one hand to my uncle's shoulder. "I'll be home late."

Charles nods once. "No problem. We were going to watch a chick flick tonight."

The hell? I do a double take, my eyes widening.

"A rom-com. Right, Charlie?" Francesca says with a wink.

I pause with the water glass halfway to my lips. My uncle Charles has never been *Charlie*. Not ever. He is Charles or maybe Chuck to those who are closest to him. He's known Francesca, what? All of a week.

"Can I have a word with you, Francesca?" I grit out through a clenched jaw.

"Sure," she says begrudgingly.

I head off toward the kitchen with her trailing a few paces behind.

I steady one hand on the island and face her. "I have no idea what it is you're up to, but my uncle is a very sweet and trusting old man."

Her pretty face scrunches up. "What are you implying?"

Tension coils in my shoulders, and I release a slow, uneasy exhale. "I'm not implying anything, I'm just saying that . . ." *Shit, what* am *I trying to say?*

Francesca, seeming to summon every ounce of civility she can find, tosses me an olive branch. "Just to be clear . . . I really like your uncle, and

I wasn't sure about this job at first, but I really think it could be exactly what I need. So can you do one thing and not mess this up for me?"

I hold up both hands. "I'm not going to mess anything up for you. But I do intend to check in on him from time to time."

She takes this information in and nods once. "Fine. I know you don't think very highly of me, but you never know, I might just surprise you." Turning, she glances back at me once before continuing back to the dining room. "If we're done here, my liverwurst is getting cold, and I highly doubt that's going to make it any more palatable."

I chuckle and follow her back to the dining room, mostly because I want to see how exactly this is going to play out.

Plating the grayish sausage, Francesca looks uneasy. "This is your uncle's favorite guilty pleasure," she says, like this is common knowledge.

"It is?" I eye the pungent and slightly metallic-smelling meat.

Charles nods. "I haven't had it in ages, though."

My body revolts at the smell. "It's even worse than I imagined. How can something so disgusting even exist?"

"Will you be nice and shut the Smurf up," Francesca says.

"Pardon?" I blink, dumbfounded.

She lets out a frustrated sigh. "I'm trying not to curse."

That's curious . . . I wonder if Charles told her it was unbecoming for a lady.

"And you thought replacing a random word in place of a swear was the way to do it?"

"Yes, I did. You have a problem with that?"

I shrug. "Suppose I did." I don't, for the record—I just . . . want to see what she'll do.

"Then I'd tell you to Frappuccino off."

I cough into my fist to hide the strange urge to laugh. *Do not encourage her,* I repeat silently to myself.

Charles ignores our bickering and cuts into his sausage, placing a bite into his mouth. I'm sure this is not part of a heart-healthy diet, but I avoid pointing that out, because he really does seem to be enjoying this.

I'm already running late, but there's no way I'm going to miss Francesca tasting the sausage on her plate.

She hesitates, staring down at the grayish-brown mass. She pokes at it with her fork, frowning.

I cross my arms and grin, watching her squirm in discomfort.

With a deep breath, she picks up her fork, mentally preparing herself for the first bite. She stabs a large piece with her fork and brings it to her lips with an expression that can only be described as "trepidation." I can already tell she's not sure what she's getting herself into.

"Are you sure you want to try that?" I ask, trying (and failing) to hide my amusement.

She shrugs. "How bad can it be?"

"It's delicious," Uncle Charles answers.

Just when I think she's going to chicken out, she places the whole thing in her mouth.

Bold move.

I wait for her face to contort as if she's just bitten into a rotten apple. And in some weird way, my respect level for her increases as I watch her chew. She's done all this for my uncle—who's clearly enjoying his dinner.

I wait for her to grab her water and chug it down, trying to rid her mouth of the horror she just experienced. I brace myself for the usual reaction—grimacing, gagging, a look of pure betrayal as she realizes just how awful liverwurst is.

But . . . she doesn't.

She just chews slowly, then . . . she smiles.

I blink.

She's still chewing, but her face softens, almost . . . content. "This is . . . really good," she says, surprising the hell out of me. "Like, I could eat this every day."

My mouth hangs open in disbelief. "Wait. What?"

She looks as stunned as I feel. "Yeah." She forks a second piece with enthusiasm. "It's like a savory mystery wrapped in deliciousness. I could definitely get used to this."

I shake my head. "You're messing with me. No one actually likes liverwurst. It's a rite of passage to hate it."

But she just shrugs and takes another bite, clearly enjoying it way too much.

Staring at her, I'm not sure if I'm impressed or horrified. "You're serious."

She grins, and I can't help my surprised expression. "Guess I'm full of surprises."

Damn. She's even more of a psychopath than I ever imagined. I'll have to keep a close eye on her. The lengths she's willing to go to to infiltrate my uncle's inner circle of trust know no bounds. *Clearly.* It's terrifying, really.

"Don't keep him up too late," I say to Francesca on my way out, certain that whatever rules I put in place will immediately be broken just to spite me.

Chapter Seven

Shake Up the Status Quo

Frankie

When I complained about Hayes, Charles assured me he wasn't so bad once you got to know him. So, I make an effort. I learn a few things. For instance, he's twenty-nine, he has washboard abs, and he writes in perfect cursive. Oh, and he eats obscenely healthily. He's also fairly nice to Charles. I still hate him, though.

Pretending to like liverwurst just to watch his face contort was almost worth it. It tasted like a rusty nail dipped in old pennies.

In addition to playing *Wordle* together, Charles and I add a few other things to our daily routine.

In the mornings, we chat over mugs of steaming coffee, and he usually gives me some type of life advice. We've gotten into playing Scrabble, and we went fly-fishing yesterday, which was more fun than I expected. But Charles did get tired out pretty quickly.

After dinner at 4:30 p.m. we watch *Jeopardy!* I'm getting quite good at it. Yesterday I got four right but missed the final *Jeopardy!* question. Charles got eight correct. He's best at the U.S. history questions. Any useless facts or anything pop culture related, I'm your girl.

All of that to say, we've found our rhythm. And in even better news, Hayes flew home.

By the start of our second week in Montana, I'm beginning to wonder how long we'll be staying here. I might need to look into joining a yoga class or something. I've already discovered the library, the best bakery, and the local farmers' market, but I need something more to do. Maybe I'll even look into the local dating scene. Living in the mountains feels very isolating. I'm not sure it's for me.

But the same morning I'm thinking about all of these things, I head to the breakfast nook where Charles is reading a magazine called *Cigar Aficionado*.

"Morning," I say.

Like every morning, he's already made the coffee and I help myself to a cup.

"How'd you sleep?" I ask, settling into a chair across the table from him. Our game of Scrabble is still spread out on the table; he gave me a thorough beating.

"Just fine."

"I'm still getting used to the dry mountain air. I still can't believe I'm here, honestly . . ." I take a sip of my coffee. "I'm still waiting for my life to settle down, instead of feeling like I'm on a roller coaster designed by a lunatic." I grin over my mug of steaming coffee.

Charles chuckles, his eyes twinkling. "I've been on this ride long enough to know it's full of unexpected loops."

I grin again. "So, what's your secret to not losing your lunch on the way?"

He leans forward. "The trick is to stop trying to drive the damn thing. Just throw your hands up and scream with the rest of us."

I laugh, shaking my head.

He smirks. "When I was your age, I had a five-year plan. You know what happened? Life had other ideas. It gave me the middle finger and sent me on some tough detours—ones I never saw coming."

I know he's talking about losing Betsey so early into their marriage.

He wraps his hands around his coffee mug and leans back. "But you know what I've learned? Even in the toughest moments, there's room to grow, to find strength you didn't know you had. And sometimes, those detours lead you to places you never thought you'd go."

I sip my coffee and give him a serious look. "So, even when it's hard, there's still something to take from it?"

"Exactly," he says, his smile returning. "Life's messy, unpredictable, and yeah, sometimes painful. But those detours—no matter how rough—can also show you just how resilient you are."

I'm reminded of a time Mom's phone had died and we were lost in the middle of nowhere with no GPS. She reassured me and said surprise pit stops were where you find the best roadside diners and the weirdest souvenirs. And it turned out, she was right.

I'm starting to wonder if I'll look back on my time working for him as one of my best detours.

"So, I should just embrace the scenic route?"

"Bingo!" he says. "Embrace the chaos, dance in the rain, and if you end up covered in mud, well, that's just a free spa treatment."

I chuckle. "So what's on the docket today?" I need to run into town and pick up more laundry detergent, and some more snacks . . .

"I'm thinking it might be time to move things along. I already called my assistant to make some flight reservations for us tomorrow."

"Oh. Okay." I blink at him. "Where are we headed?"

"Hawaii."

"Really?" My voice betrays my excitement. If he's tricking me, I'm gonna sucker punch him.

"It's one of my favorite places."

Another detour . . . but this one, I'm excited about.

Still, I can't help wondering—*is this what life is like now?* Just picking up and flying somewhere on a whim?

Before this trip, I couldn't make it through a Tuesday without tripping over my own shoelaces or setting off a fire alarm. But ever since I got on the plane with Charles . . . nothing. No disasters.

No spills. No flaming embarrassment.

Maybe he's my good luck charm.

Or maybe being absurdly rich just cushions you from chaos. Either way, I'm not complaining.

Chapter Eight

Make Amends

Hayes

My cousin Hart texted that he had a suite for tonight's Rangers game and invited me along. I don't follow hockey, but I do enjoy it. And since Hart and I haven't always seen eye to eye, him inviting me feels like an olive branch being extended.

"How do you feel about going to a hockey game tonight?" I ask Maddie, who's making me another of those friendship bracelets. I already have sixteen of the things, so I have no idea what propelled me to buy her even more supplies.

She scrunches up her nose. "I've never been to a hockey game. Will I like it?"

I shrug. "They have cotton candy, so I'm going to go with . . . *yes*, you'll like it."

The kid's a complete sugarholic.

"Okay. I'm in. Do I have time to finish this bracelet first?"

I nod. "Take your time. We'll leave in an hour."

Getting out of my own head might be a good thing. A fast-paced and violent sport like hockey should do the trick.

I'm unsure if it's my approaching thirtieth birthday or what, but I've been all kinds of in my head lately. And it might seem like I've lived a charmed life, but I've weathered many storms.

My parents' separation when I was nine.

Dad's rehab stint when I was twelve.

Mom's shoplifting scandal the year after.

Dad's relapse and rehab take two when I was fifteen.

Mom getting hooked on prescription pills.

Dad's affair and the birth of his so-called love child.

The media finding out about said love child and Mom threatening to divorce him.

Another trial separation that my parents announced on my twentieth birthday. Those are just a few of the highlights. It's been one thing after the next.

Now I've almost come to expect a disaster around every corner, and I'm finding it harder than ever to just enjoy the good times. I'm always waiting for the other shoe to drop.

Maybe that's why I've been so on edge about my uncle Charles and his new travel companion. I assume the worst is going to happen, and I'm constantly bracing for the fallout.

It must be some defense technique where I don't allow myself to be happy. I wouldn't even know the emotion if it slapped me upside the head.

Maddie decides to change into a purple sweater and glittery jeans for the hockey game. I pull a seldom-worn Rangers hoodie from the back of my closet, and we set out. Hart texted me a parking pass for the underground garage at Madison Square Garden, so it's easy to get there in time for the puck drop.

Hart and his wife, Alessia, are here when we arrive, but so are a few of his longtime friends. I recognize Monty, a genius computer programmer, and go over to say hello.

I also help myself to a beer.

"Go easy on that neon-yellow cheese, yeah?" I say to Maddie, who's fixing herself a giant plate of nachos from the taco bar in the suite—complete with that liquid yellow goo they have to call *cheez* because it's certainly not *cheese*.

Hart approaches. He's wearing a Trocheck jersey and a big smile. "You made it."

"Yeah, thanks for the invite." We shake hands. My relationship with my cousin has evolved a lot over the years. Mostly because he's grown up a lot—it forced me to take stock of my own life and where it was headed. In the last few years, my cousin went from an aimless affluent heir the tabloids liked to paint as a playboy to a family man with two small kids.

I dare a glance over at his wife. She's sitting alone with a glass of red wine, watching as the Zamboni makes slow, but steady, passes across the ice. I'd treated her poorly when she and Hart first started dating. There's no denying it. I figured they'd never last—she was at least a decade older than him, so I figured I'd speed the inevitable breakup along by pointing out how disastrous an idea they were. Maybe it was my own insecurities bubbling to the surface. Hell, maybe I'm just used to family drama and needed to invent a reason to cause some of my own. Regardless of the reason, it's obvious I was very wrong about them together. Hart has never looked happier. He's showing Monty photos on his phone of a humanitarian project they just completed in Namibia.

They've been married, quite happily, for three years now and have two kids under the age of two. I attended their wedding and saw them at various holiday gatherings, but I never actually said those two little words to her that I should have.

Somewhere in the back of my mind, I see Frankie. Not saying anything in particular—just *being* who she is. Blunt. Brave. Unafraid to speak her mind, even when it terrifies her.

I'd never admit it, but maybe she's rubbing off on me.

I excuse myself and wander over to where Alessia is sitting alone. I take a breath and lower myself into the seat beside her.

"I have something I need to say."

Her eyes dart around me, like she's plotting her escape. I really can't blame her. I cornered her once before like this and tried to convince her to break things off with Hart.

"I was an absolute and total dick to you. And I know this apology is a little late, but for what it's worth, I'm sorry. Truly. I'm man enough to say I was wrong about you and Hart."

Alessia looks taken aback, almost stunned by my words. Her lips, which are painted a pretty shade of red, turn down. "I'm not sure what to say, other than yes, you were a total dick to me."

My chest tightens. "I'm sorry. And I sincerely hope you can forgive me, but I'll also understand if you can't."

"I forgave you a long time ago. Dwelling on the past wouldn't have served me, and you're Hart's cousin."

"Wow. Well, thank you." I'm not sure I deserve her kindness, but I'm grateful for it all the same.

"Doesn't mean I have to like you," she says with a smile that is most likely fake.

"Obviously," I say. After the way I behaved, I can't expect we'll suddenly be best friends. "Well, enjoy the game."

"Will do." And with that, she stands and heads over to Hart, who's wearing a curious expression, no doubt wondering what we were discussing.

I down the rest of my beer and glance over at Maddie, who's helping herself to a second plate of nachos. Since I don't want her puking in my Land Rover on the way home, I decide to go over and intercept.

I might have matured a little tonight, but let's not get carried away.

Chapter Nine

Take the Scenic Route

Frankie

Who knew the Big Island was actually just called Hawaii? I'd bought myself a couple of travel guides to read on the long flight over the Pacific and learned each island has its own name. Collectively, they are referred to as Hawaii, but Charles and I are actually going to the *island* of Hawaii—the Big Island. In my reading, I learn it's arguably the most laid-back and least touristy of the islands. It sounds great to me.

When we land, I have two thoughts:

1. Wow, it's beautiful.
2. I should've packed more deodorant.

It's the most majestic, breathtaking place I've ever seen. Sun-drenched, with palm trees gently swaying in the warm breeze, and then parts of it look like I've landed on Mars—big swaths of earth scorched by lava, which has hardened into twisted black rocks where nothing will grow—maybe ever again.

Instead of Wincock, our sign says Hardcock this time—thanks to me. I chuckle to myself, waiting for Charles to notice.

"I said inconspicuous, Frankie. For heaven's sake," he scolds me, but I can tell he finds it the tiniest bit funny. Turns out I like keeping the old man on his toes.

Our driver drops us off inside another gated development. I can see the ocean in the distance, and the electric golf cart in the garage is how we'll get around. It's magical. The house is four bedrooms, four and a half baths, with a large back patio with a private pool and spa. There's a distant view of the water. I sincerely hope we'll stay here for a long, long time.

I spend my days snorkeling while Charles sits in the shade and watches me. We eat lunch together alfresco, and sometimes I have to pinch myself that this is actually my *job*.

"I don't think we should ever go back home," I tell him on our fourth day.

We're seated under the shade of an umbrella at my new favorite beach club—Mauna Lani, watching kids build sand castles and tourists learn to surf.

But it's not just the view. It's the quiet in my chest.

No email notifications. No awkward job interviews or spreadsheets. No empty apartment.

Here, I don't miss my mom quite as much. Or maybe I do—but it doesn't ache the same way.

And for once, I'm not scrambling to hold my life together.

He chuckles. "I agree, let's stay put for a while."

Later that evening, we're on the patio, enjoying a light dessert as the sun sets. Well, Charles is enjoying a light dessert. My own bowl of passion fruit mousse is heaped with a mountain of whipped cream. The warm Hawaiian breeze rustles the palm trees, and for maybe the first time ever, I feel totally and completely relaxed.

Charles sets his dish down and looks at me with that same calm intensity he always has when he's about to share one of his nuggets of wisdom.

"Frankie," he begins, "do you know why I like *Jeopardy!*?"

I smirk. "Because it makes you feel smart?"

He laughs, shaking his head. "No, though that doesn't hurt. It's because it teaches you how to frame questions. Most people think life is about having the answers, but I've learned sometimes it's about asking the right questions. Answers might change as we head into a new season, but the right questions? Those guide you to places you've never thought to go."

I mull this over, stirring my coffee. "So, what's the right question I should be asking myself right now?"

He leans back, gazing out at the horizon, where the last streaks of orange fade into purple. "Ask yourself what you're holding on to that might be holding you back. Sometimes, it's fear. Sometimes, it's a person. Sometimes, it's the idea of who you think you should be."

I feel a twinge in my chest. Charles always knows how to get under my skin in the best and worst ways. But before I can respond, he grabs the remote and flips on the outdoor TV. "Come on," he says, grinning, "*Jeopardy!*'s starting."

We spend the next thirty minutes yelling out answers—or, rather, questions—at the screen. Charles is unbeatable, of course, but I balance him out on the pop culture side. It's easy and fun, and for a moment, I feel like we're in our own little bubble where nothing can touch us.

But bubbles always burst.

The next afternoon, I'm texting with Tessa when I hear the sound of tires crunching on the driveway. I glance out the window and freeze. Hayes is here. And this time he's not alone.

A stunning blonde steps out of the car, her legs impossibly long and tanned, her outfit so perfectly tropical it could've come from a resort catalog—white linen shorts, a citrus-colored crop top, and a floppy straw hat she doesn't even need. She leans into Hayes, laughing at something he says, and my stomach twists. A darker-skinned guy wearing a floral shirt climbs from the back seat of the SUV, dark sunglasses covering his eyes.

Charles tells me he forgot to mention Hayes is coming in today with some friends.

Forgot to mention? Do I need to check this dude into memory care? This is going to change everything. My happy bubble has just been popped.

I plaster on my best fake smile and step into the foyer. "Hayes. What a surprise."

"Isn't it?" he says, grinning as if he doesn't have a care in the world. The woman—who looks familiar to me as she gets closer—steps beside him, her hand casually resting on his arm. "Guys, this is Olivia. And Charles, you know my friend Malachi."

"Of course," Charles says, shaking Malachi's hand.

"And this is Francesca," Hayes adds stiffly. "She works for my uncle."

"Frankie," I correct him.

"Pretty sweet work trip," Malachi says, smiling at me. He's pocketed the sunglasses, and he's very cute, but if he's friends with Hayes, it probably means he's a walking red flag.

"Yeah, it's not bad," I say, returning his smile.

I realize why I recognize Olivia. Liv Holloway was a famous child actress who starred in a bunch of movies alongside other A-listers. But aside from a few bad teen comedies, she sort of faded from public view. At least, I haven't heard anything about her in years, so I have no idea what she's doing these days.

"Nice to meet you, Olivia," I manage, extending my hand. Her grip is delicate, and her smile overly rehearsed, probably from hours spent in front of a camera.

"I've heard so much about you," she says sweetly, and I have to fight the urge to roll my eyes. That's obviously a lie. Why would Hayes have said boo about me?

Charles clears his throat, breaking the tension. "There are drinks and snacks in the kitchen if you'd like."

"Perfect," Hayes says, leading Olivia and Malachi toward the kitchen as if he owns the place.

I retreat to my room and continue texting Tessa.

Frankie: Ugh! You will not believe this. Guess who just showed up to ruin my island paradise?

Tessa: Literally no idea . . .

Frankie: Hayes :(

Tessa: What's his vibe? I picture a beta male. An entitled dweeb

I laugh so hard I snort.

There's nothing beta about him. I actually wish there was. He seems to take over every room he's in and manages to suck all the oxygen out in the process.

Frankie: This is him.

I send Tessa a photo I snapped of Charles and Hayes in Montana. I sketched devil horns on top of Hayes's head.

Tessa: Holy main character energy. He's a total snack!

Frankie: He's a jerk

Tessa: If he were an apple, he'd be a delicious

Frankie: And a control freak

Tessa: He looks AI generated

Frankie: He's insufferable!

What does she not understand about this? I just want someone to make it make sense. How is life fair that Hayes gets to be gorgeous *and* rich *and* charming . . . all while having the heart of a shrew.

Tessa manages to remove the devil horns and crops Charles out of the photo before sending it back to me.

Tessa: 10/10 would ride this ride

Sadly, she's not done.

Tessa: For real though, that man is next level hot! He's a walking fire emoji.

Frankie: Gross. If you're done drooling, I need to figure out a way to coexist with him and his little girlfriend. I don't know how long they'll be here. Maybe I need to end my boy-ban and get on some dating apps here—meet someone myself.

Tessa: Why am I getting the impression you're jealous?

Frankie: Jealous? Ewww. No

I continue typing.

Frankie: More like annoyed

Yes, annoyed and frustrated. This is supposed to be my job, and that's something that I take seriously. I actually think I'm damn good at it, and I'm pretty sure Charles agrees. And now we're two for two with Hayes barging in and making everything about him.

If this is my story, he's the villain. The way he watches me from a distance, scowling and frowning when Charles and I share an inside joke. Does he not want his uncle to be happy? I can't understand his anger, it's so misplaced. But there's nothing I can do besides live with it, because everywhere I turn, there he is.

> **Tessa:** Okay because I was going to say, Hayes is not your type and based on everything you told me—a complete tool.

"Francesca?" The sound of Hayes's voice comes through the closed bedroom door.

I open it and peek out. "Yes?"

"What's the Wi-Fi?"

I bite the inside of my cheek. I don't know what possessed me to actually follow through on that dumb joke from earlier—but when we got here, I changed the network name.

It made me smile. And honestly? It kind of felt like something Charles would secretly appreciate.

"ItHurtsWhenIP."

Hayes remained stone faced. Not a chuckle, not the crack of a smile. Nothing. Nada. This man probably thinks I'm certifiable.

"The password is HideYoKidsHideYoWi-Fi."

"Great. Thanks." He turns to leave, and I release a slow groan.

It's funny, dang it! Why can't he just be normal?

Chapter Ten

Expect the Unexpected

Hayes

Why can't she just be normal?

That is the question that lingers in my brain long after my encounter with Francesca. But I don't have time to dwell on my uncle's odd new assistant. I have friends to entertain.

That first evening, I take Olivia and Malachi out to see the sights. The sleepy tourist town of Kona is certainly not known for its nightlife, but it's the best shot for finding beach bars open past nine. We drink mai tais and dine on poke bowls at an ocean-side bistro.

We spend the following day at the neighborhood beach club. It's a short golf cart ride down to the water. Malachi and I took the bikes so there was room for Olivia to ride down with Francesca and Charles.

Olivia suns herself in a barely there bikini, and Malachi and I spend most of the afternoon surfing.

Francesca seems attentive to my uncle, which is good to see. I honestly wasn't sure. They spent the morning playing a very relaxed game of pickleball, then they competed head-to-head in something called *Wordle*, and now they're doing a crossword puzzle while she sips a mai tai.

"Should we get some lunch?" I ask.

Olivia pops one earbud out. "Did you say something?"

"Lunch?"

She nods.

"I'm in," Malachi says.

"Charles?"

He exchanges a look with Francesca and frowns. "You should join them. I'm going to nap right here." He pats the lounge chair and leans back, placing a large straw hat over his head.

Francesca hesitates, but I nod my approval. "You're more than welcome."

"I'll bring you back something," she says to Charles, who only waves her off. He does seem quite tired, and I've got to say, this is probably a lot of activity for him. Though I do think it's good for him. The man has worked long hours for decades, ensuring the family trust funds are performing above market expectations. He deserves some R & R.

It's a short walk to the beach bar, and after Olivia dresses in a long flowing white dress, we set off.

I follow Malachi and Francesca, walking barefoot along the shoreline with Olivia at my side. The waves roll in lazily, licking at the sand before retreating. It's perfect and beautiful here, but something feels off between Olivia and me.

Inviting her on this trip was a bit impulsive—which isn't like me. I guess I wanted to see if there was more beneath her perfect exterior. We'd been dating for a few weeks, but the more I got to know Olivia, the more doubts I had.

"Pretty incredible out here, huh?" I say, motioning to the water. The sunlight glints off the waves, casting everything in a golden glow.

She follows my gaze, squinting behind her shades. "Yeah, totally. I mean, the light is amazing. Imagine how good a photo would look here. Do you think the lighting would hit me right if we faced that way?" She gestured toward the setting sun.

I stop walking and stare at her, half expecting her to be joking. She isn't.

I nod slowly.

"Good, because I was hoping to do a little photo shoot. If you're up for being my photographer later?" She pouts slightly, tugging her sunglasses off and hooking them in the neckline of her bikini top. It feels like a practiced move—calling attention to her breasts in order to get what she wants.

"Uh, I guess so."

"What? I'm just saying, it's good content. Not everyone gets to be here, you know."

I sigh, running a hand through my hair. Olivia seems to have a way of making me feel like I need to loosen up, to stop overthinking everything and just be cool. More laid-back. More like her.

After that we walk in silence for a few minutes. Malachi and Francesca seemed to be deep in conversation ahead of us. Malachi lets out a deep laugh at something she says, and they're both nodding and chuckling now. Francesca's beachwear leaves a lot to be desired—instead of Olivia's matching bikini and cover-up, fashionable sun hat and shades, Francesca is wearing a simple one-piece black suit and an oversize T-shirt, which she manages to pull off, honestly.

Realizing that Olivia is still talking, I try to focus.

"And when we get back, I hope you're ready for a night of the most ridiculous people you'll ever meet," she said. "The gallery crowd is so over the top."

I glance over, realizing she's head down as she walks, scrolling on her phone. "Gallery?"

She looks up. "My friend Gianna is having this exhibit thing when we get home. It's all, like, made out of recycled trash. Very trendy."

"Sounds interesting," I say, stepping over a sand castle that some kid has abandoned. "What's the theme?"

She waves a hand dismissively. "I don't know. Something about consumerism? Honestly, I don't even get half of what she does, but it makes for good Instagram content."

I pause, shielding my eyes from the sun. "Do you like her art?"

Olivia shrugs, still glued to her phone. "I mean, it's fine. Not really my thing, but she's my friend, so I have to go, right?"

"Right," I murmur, feeling a flicker of discomfort. "So, what is your thing?"

She looks up, confused. "What do you mean?"

"Like, what are you passionate about? What gets you excited?"

The question slips out before I can stop it. But it's been on my mind more lately—this need to understand what drives the people around me.

Maybe it's because I've seen what it looks like when someone goes all in on something—

Frankie comes to mind, uninvited. Again.

Maybe we should've had this conversation earlier, but everything between Olivia and me has always been surface level. Until now, I hadn't noticed how thin that surface really was.

She tilts her head, as though the question itself is strange. "Well, I guess I like . . . nice dinners? Traveling. Fashion, obviously." She gestures to her dress with a self-satisfied smile. "And, you know, just enjoying life. Why stress about deep stuff when you can have fun?"

Her words land like a dull thud, but I mask my disappointment with a smile. Most of my past relationships were built on banter, convenience, and knowing when to leave well enough alone. This—whatever this is—feels different. And I'm not sure what to do with that.

"Fair enough. Do you ever want to do something bigger? Like—" I hesitate, realizing how earnest I sound. "Like make an impact somehow?"

"People are too serious about everything these days. Like, oh, let's save the turtles or whatever." She rolls her eyes. "Not that I'm against turtles, obviously, but does it really matter in the long run? We're all just specks in the universe."

I frown, caught off guard. "Got it."

She laughs, light and carefree, like I'd just told a joke. "Hayes, not everyone's wired like you. I'm just here to enjoy life while it lasts. No offense, but worrying about everything sounds exhausting."

Her words hit me like a rogue wave, cold and unexpected. I never suggested she worry about everything—only that she maybe look up from her phone once in a while—care less about taking selfies and more about being there for other people.

For the first time since we started seeing each other, I'm not sure if I like what I see beneath her polished surface.

I shove my hands in my pockets, staring out at the horizon. "I guess we see things differently."

She shrugs, oblivious to the shift in my mood. "Guess so. But hey, that's what makes life interesting, right?"

I don't answer. For now, I need to do what I do best—put on a mask of indifference and deal with it internally.

I'll probably give myself an ulcer by thirty, but whatever.

Chapter Eleven

Stand Up for Yourself

Frankie

Hayes seems even grumpier than usual. I wonder if something's wrong between him and Malibu Barbie. The Grumpillonaire and the Barbie . . . it sounds like the title to a cheesy romance novel. I decide not to dwell on their drama. Not my circus, not my monkeys.

Malachi's nice at least. He told me a story on the walk over about his last trip to Hawaii—it was right before he graduated from high school—and he got stung by a jellyfish in a very unfortunate spot on his body. His mother insisted on helping him, which was awkward, to put it mildly.

After we place our lunch orders at the counter, Malachi and I find a picnic table to sit down at to wait while Hayes and Olivia are still in line.

"What's their deal?" I ask, tipping my chin toward them.

Malachi shakes his head. "That?" He glances to where they're standing. "That is a result of bad parenting—probably on both sides—and little to no self-awareness. Neither of them is fit to date, especially not each other."

His assessment is interesting, to say the least.

"Watching how Hayes was raised, it's no doubt he has issues," Malachi adds.

Charles kind of said something similar when I complained about his nephew. I'll admit, I'm curious, but Hayes is a twenty-nine-year-old man. It's like—grow up, dude. Get over it.

"So you two grew up together?"

He nods. "We met in the fourth grade. Best friends ever since."

Hayes and Olivia make their way over to us. The way they're sitting—a wide expanse between them and her glued to her phone—gives me another clue that they're not quite the happy couple I first assumed they were.

A server delivers our food, and I'm so hungry that I dive right in.

Olivia delicately picks at her salad, pushing the croutons to the side like they've personally offended her. Meanwhile, I take a massive bite of mahi mahi and grin at her.

Hayes gives me a hard look, uncertainty painted across his features.

"What?" I ask.

"You seriously ordered grilled fish and spinach? When there's a walking taco on the menu that's literally just a bag of FRITOS with that horrible, processed meat you like?"

Don't rub it in.

"I'm trying to make better choices." Now that I have to be seen next to your waif-thin toy in a bikini.

"How's that going for you?"

"I'm one day in."

He laughs.

Him laughing is such a rare occurrence that I pause to appreciate it. He actually has a nice laugh—it's warm, rich, and genuine. He doesn't do pity laughs or fake smiles, so if you get one, it's because you earned it.

Our eyes meet across the table. His expression is curious . . . a little sad, a little hopeful. I'm not sure what to make of it.

I really wish I hadn't shown his photo to Tessa. I also really wish Tessa hadn't pointed out how attractive he is.

"Here's a serious question for you," I say, watching Hayes stab aimlessly at his plate. He looks up and meets my eyes. "Are you angry at that piece of salmon?"

He grumbles and nearly snaps the plastic fork in two. "This thing is worthless."

"It's a *fork*, Hayes, chill." Is he seriously so pampered that he can't use a plastic fork?!

He holds it up. "This is not a fork. Cutlery shouldn't be biodegradable."

"Excuse me," I say, pointing a plastic knife at him. "Think of the environment."

"I am," he insists. "Surely it wouldn't take much extra work to offer actual silverware and throw it in the dishwasher."

He has a point. And here I thought he was just being snooty about eating with flimsy flatware. Though to be fair, he probably is.

"So where are you and the old man headed next?" Malachi asks me, trying to make conversation.

"I'm actually not sure. I've just been taking things one day at a time."

Olivia sips her cocktail and tilts her head, like she's weighing something over in her mind.

"You know," she says, turning her attention to me, "it's almost *impressive* how well you've managed to keep up. I imagine all of this"—she gestures vaguely at our idyllic surroundings—"must feel a little overwhelming for someone like you."

I blink. "Someone like me?"

"Stop, Olivia," Hayes warns.

She tilts her head, lips curving in a faux-apologetic smile. "Oh, you know. It's just . . . not exactly your world." She gestures vaguely around us—the cabanas, the designer resort wear, the kind of wealth that doesn't check price tags. "I imagine it's a little overwhelming."

There it is. The little dig wrapped in a velvet glove. The old me—yesterday me—would have just laughed it off, maybe even agreed. This isn't my world. But today? Today I'm tired. Tired of pretending I don't notice when people like Olivia talk down to me like I'm some kind of charity case.

I set my drink down, meeting her gaze with a look that says *not today, Satan*.

"You're right, Olivia. This isn't my world. I don't usually vacation in places where a round of cocktails costs nearly as much as my monthly car payment. But you know what's funny?" I smile sweetly. "I'm still here. Turns out, you don't have to be born into privilege to exist in a space like this. You just have to be invited."

Her lips part slightly, caught off guard.

I lean in a fraction. "And before you say it—yes, I *was* invited. By Charles. Who, last time I checked, doesn't throw around pity invites."

Olivia blinks, her smile faltering just slightly. "I didn't mean—"

"Oh, I think you did." I say, enjoying this far more than I probably should. "But it's okay, Olivia. I'd hate to take up any more space in your *exclusive* little world."

I grab my trash and rise to my feet, feeling an unfamiliar, almost heady satisfaction roll through me. *Huh. That felt good.*

I head back over to the beachside shack to order something I can bring back for Charles. And maybe a walking taco for me, because Hayes was right—what the hell was I thinking?

While I wait at the counter, I can't help but see Hayes and Olivia from his vantage point—they're in a heated conversation behind the bathrooms. She puts her hand on her hip and gives him a mocking look. Hayes looks down and shakes his head.

When he looks up at her, he says something—calm, controlled—but she throws up her hands like he just suggested she throw her designer handbag in the ocean. A tense silence stretches between them before she turns on her heel and struts away, leaving Hayes staring after her, hands shoved deep in his pockets.

Anger rises inside me. I don't know why I care, don't know why her mere existence should annoy me so much.

"I'm sorry my breasts didn't come with receipts," I mutter.

"What?" Hayes approaches from behind, and his gaze drops to my chest.

"Nothing!" I blurt. I didn't realize I was talking to myself *out loud.* We both watch as Olivia storms off, her white dress floating behind her. "Trouble in paradise?" I ask, hoping to steer the conversation away from my boobs.

"Something like that. It's fine, though." There's an edge to his voice, and I sense I've touched a nerve.

"Order up for Frankie!" the cashier shouts.

I grab Charles's lunch and return to Hayes's side.

"It's okay to feel your emotions." He glances over at me like this is a foreign concept. "Hasn't anyone ever told you that?"

He shrugs. "It doesn't matter."

"Except maybe it does." Maybe I can impart some of the wisdom Charles is bestowing upon me. What was our last conversation . . . something about asking the right questions. "Does she make you happy?" I grab a stack of napkins and some ketchup packets for Charles.

"I broke up with her," he says flatly, looking out at the water.

Oh. *Is this because of me?* But I'm not brave enough to ask him.

"She'll be flying back to New York this afternoon."

"Okay." I wish I sounded even a teensy bit sad about that, but let's be honest . . . I couldn't care less about some entitled D-lister getting sent home.

~

"I need to go to the grocery store. Pick up a few things." Charles gave me a list.

He needs stool softener, apparently, and some special type of toothpaste.

"I'll join you," Hayes announces, rising from his chair.

I'd rather he didn't, but what can you do? Maybe he's just bored. The house is quiet because Olivia's cab took her to the airport an hour ago, and Charles is napping. I'm not sure where Malachi's gone off to.

Since the neighborhood market is only a mile away and doesn't require any main roads, I talk him into taking the golf cart.

"You sure this thing is street legal?" He examines the electric golf cart, which has been painted an adorable shade of mint green.

"It's fine, Hayes. Come on."

We cruise along in silence, just the hum of the road noise as our backdrop since there's no radio.

"Meet back up in five?" I suggest just inside the store. I don't fancy the idea of wandering the aisles together like some cozy couple.

"Fine by me," he grits out.

Six and a half minutes later, Hayes is waiting for me in the front of the store, standing impatiently near the self-checkout lanes.

"Find everything?" he asks, examining the contents of my overflowing shopping basket. Somehow between my plus-size tampons, Sour Patch Kids, stool softener, frozen chicken nuggets, and green tea eye masks, it feels too revealing, like he has a snapshot not just into my grocery choices, but into my *life*. His own basket, in contrast, offers me a look into his. Organic mixed greens. Vegan protein powder—unflavored. And the latest issue of a magazine called *The Economist*. We couldn't be more opposite if we tried.

Oh my God, the stool softener!

"Some of this is for Charles, you know."

He eyes the tampons again. "I'm sure."

Ugh! He drives me insane. Just as I'm beginning to wonder what the state laws in Hawaii are like for assault, he takes my basket and hands it to the cashier before I have time to protest.

"I've got it."

Chapter Twelve

How to Accidentally End Up on a Date

Frankie

I don't know how I end up in these situations. One minute, I'm just trying to get through my day, and the next, Charles is roping me into some errand that holds zero appeal.

"I just need you to check it out," Charles says, leaning back in his chair like he's asking me to grab him a coffee and not go scope out a multimillion-dollar real estate deal. "Tell me if the place has good bones."

I squint at him. "I have no idea what *good bones* look like. I live in an apartment where the sink leaks if I breathe too hard."

He waves a dismissive hand. "You have instincts. Just go see if it feels right."

"Then why is *he* coming?" I jerk my thumb toward Hayes, who is standing near the window, scrolling through something on his phone, looking predictably unimpressed with this conversation.

"Because Hayes actually knows real estate," Charles says. "And because he was standing here when I had the idea, which means he's now involved."

I turn to Hayes, arms crossed. "You don't have to go."

He doesn't even glance up from his phone. "Believe me, I wouldn't if I had a choice."

"Well, *great*." I sigh. "This'll be a blast."

And that's how I find myself standing in an absurdly fancy house with Hayes Winters, being mistaken for his *wife*.

"This would be perfect for you two," the real estate agent chirps, beaming as she gestures toward the massive living room. "It's so open and inviting. Great for entertaining."

I blink. "Oh. We're not—"

"We're not entertaining anyone," Hayes cuts in, giving me a look.

The real estate agent giggles, because of course she does. Hayes has that effect on people. He could mutter something about *property taxes* and women would still twirl their hair and ask him to repeat it more slowly.

"Well, even if you're more private," she continues, undeterred, "the chef's kitchen is stunning. Top-of-the-line appliances." She nudges me playfully. "Bet your husband loves to cook."

I choke. *Husband?!*

"Oh, he's just the absolute best," I say with all the saccharinity I can muster, slapping a hand on Hayes's arm before he can correct her. "Nothing like a man who can whip up a five-star meal after a long day of brooding over the stock market."

He slowly turns his head to look at me, jaw tightening.

This is actually kind of fun, messing with him. I bat my eyelashes. "He's probably too modest to admit it, but he actually has a knack for whipping up fancy dishes using only gas station ingredients. Don't you, sweetheart?"

His nostrils flare. I can tell he's debating whether to argue or just let me dig my own grave.

"Hmm." The real estate agent tosses her hair over one shoulder. "Like what?"

"Oh, like give this man a packet of coffee creamer, some tortilla chips, and a can of spray cheese, and look out."

"Sweetheart," he says, a hard edge to his voice.

"Babe. The world needs to know." I plant my hands on my hips and glare at him, signaling that I mean business.

The real estate agent practically swoons. "That's so romantic. A man who cooks *and* buys his wife beautiful homes? You are one lucky lady."

Hayes exhales through his nose, clearly regretting every decision that led him here.

I smirk up at him. It's not my fault he's fun to mess with.

"Yeah." I shoot him a grin. "I guess I am," I say, gathering momentum. This is the most fun I've had since arriving in Hawaii.

He scowls at me hard, clearly exasperated, before wandering out to the pool alone. I mentally pat myself on the back. I may have won the battle, but I wasn't cocky enough to think I'd won the war.

"Just wait until you see the primary bathroom. His and hers bidets," the real estate agent says, leading the way.

"Oh, just wait until you hear about Hayes's love for a good bidet . . ."

What could I say, other than it was fun to mess with him. He was always so buttoned up. It was annoying! Which meant there was something deeply satisfying about riling him up.

"What do you say we call a truce and stop and get a drink on the way back," Hayes asks as we pull out of the driveway.

His offer surprises me, but I don't let on. Instead, I give the most beautiful house I've ever stepped foot in a wistful look from the window and shrug. "Sure, why not?"

A few minutes later, he pulls the car into a restaurant called The Drunken Coconut.

The menu is sticky and plastic, and I don't miss the way our server practically swoons over Hayes. *Gross.*

After we order our drinks—a vodka tonic for him and a strawberry daiquiri for me—I peruse the appetizer menu. I find all the usual suspects—chicken wings, sliders, onion rings, and poke bowls—but I'm in the mood for something else . . .

When our drinks are delivered, I smile and pull mine toward me. She's glorious in a tall, fluted glass adorned with a fresh strawberry garnish.

"Anything else I can get you?" the server asks, batting her eyelashes at Hayes.

He motions to me. "Anything she wants."

Okay, that was kind of nice. I'm not used to Hayes acting like an actual gentleman. "The fried mac 'n' cheese bites, please."

"Sure thing," she says, before turning to waltz away.

I realize I've never sat like this—one-on-one—with Hayes before. He's very tall with broad shoulders, and he has a certain presence about him. His skin has a sun-kissed glow, thanks to our time spent at the beach these past few days.

Objectively, he's cute.

There, I said it. Tessa would be so proud. And if he weren't such a total goober, I might feel tingly and intimidated. Thankfully, I don't, because it's *Hayes*. And that would just be weird.

I take a sip of my drink and moan. "This is soo good, you want to try it?"

Hayes shakes his head.

"So, what was it like, growing up being you?"

"That's a loaded question." He barks out a laugh. "What would you like to know?"

Based on his reaction, I suddenly feel a bit foolish for asking, but I'm already in this deep, I might as well forge ahead. "I mean your family has capital *M* money."

He removes the straw from his drink. "We do."

"And I guess I'm just curious . . ."

He shrugs. "It's nice. I'll never complain about that." He takes a sip of his cocktail. "It means having the world at your fingertips, but it also means you're never really your own person—every move is a reflection of the family's legacy."

I never considered there were downsides, so that's interesting. "What are your parents like?"

He laughs, a short humorless sound. "They're a complete mess."

All of this comes as such a shock that I'm momentarily speechless. I figured his family, on the cover of countless magazines, would have it all together. In my head, I'd built it up that they were the perfect family.

"My parents met in the nineties. Dad had a brief stint as a drummer in Cradle to Grave."

I knew that band. They had one or two massive hits that got significant radio play in my youth. "They had that one song . . ." I tap my knee, trying to remember the catchy beat.

"Exactly. They were a one-hit wonder."

"'Velvet Riot,'" I snap, proud that I remembered.

"That's the one."

"It's a cool song."

He shrugs. "Anyway, my mother went to one of their shows and talked her way backstage—which wasn't difficult. She was Evelyn Winthrop—she was used to getting what she wanted."

"And what she wanted was a fling with a rock star?"

"Yes. Or more precisely a drummer. Maybe it was some rebellious thing to piss her parents off, who knows."

"Well, what happened?" I take another sip of my drink.

"What happened was that they hit it off and started dating. Dad was never in love with her or even ready to be a husband. He was young and getting his first taste of success. Then his best friend and bandmate overdosed and died, and it struck something in him. He realized how short life could be and didn't want to waste any more time. They were married within two months and pregnant with me weeks after."

"I think I read about that at some point—their lead guitarist—heroin, right?"

Hayes nods. "The band broke up shortly after that. The rest is history."

"Well, this is a revelation. I always imagined you having this perfect upbringing."

"Not hardly. My parents can barely stand each other, and my dad fathered a secret child. Maddie—she's eight now. But they'll never divorce."

Did this explain—at least in part—why Hayes was so cranky and jaded? Maybe. I'd need to investigate it further.

But the server takes that moment to deliver my mac 'n' cheese bites, so any further introspection has to wait. I dig right in—like a voracious trash panda. Hashtag no regrets. The outside is crispy, and the inside is cheesy, gooey goodness.

He tells me a little more about his half sister, Maddie, while I eat, and I'm surprised to learn that they actually hang out. He takes her to the mall and out to eat. He shows me a friendship bracelet she made him. In my brain, Hayes is so one dimensional that it takes me a full minute to comprehend it.

"What about you?" he asks, passing me a stack of napkins. "Family back in New Jersey, I suppose?"

I wipe my hands and shake my head. "Sadly, no. Not anymore." I fill him in that I was raised by a single mom and that I didn't know my dad.

Hayes looks somewhat shocked, his brow furrowed in confusion.

"I know. It's a shock I'm so well adjusted and sweet." I grin and take another sip of my drink.

He leans forward, placing his elbows on the table. "Doesn't it bother you that your father couldn't even be bothered to stick around?"

I raise one shoulder. "Not really. Everyone's on their own path. He had to follow his. My mom took good care of me. Why should I complain? Others have it much worse."

Hayes doesn't seem to have a response to this, but his jaw tightens.

"Where was your first kiss?" I ask him. "Mine was at a middle school football game."

He smiles at my rather abrupt topic change. "Paris."

I gasp. "That is incredibly romantic!"

He chuckles and shakes his head. "Believe me, it wasn't. My braces got in the way, and I was terrified I had bad breath. And I probably did. I'd just tried escargot for the first time."

I laugh. "Okay. Gross. But I feel like I could go toe-to-toe with you on who's had it worse in the dating realm, though. Trust me, I have gone out with some doozies."

He takes a swallow of his drink, considering this. "I don't know, I feel pretty stupid for bringing Olivia here."

"Why?"

"Because I hardly know her. Because she was all wrong for me." He shrugs.

I could just nod and sympathize, but something in me pushes back.

"Listen, as someone who's made a lot of questionable dating choices, you could just take a break from dating altogether."

He frowns. "A break?"

"Yeah. Stop looking and actually figure out what you want. Maybe the problem isn't them. Maybe it's you." I give him a playful smirk to soften the blow, but the words land more heavily than I expected.

Maybe because I've been thinking about this myself.

About all the times I rushed into something just to feel less alone. About how easy it is to keep blaming the other person when you haven't really looked inward.

He exhales, shaking his head. "Gee thanks."

I shrug. "Hey, I'm just saying, maybe if you quit chasing after the wrong women, the right one might actually have a chance to find you."

He rolls his eyes, but his silence tells me that he's wondering if I have a point.

Since it's possible I've offended him by basically saying he's the problem, I decide to be a little bit vulnerable. "I've actually been on a boy ban for a while now. It's allowed me to sort of figure myself out."

"I'll consider it. Thanks. And how do you know so much about all this?"

"A lot of therapy," I answer, probably too quickly. "You pick things up."

"Why have *you* had a lot of therapy?"

My mouth drops open. "Seriously? I'm a walking disaster. Don't try to tell me you haven't noticed." I give him a hard look, and Hayes doesn't argue. "Anyway, it starts to get to a person."

He looks at me, his gaze softening, and the way his eyes linger on mine seems to communicate something that even words can't say. It's like he sees beyond all the layers I hide behind, sees not just the girl sitting in front of him but the strength and the vulnerability that I guard so fiercely. The way that I want to be the best version of myself, but something—namely me—holds me back.

"Anyways . . ." I draw out the word, needing to break whatever weird connection this is. "We should go. I promised Charles we'd have a Scrabble rematch when I got back."

"Sure. Of course," he says, blinking.

Chapter Thirteen

Let Your Freak Flag Fly

Frankie

Tessa calls me that night. "Why are you home? I figured you'd be out."

It's Friday night. I *should* be out. So naturally, I lie.

"I did a self-tanner. It's important that it develops under the right conditions." It's not a complete lie. I did put on self-tanner—yesterday. I'm home because I have nowhere else to be.

We talk for a few minutes more, but she has plans and needs to head out.

Charles is sleeping. And Hayes is out with Malachi. Who knows what they're up to. They could be picking up women, for all I know.

Meanwhile, I'm home in my pajamas and it's not even nine. I haven't had an adult conversation since Hayes and I called a truce and shared a happy hour cocktail. I can't sit around the house every night. Charles is often in bed by 7:30, and I'm more of a night owl. I'll go insane if I don't get some human interaction.

That's it. I've decided. I'm going to set up a profile on one of those dating apps. I could meet someone and have a fling. Maybe a cute local.

I grab my laptop and begin typing. The key is going to be sounding normal. Bland. Vanilla. Maybe that will attract a nice, normal guy. Tessa seems to think I'm a walking billboard for red flags.

I start typing, and it's much harder than I thought to write an engaging bio. And who am I kidding? I'm *not* normal.

I delete everything I've written and open a new window.

> ChatGPT write me a dating profile.

I click enter and stare hard at the screen.

The dating profile it comes up with is even worse! I might be vanilla, but I ain't *that* vanilla.

I close out of ChatGPT and make up my own, letting my creativity fly, because why not? Life's too short to be boring.

> Frankie: 30, currently globetrotting
> *Swipe right if you enjoy sarcasm, unsolicited snack recommendations, and watching me aggressively parallel park while laughing hysterically.*
>
> Location: Somewhere between *thriving* and *needing a nap.*
>
> Special Skills:
> - Can turn any situation into a sitcom episode.
> - Once won an argument with a seagull (he started it).
> - Expert at pretending I know things about wine.
>
> Red Flags:
> - Will absolutely judge your taste in gas station snacks.
> - Might refer to you as "buddy" just to keep you on your toes.
> - Laughs at my own jokes (because someone has to).

Looking for: Someone who won't question my choice in snack foods. Bonus points if you can assemble IKEA furniture *without* crying.

Let's make questionable life choices together!

Satisfied with myself, I post it to the site Tessa is always telling me about. The one where women get to make the first move. Once my profile is live, I begin sifting through the options.

Too old.

Too bald.

Too . . . political.

After searching for twenty long minutes, I find someone who looks promising. He's thirty-one and a surf instructor, and his profile picture is him carrying a fluffy apricot-colored dog while riding a skateboard . . . I mean bonus points for the multitasking alone. He also has really pretty blue eyes and sandy-colored hair.

I read over his bio with a discerning eye, searching for red flags in a way that I hope would make Tessa proud.

Ryder, 31

Professional wave chaser | Mediocre skateboarder | Certified Alpha Male

I spend my days teaching people how to surf and my nights wondering if my dog is proud of me. If you like sunset beach walks, questionable life advice, and spontaneous road trips to find the best fish tacos, we'll get along just fine.

Looking for someone who can keep up, and won't judge me for eating cereal straight from the box. Bonus points if you can name at least three types of clouds.

I cannot, in fact, name even one type of cloud, but I click on the message icon and type out something that I hope is cute and friendly-sounding, since according to Tessa I am *monumentally* bad at this.

Frankie:

Okay, first of all, I'm *very* impressed by your multitasking skills—carrying a dog *and* riding a skateboard? That's a whole new level of impressive. Are you secretly training for the "World's Coolest Human" competition, or is this just your everyday thing?

(Also, is the dog in charge or are you the one calling the shots here?)

Looking forward to your answer, pro skateboarder/dog whisperer.

Ryder:

Haha, you caught me! I *am* training for the "World's Coolest Human" competition. It's a tough field, but I'm in the running for *most likely to have a dog who's cuter than me*.

As for the dog . . . yeah, she's definitely the one in charge. I'm basically just her personal chauffeur. But hey, I get a good workout in, so it's a win-win.

How about you? Any hidden talents, or are you just here to judge people's snack choices and laugh at bad puns?

Okay so we're off to a promising start. Why is Tessa always warning me away from dating apps? This is actually kinda fun.

I recall a conversation we once had. She all but scolded me.

"Sweetie. I've spent so much time on that site, they made me a mod."

"Oh good, then give me all your best tips," I demanded.

"The differences in our dating pool are vast. Women are flagged for having included too much personally identifying info—like them in a uniform in front of the restaurant where they work. Guys are being flagged for ahem . . . other pics."

"Like?" I prompted.

"I've seen things, baby girl, let's leave it at that."

"Tell me. Quit being weird."

She did tell me, and I've never been the same. Ick! But so far, Ryder hasn't assaulted me with any photos of his genitalia, so that's a plus. *See?* I can do the whole dating thing. Look at me, functioning like a normal human.

I roll up my sleeves and get to work coming up with a witty reply.

Frankie:

Well, you and your tiny, four-legged boss are truly redefining *transportation efficiency*. Next up: surfing while carrying groceries?

As for hidden talents . . . I have an *elite* ability to trip over absolutely nothing, I can recite the entire menu of my favorite taco truck from memory, and I once won a staring contest with a cat. (He blinked first. It was a proud moment.)

Now, tell me the truth—does your dog approve of your dating choices? Because I feel like she has *very* high standards.

I almost want to brag about my ability to come up with witty Wi-Fi names, but Hayes didn't seem impressed, so I opt to leave that out.

Ryder:

Oh, Sunny would love you, I'm sure. She likes everyone. Taco truck, huh? That's impressive. If you're up for it, there's a killer beach bar that has a great happy hour. Live music and everything. You up for? Tomorrow maybe?

And just like that, I have a date tomorrow.

Chapter Fourteen

Out of Sight, Not Out of Mind

Hayes

I barely look up from my laptop as Charles greets Francesca the following morning. "Someone's in a good mood today," he says, folding his copy of *The Wall Street Journal* to watch her as she moves around the kitchen, humming.

She's standing by the espresso machine, grinning as she adds sugar to her coffee. "What? Am I not allowed to be cheerful?"

"I didn't say that. It's just noticeable for someone who's self-professed 'not a morning person,'" Charles says, shooting me a look like he expects me to chime in. I don't. Instead, I click aggressively at my keyboard, though I have no idea what I'm even typing anymore. Something about her energy is irritating today. Too bright. Too . . . distracting.

"Fine, if you must know, I have a date tonight." She turns, her face practically glowing with excitement. "His name's Ryder. And he's a surf instructor."

My jaw tightens. Ryder. Even the name annoys me. I can already picture the guy—sun-bleached hair, that lazy, easygoing confidence, the kind of guy who calls everyone "dude" and never wears shoes.

Charles lets out a low laugh. "Got it. Well, you deserve to have a little fun."

"Thanks. He seems really cool."

Cool. Right. I clench my fists under the table, irritation prickling at the edges of my mind. I have no reason to care who Francesca goes out with. None at all. It's not like I pay attention to the way she smiles or how her laugh has this ridiculous way of making a room warmer. It definitely isn't that I have, on more than one occasion, caught myself looking at her when I thought no one would notice.

And yet, here I am, annoyed as hell over the fact that she is happy. That makes no damn sense.

"So, where's he taking you?"

"Hmm. Oh, some beach bar. Low Tide or something, I think."

The Low Tide Lounge. I know it well. It isn't what I'd call a first-date kind of place, but whatever.

She takes her coffee and turns toward the door. "I'm going to sit on the lanai."

Maybe things between us are weird ever since our happy hour yesterday. I kind of stared at her in awe. She's dealt with so much and has basically zero family. Yet, she's still cheerful. A glass-half-full kind of person, even though she has no reason to be.

Malachi rounds the corner and enters the kitchen. "Last night in paradise. Should we go out?"

I nod absently. I forgot he's leaving in the morning. It seems Francesca has snatched all my focus. It's irritating.

~

Later that afternoon, Francesca wanders from her bedroom, wearing an oversize bathrobe—her facial expression one of outright horror. "I have an enormous pimple."

I glance up from my laptop. "Tragic. How will we go on?"

It takes me a second to even find it—a tiny pink bump on her chin—but judging by her expression, we need to call in a crisis team.

"It's gross, right?"

I force a frown. "It's brutal. I can barely look at you. You should probably cancel your date."

She lets out a deep, cathartic exhale. "No, you know what? I'm not canceling. First, I've solved much bigger problems than this. Second, I'm nothing if not crafty. When my mom told me we didn't have the money for a Barbie Dreamhouse, I solved that problem with cardboard, tape, and finger paint. I've got this." She hums to herself, tapping her chin. "An ice cube and extra concealer, that's all I need."

I blink. Her ingenuity is admirable.

She marches off with the resolve of someone about to perform surgery—not hide a zit.

I try to focus on the spreadsheet on my laptop, but I'm too distracted.

Why did I hurt her feelings and tell her she looked gross? Maybe because I'm annoyed about her date with some surf hippie. I know nothing about him, but I already know he's not good enough for her.

She's supposed to be here, helping my uncle, not out flirting with randos.

So later, when I catch up with Malachi, I say to him, "It's your last night here, let's go out."

My delivery could have used some finesse. It's less of an invitation and more of an order, but Malachi doesn't seem to notice.

"Sure," he says. "Where to?"

"The Low Tide Lounge."

When we walk inside thirty minutes later, I do a double take when I spot Francesca.

She's wearing a red mini dress that skims along her curves in a way that makes my mouth water. She looks like a piece of candy that I desperately want to bite into.

Where the hell did that thought come from?

This is Francesca. Who eats processed garbage and drives me absolutely bonkers.

I shake the thought away. I must be losing it.

"Is that *Frankie*?" Malachi asks, eyes wide and locked on to where she's leaning against the bar.

I don't mean to look, but it's impossible *not* to.

The dress is red—*bright* red—like she wore it specifically to be noticed. And it's not just the color. It's the way it fits, hugging curves I've somehow never paid this much attention to before. The smooth line of her waist, the way the fabric clings to the curve of her hips. It's difficult to keep my eyes off her.

Her date has shaggy, sun-bleached hair, blue eyes, and an easygoing grin that probably lets him get away with *way* too much.

He's leaning against the bar, one forearm resting casually on the counter as he chats with Francesca and the bartender. His other hand fidgets with a cocktail napkin, absentminded, like he's not good at standing still. He laughs at something—a loose, effortless sound—and tosses back a sip of his drink like he has *nowhere* to be and *all* the time in the world to enjoy it.

It's annoying, really. Watching Ryder like some kind of case study in laid-back, surfer-bro charisma.

Ridiculous.

"Let's get a drink," I grumble.

Malachi leads the way to a table that's tucked into the farthest back corner of the bar and is perfect for observing from a safe distance.

Francesca is explaining something to her date with a lot of laughter and exaggerated hand gestures.

Malachi seems transfixed.

"You're staring," I point out.

He shrugs. "I've never seen her look so . . . put together."

I clench my jaw and look away, irritated with myself. It's *Francesca.* The same woman who gives me grief at every turn and has an entire section of her brain devoted to ranking gas station snacks.

Malachi drums his fingers on the table, eyes flicking to mine. "Serious question—if you had to pick one theme song that plays every time you walk into a room, what is it? And before you say something boring, just know mine is 'Return of the Mack.'"

"What?" I blink at him. My gaze betrays me again, dragging back over to her just as she leans over the bar to grab a cocktail napkin, the dress stretching *just* enough—

I exhale sharply and down the rest of my drink.

This is a problem.

I signal our server for another drink since mine seems to have disappeared.

Thankfully, our server appears at just the right moment, and after we order another round, Malachi does his best to steer the conversation away from Francesca. And I've never been more grateful. Soon though, he catches me staring again.

"I love humans with golden retriever energy." He chuckles.

I glare at him. "This conversation would be even better if I knew what you were talking about."

"Frankie. She's fun and adventurous. And don't try and tell me you haven't noticed how cute she is."

"Stop. She's not cute, she's ridiculous," I all but snap at him.

"She could be good for you," he muses, tapping his chin.

I rub at my temples, where a sudden headache is forming.

He gives me a look, grinning like he's got a secret. "You have a crush on this girl."

"I'm not going to answer that."

"So that's a yes."

"Why are you still talking?" I snap.

"If you don't stop scowling at them like that, you're going to age yourself prematurely."

"Will you stop? I'm not scowling. My face still moves because I haven't had any of that toxin you insist on injecting into yours."

Malachi flings a straw across the table that hits me in the chest. "It's called Botox, and you need it."

"Whatever."

Chapter Fifteen

Break Out of Your Comfort Zone

Frankie

Ryder is much shorter than I anticipated, but he's just as cute as his photos.

"Are you new here? I haven't seen you around" is the first question he asks, after greeting me with a friendly hug.

Since I didn't know if he was referring to the island or the dating-app scene, I settled for a simple "Yes."

From there, things were a little iffy. The conversation was difficult to come by—like pushing a boulder uphill. I asked about his work—he was currently unemployed—and about his family—he merely said they live in Ohio. His one-word answers weren't helping.

Behind the screens of our phone, we were magic. In person, we have less to say. Even if the vibes are slightly off, I've assured myself that tonight will be more fun if I just roll with it.

So that's what I do. In typical Frankie fashion, I laugh and tell him about Tessa and Charles, and generally work to keep the conversation flowing.

When we finally get our drink order, I lift my glass in a toast. "To whoever invented stretchy pants—your contribution to society will never be forgotten."

Ryder's eyes crinkle, and he gives a weak chuckle.

After we finish our drink, Ryder gets strangely fidgety. "Are you good?"

I figured we'd stay awhile, make an evening of it. But hey, I'm not going to force it if he's not. "I guess so."

I inhale and try not to feel let down. But something isn't adding up . . .

One second, we're finishing our drinks, Ryder laughing at something stupid I said, looking every bit like a guy without a care in the world. The next, he's standing up, clapping a hand on my back like we've got *places to be*.

"All right, let's bounce," he says, already steering me toward the exit.

I blink. "Uh. The check?"

"Don't worry about it," he says, flashing that effortless grin. "I know the system."

I don't know what that means. But I do know the check is still sitting there, untouched, and that Ryder is moving *very quickly* for a guy who has been acting like time doesn't exist.

We step outside, and he stretches his arms over his head like a man *free* of responsibility. Meanwhile, my brain is doing urgent calculations.

Did he leave cash while I wasn't looking? Did he start a tab? Did I just unknowingly become an *accomplice* in a dine-and-dash?

Oh God. I think I did.

I stop in my tracks. "Wait. Did we—"

"You hungry?" he interrupts, like we didn't just flee the scene of a financial crime. "There's a taco truck down the street."

I stare at him. He grins like this is just another night, just another casual stroll through life, where money is optional and bartenders don't need to get paid.

I pinch the bridge of my nose and sigh. "Great. Now I have to come back in the morning and pay our bill."

Ryder claps a hand over his heart, mock wounded. "Frankie, Frankie. Where's the trust?"

“Somewhere back at the bar, along with our tab.” I jerk my thumb toward the bar.

He just shrugs. “I’m a little low on cheddar right now, but it’s fine. I’ll get them back next time. I’m sure it all evens out in the end.”

That’s not how this works. That’s not how any of this works.

“So that’s a no to the taco truck?” He gives me a hopeful look.

“It’s a no to the taco truck.” It’s a sentence I never anticipated needing to say.

He flashes me a peace sign and strolls away without a care in the world.

I make it back home a short time later, and unsurprisingly, Charles is asleep. I have no idea where Hayes and Malachi are. I decide emergency carbo-loading is in order. First, I change out of my dress, opting for leggings and an oversize T-shirt.

Once I’m cozy, I raid the pantry and grab anything that looks good—FRITOS and canned bean dip, Swedish Fish and a bag of trail mix that I don’t remember buying. Then I begin filling the void, one chip at a time. What? It’s a totally reasonable coping mechanism.

From the foyer, I hear the front door open and then close, then male voices. Hayes and Malachi are home, it seems. They must have also called it an early night. It’s not even nine.

Footsteps move closer, and Hayes appears in the kitchen doorway. He seems surprised to see me here.

“You’re home.” His tone isn’t judgmental, and for that I’m grateful. I’m not exactly feeling the best about myself right now.

“We decided to call it a night.” I wash my hands at the sink and grab a dish towel.

“Gotcha.” He stands there, sort of staring at me in an odd way.

“Anyways, I skipped dinner, and I’m hungry.” I don’t know why I feel the need to explain my snack-attack. I don’t owe him an explanation.

But he's still just standing there, watching me.

"I could eat," he says, pocketing his phone. "Do you want me to make you something? A sandwich or an omelet or something?"

"Um . . . sure?" Hayes being nice to me is a new development that my brain is struggling to comprehend.

He must sense my hesitation, because he's still just watching me. "Unless you prefer to be alone?"

I shake my head. "Not at all."

"Great. Omelets? I think we have some bacon leftover from breakfast . . ."

"That sounds great, actually." At the mention of real food, my stomach perks up in interest.

Hayes begins looting the fridge for ingredients. He finds a block of cheddar cheese and a bunch of green onions, along with butter, milk, and a carton of eggs.

I heft myself up onto the counter to watch while he heats a pat of butter in a sauté pan. "I love that you cook. I can't even crack an egg."

"Sure you can. Here, try it."

I slide down from the counter, and Hayes places a small bowl for me on the counter, then he hands me an egg.

I let out a sigh. "You asked for it." *Here goes nothin'* . . .

I crack the shell against the side of the bowl, and several things happen at once.

The yolk lands on the floor between our feet, and somehow the egg white ends up on his shirt. The only thing in the bowl is the cracked eggshell.

"Told ya."

"Damn. Okay, fair. You were right. You suck at this. Let me handle it."

I step aside. "Be my guest. Feed me."

"Is that why you live on gas station snacks?" He smirks like he's got me figured out.

I shake my head. "No, I just genuinely love junk food."

"Fair enough."

While Hayes begins cooking, I clean up said junk food, because despite his chill attitude, I'm pretty sure he's still secretly judging me. He side-eyed the canned bean dip pretty hard, though to be honest, it does look weird. Tastes *amazing*, but yeah, it looks weird.

While he works, I'm transfixed. There's just something about a man who's volunteered to cook for you. Even if that man is *Hayes*.

He moves around the kitchen with the kind of efficiency that shouldn't be attractive but *is*. Sleeves rolled up, his hair slightly mussed, he tilts the pan, giving it a quick flick of his wrist, and the omelet folds over perfectly.

I prop my chin on my hand. "You know, this is almost disorienting. You being . . . nice."

"I can take it back."

"No, no—by all means, keep the omelet coming."

He smirks but doesn't argue, sliding the food onto a plate before setting it in front of me. "So. How was your date?"

I stab my fork into the eggs, debating how honest I want to be.

"Let's just say, if I never go out again with a guy who describes himself as an 'alpha' in his dating profile, it'll still be too soon."

Hayes exhales through his nose. It's dangerously close to a laugh. "Noted." He plates an omelet for himself and looks over at me. "And for the record, if a guy has to tell you he's an alpha, he's definitely not one."

"Seems like a low bar for self-awareness."

"You'd think. And yet."

I take a bite, chewing thoughtfully. It's . . . annoyingly good. The bacon is perfectly crisp, the cheddar rich and melty.

Of course Hayes would nail something as deceptively simple as an omelet.

I glance up, expecting smugness, but he's just leaning against the counter, watching me with that unreadable expression.

And for once, the silence between us doesn't feel like a contest.

"You know, this is weird," I say.

He lifts a brow. "What is?"

"Us. Not fighting. I'm not saying I miss the bickering, but . . . it's kind of our thing."

He tilts his head. "Maybe we just needed a ceasefire."

I poke at my omelet. "Or maybe we're too tired to keep our knives out."

His lips twitch like he wants to argue, but instead, he just nods. "Maybe."

And weirdly, that feels like progress.

Out here, I have no one. And sometimes, you just need a friend. Someone to talk to about a bad date. Someone to eat late-night eggs with.

I guess Hayes will do.

Our friendship might be a bit . . . bumpy.

But for now, it's a road worth traveling.

When we're finished and he's loaded our plates into the dishwasher, he turns to me.

"I have a confession to make."

We're only a foot apart now, and he's towering over me—his jawline distractingly chiseled, hair tousled in a way that feels unfair to the rest of humanity. I force myself not to notice.

"I was there . . . at the Low Tide Lounge."

I blink. "You were spying on me?"

"Not spying. Just . . . observing."

"Then you must've noticed how painfully awkward it got. How abruptly it ended."

He shakes his head. "When you left together, I figured you were going home with him."

Now I'm really blinking. "I'm not that kind of girl, Hayes."

The words come out soft, a little breathy—and I instantly regret how flirty they sound. But it's too late. The air has shifted.

He steps closer. Not much, just enough.

His hand comes up, brushing a loose strand of hair behind my ear, and then he lingers—his fingers trailing lightly down my cheek, like he doesn't want to stop touching me. "You were too good for him." His voice is low. Rough around the edges.

A breath escapes me. Slow. Unsteady.

It does nothing to calm the wild thrum in my chest.

For a second, I think he might kiss me. And worse—I think I might let him.

I step back, murmur a quiet "Good night," and bolt from the kitchen on shaky legs.

Chapter Sixteen

Learn to Let Go of Control

Hayes

The following day, I drop Malachi off at the airport, knowing my own time in Hawaii is also quickly coming to a close. I fly out late tomorrow afternoon. Back to New York. I've worked while I've been here, sure, but there's a long list of things waiting for me back home.

As I drive back to the house, I catch myself replaying last night. The way Francesca sat on the counter—tired but slightly amused, like she hadn't completely given up on the night. Like being there, with me, wasn't the worst possible outcome.

It was . . . easy.

No sharp words. No power plays. Just quiet back-and-forth. And damn it if I don't find myself thinking—I wouldn't mind doing that again.

When I walk through the door, it's quiet, except for the low hum of the TV. I assume Frankie and my uncle are having a low-key night, and I debate whether to join them.

A thunderous fart rings out from the living room. I have no way of knowing if it was Charles or Francesca, but either way, I give it a few minutes to clear. I have my limits.

I take a breath, compose myself, and casually stroll in. "Hey."

"Shh," Francesca whispers, pointing toward Charles.

He's passed out in the recliner, mouth wide open. I really hope that noise came from him, because the alternative is a little too traumatizing to consider.

Francesca rises and gently removes his shoes, setting them beside his chair. It's oddly endearing, watching her fuss over him like that. He's been alone so long. I've never seen anyone care for him this way.

He never remarried. No kids of his own. It always struck me as a little sad.

But now? Now he has Francesca.

With each passing day, I find myself slipping deeper under whatever spell she's cast. Even my uncle is smitten.

Sure, she sits cross-legged in dining chairs and eats an entire bag of something called Zombie Fajita Takis without flinching. The smell alone sent me to the other side of the house.

But in a plot twist that would shock even Agatha Christie, Frankie's growing on me like an unwanted rash.

She's not the type of girl I was raised to expect. Nothing like the prim and proper girls I'm accustomed to from my prep school days. Not polished. Not Ivy League. She's just . . . real.

She's the kind of girl you spend a fun, forgettable night with in college.

Except . . . I don't see how you could possibly forget about a girl like Frankie.

The next morning, I wander into the kitchen for coffee and immediately catch the vibe—Charles and Francesca are mid-conversation and go quiet when I appear. They're huddled over the table, surrounded by a stack of travel guides.

I pour a mug of coffee and nod toward the books. "Are you planning your next escape?"

Charles nods. "I suggested the *Elysium*. Frankie suggested Las Vegas."

"Vegas?" I cock an eyebrow at her.

She bristles. "What? It's fun there, dang it."

"Oh yeah, nothing screams 'vacation' like dragging an eighty-two-year-old to Vegas."

Frankie sticks her tongue out. "There are shows. Restaurants. Lots to do, actually."

Charles shrugs. "Yes, but *Elysium* is . . . well, it's Elysium."

From the look on her face, Frankie has no idea what that means.

I crack a smile. "I'm headed out this afternoon. Just let me know where you end up."

Charles nods.

"Have a safe flight," Frankie says, stacking the guides.

I nod, but something twists in my chest.

I expected to leave Hawaii the same way I came—untouched, unmoved, counting the minutes until I could get back to a world that made sense.

Instead, I find myself searching for answers I don't have.

My bags are packed. My first-class ticket is booked. But for the first time in a long time . . . I'm not sure I want to go.

And that? That's the part that knocks the breath out of me.

~

Back home, I slide quickly into the usual routine: work, gym, the occasional dinner out.

Now, I've got Maddie for the weekend. She's cross-legged on the floor, brow furrowed in concentration as she lines up plastic horses in what appears to be some kind of epic standoff.

I don't ask. Last time I questioned the logic of her games, she gave me a full TED Talk on why unicorns would absolutely destroy medieval knights.

Instead, I lean back on the couch, arm slung over the backrest.

"What's the situation here? Should I be worried about a pony uprising?"

She rolls her eyes but grins. "No, Hayes. This is a rescue mission. The ponies are saving their friend from the evil king."

I nod, solemn. "High stakes."

She sighs. "Obviously."

She moves one of the horses forward, then glances up, her tone shifting.

"You were gone forever."

I exhale, raking a hand through my hair. "It wasn't that long."

She shrugs and twists a tiny unicorn between her fingers. "Long enough."

I don't know what to say to that. It's not like I was avoiding home. But I also wasn't racing back.

Still, sitting here now, watching her launch a magical battle with plastic ponies, something inside me settles.

I pick up a tiny knight and flip it over in my palm. "Think there's room for one more in this rescue mission?"

Her eyes light up. "Only if you don't make your guy annoying."

"No promises."

She giggles, shaking her head.

And just like that, I realize—I missed this. I missed her.

And maybe, just maybe, I'm done keeping the things that matter at arm's length.

Chapter Seventeen

Make the Most of It

Frankie

"Are you sure you're feeling okay?" I ask Charles for the third time.

He looks more tired than usual, a little pale around the edges. Though to be fair, I'm probably not winning any beauty contests either.

We flew from JFK to CDG—that's New York to Paris, for the uninitiated—on an overnight flight. And we are now sitting in the charming hotel lobby, picking through the complimentary continental breakfast.

It's one of the many things I've come to appreciate about Charles. You'd think he'd be more snooty for a billionaire, but he's perfectly content with a free breakfast spread. And obviously, so am I. Why wander the streets in search of a boulangerie when there are perfectly good croissants downstairs?

He waves off my concern. "Not you too."

"Just asking." I smile and take a sip of my café au lait—just coffee with milk, but it sounds far more romantic in French. It's also out-of-this-world good. And my pain au chocolat croissant is so flaky and delicate, it basically evaporates on my tongue.

"I'm doing just fine," Charles says, patting my hand.

The quiet hum of morning conversation blends with the soft clink of porcelain cups. The boutique hotel lobby is elegant, downright cinematic. Sunlight filters through tall, arched windows, casting a golden glow over the black-and-white checkered marble floors. Deep emerald velvet chairs surround gold-trimmed round tables, each topped with a single fresh flower in a delicate vase. The air smells like espresso and warm pastries. I've been here all of a few hours, and I already love Paris.

"Did you get today's *Wordle*?" he asks, glancing toward my phone.

I'm mid-text to Tessa, who I saw once for a wine-and-wedge after returning from Hawaii. Now she's apparently in crisis mode.

Tessa: I need you to remain calm.

Frankie: That's never going to happen, but continue.

"I haven't played yet, so don't spoil it for me, Charlie boy." I grin.

"I'm stuck on the last guess. There's a *P* and a *T*, that's all I've got."

"La la la," I say, sticking my fingers in my ears. "I can't hear you."

He frowns, then laughs, shaking his head. I go back to texting.

Tessa: I may or may not be dating a man who unironically calls himself "Big D."

I nearly choke.

Frankie: . . . Please tell me that's just a dumb nickname.

Tessa: His actual name is Darren.

Frankie: Oh, thank God. For a second, I thought you were dating a walking meme.

Tessa: Well, I haven't ruled that out yet.

Frankie: How did this happen? Why did this happen? Is this a cry for help?

Tessa: He's hot. He has a motorcycle. He makes me laugh. And he once saved a duck from a storm drain.

Frankie: Damn it. That's distressingly charming.

Tessa: I KNOW. This is why I texted you. Am I being delusional, or is this fate?

Frankie: Honestly? Fate. Or a very well-orchestrated mistake. Either way, I support the chaos.

Tessa: That's why you're my best friend.

Frankie: Right back atcha, girly.

Tessa: So, where are you these days? France, right?

I glance up. Charles is still frowning at his phone. "Pitch? Party? Patio?" I offer.

He shakes his head. "It doesn't start with a P. It's the third letter."

I chew my lip. "I'll keep noodling."

Frankie: Yes, we're in Paris for a few days, then heading to Nice. I think we leave from Antibes?

Tessa: Oh la la, so fancy. Have a blast. Send pictures.

Frankie: Will do.

"Input!" I blurt out.

A server in a crisp white shirt shoots me a look.

Sorry, I mouth, realizing I don't know the French word for "apologies." I'd studied the basics: Bonjour. Merci. S'il vous plaît. Fromage.

"That's it," Charles says, typing the word with a grin.

"Happy to be of service."

"So what would you like to do today?" he asks.

I shrug. "Something touristy? Or is that totally boring for you?"

He told me on the flight that he's been to Paris more times than he can count. I worried that meant he'd reject doing the touristy things like the Eiffel Tower—which is at the top of my bucket list.

"I'd be happy to show you some of my favorite spots," he says with a warm smile. And, not going to lie, that smile makes me irrationally happy. This trip? Kind of a once-in-a-lifetime thing for me.

"What are some of your favorites?"

"Montmartre. I can't do all the steps, but you could explore the area, visit Sacré-Cœur. We could get our portraits sketched by a local street artist. We'll definitely see the Eiffel Tower, though I'd skip the observation decks. The view's better from the Arc de Triomphe anyway."

I nod, excited. "What about the *Mona Lisa*?"

He removes his glasses, setting them on the table. "We can do the Louvre. I won't last long walking around, but we could see the *Mona Lisa*, maybe a few other pieces."

I've read about so many spots—the Catacombs, the Panthéon, Notre-Dame—but I know we won't hit them all. Still, the day already feels wide open with possibility. And best of all, Hayes isn't here to annoy me.

Winning.

Chapter Eighteen

One Step at a Time

Frankie

I have to admit, Antibes is stupidly beautiful.

The kind of beautiful that makes you question your entire life's trajectory—like, maybe I should have gone into *art dealing* or *diamond smuggling* or whatever it is rich people do to afford places like this. The air smells like salt and sun-warmed stone, and the buildings lining the harbor are straight out of a watercolor painting.

After a few fun-filled days in Paris, Charles and I jetted off to the Cote d'Azur—the South of France.

It's apparently a playground for the rich and famous. My research revealed that the likes of Leonardo DiCaprio, the Beckhams, and Beyoncé and Jay-Z had all vacationed here.

All this time when Charles was telling me about this trip, and that we'd be spending time on *Elysium*, I thought it was a place. Maybe some fancy private island off the coast of Spain or something. I had no idea it was the name of his yacht.

When I googled it, I discovered that in ancient Greek mythology, Elysium was a paradise for gods.

Still, when we arrive at the marina, I'm unprepared for the stunning marvel before me.

This isn't a yacht, it's a floating, multistory mansion that could probably survive the apocalypse.

"Charles," I mutter, staring up at the gleaming white vessel. "This thing has a helipad."

He barely glances up from his phone. "Mmm."

I narrow my eyes. "Are we expecting someone to drop in via *helicopter*?"

"No, but it's nice to have options."

I want to argue that *normal* people's options are, like, economy vs. extra legroom, not *which airborne vehicle should I descend from today?* But before I can, a sharply dressed man in a crisp white uniform approaches.

"Welcome aboard *Elysium*," he says, flashing the polished smile of a man who has *never* been overwhelmed by an eight-figure boat. His accent is hard to place. European, though. "I'm Captain Laurent. I trust your journey was smooth?"

Before I can answer, Charles says, "Lovely, thank you."

"Allow me to introduce Colette, miss," Captain Laurent continues, gesturing to a petite brunette with effortless grace and a clipboard that suggests she means business. "She's our chief stewardess and will ensure your stay is exceptional."

Colette beams. "Welcome! If there's anything you need, just let me know." She's very pretty, and I'm momentarily distracted by how porcelain her skin is.

A guest services specialist named Melisse had contacted me ahead of our departure to arrange for the provisions we wanted on board, which were apparently groceries. *Provisions* sounds so pretentious. I had to tell her about my allergies and preferences. She already knew Charles's favorites, but I made sure to remind her about his love for liverwurst.

But other than that, I feel a little clueless about how this whole thing works. Charles only mentioned that we'd be visiting different ports and to have my passport on board with me.

"Uh, yeah, quick question." I glance between them. "Where exactly do *I* stay? Do I get, like . . . a bunk bed situation, or are we talking a *Titanic*-style *steerage* scenario?"

Colette's eyes widen slightly. "You . . . have a full suite, Miss Francesca."

Charles sighs. "Frankie, it's a yacht, not a *hostel*."

"My bad," I deadpan. "I'm just adjusting to the concept of a floating five-star hotel."

Colette laughs politely, but the captain is clearly debating whether or not I'm a liability.

"Well, welcome aboard and feel free to explore the vessel," he says diplomatically. "Dinner will be served on the aft deck at sunset."

"Sounds great," Charles replies.

"Wait," I interrupt. "Do we need to, like . . . *help* with anything?"

Now Colette looks genuinely alarmed. "Help?"

"Yeah, you know, hoist sails? Swab the decks? Batten down hatches?" I wave vaguely. "Nautical things."

Captain Laurent clears his throat. "*Elysium* is fully crewed. We don't have sails since it's a motor yacht. And you won't need to, uh . . . batten anything."

Charles pinches the bridge of his nose. "Frankie, for God's sake."

I shrug. "Just checking."

The captain wisely decides to move on. "Well, then, enjoy your time aboard *Elysium*. We hope to depart in a day or two, and until then, make yourself comfortable. We're glad to have you aboard again, sir."

As Charles steps onto the yacht like he was *born* for this, I take one last look at the impossibly blue water and the kind of luxury I will *never* be used to.

Then I square my shoulders and board the yacht—mentally promising myself I won't fall overboard or, worse, make an absolute spectacle of myself.

Probably.

~

My guest cabin is dreamy—plush bedding, buttery-soft linens, and a window with a view so perfect it almost looks fake. There's a private en suite bathroom with gold fixtures, a rainfall shower, and towels that feel like they were spun from actual clouds. Everything smells like lavender and luxury.

I wander from my cabin, strolling along the deck toward the front of the vessel.

There are names for things I'll probably never get used to. The kitchen is the galley. The balcony is an aft deck. The mess is part of the crew quarters.

There's also the poop deck and the flybridge, which sound made up but aren't.

It's more than I need. Way more than I'm used to.

And for a second, I wonder—not for the first time—what exactly I'm doing here.

In addition to meeting Captain Laurent and Colette, I've been introduced to several other crew members. An engineer. Someone called a stew. A couple of deckhands. And a private chef.

It's dizzying, watching them all move about the yacht with purpose and precision—like they belong here.

I'm still figuring out if I do.

We won't depart from our slip in the marina for a couple more days because, apparently, we're still waiting for one more member of our crew who got held up in immigration.

I lean against the railing, the salty breeze cooling my skin as the sun melts into the horizon. The stone walls of the city darken into shadow as lights come on in the old town above them—forming the kind of view people write poetry about. Or, I don't know, put on their vision boards. But instead of feeling inspired, all I can think about is how I feel like I don't belong here. Not really.

Olivia said something similar to me back in Hawaii, noticing how out of place I was. I reveled in putting her in her place then, even if I'd been left with remnants of doubt circling in my head.

I stuck my foot in my mouth with Laurent and Colette, and let's be honest, I doubt it will be the last time.

Though this isn't really about Laurent and Colette—it's about me. Is this really what I'm supposed to be doing with my life? Should I pack it up and head back to Jersey and find a real job?

I never expected to feel so unsettled vacationing in the French Riviera, but here we are.

Charles steps up beside me, setting his drink down with a quiet clink. "Beautiful, isn't it?"

I nod.

He turns to me, probably not used to me being so quiet and withdrawn. "Are you doing okay?"

"Honestly?" I squint at him.

"Always," he assures me.

"I don't know. I feel like I keep waiting for someone to tap me on the shoulder and tell me I don't belong here. That I took a wrong turn and ended up in the wrong life."

"Is this about earlier?"

Even the perpetually composed Charles seemed somewhat embarrassed by my comments.

"Maybe."

"You know, you sell yourself short."

A laugh escapes me—quiet and a little shaky. "You say that like it's a bad thing. I prefer to think of it as being realistic."

He side-eyes me. "No, it's self-sabotage. There's a difference. Do you think I had everything all figured out on day one?"

I give him a hard look. "Of course. You're *you*."

Charles laughs. "Fair point. But I promise you, there have been times when I don't know what I'm doing either. I just decided to show up anyway. Confidence isn't something you wait for—it's something you build by doing. By showing up, even when you feel like an impostor."

I scoff. "Easier said than done."

"Then fake it. Walk in like you own the place, even if inside, you're still figuring out where the bathroom is."

"So . . . just lie to myself?"

"No. Borrow confidence from your future self. The version of you who already knows she belongs. You're her. You just haven't caught up yet."

The words hit like a flick to the forehead—annoying and impossible to ignore. I grip the railing and release a slow exhale.

Charles shifts, leaning one elbow on the railing. "All I'm saying is don't discount yourself."

"I'm not," I say quickly. I know I'm pretty great, I just don't know if I'm great in this role or with these kinds of people.

"Aren't you, though? You don't think you deserve to be in certain rooms, so you keep yourself out of them. You don't think you're good enough for certain people, so you keep your distance."

My grip tightens around the railing. I don't like where this is going. Mostly because he's not wrong.

"Okay, Dr. Phil," I say, forcing a smirk to disarm him. "And what exactly am I supposed to do? Just wake up one morning and decide I'm the main character of my life?"

Charles grins. "Yes."

I roll my eyes, but his words stick like gum on the bottom of my shoe. I've spent so much time keeping my head down, playing it safe, assuming that people like me—people who fumble through life, who aren't all put together—don't get to be the ones who *win*. But what if I've been wrong?

"I'm me, Charles. I'm probably still going to make an ass of myself sometimes." The words are quieter than I mean them to be.

Charles doesn't hesitate. "Yeah, you'll have some mess-ups from time to time, that's life. And then you try again."

I'm quiet for a moment, then smirk again. "Okay, fine. But if I get called out, I'm blaming you."

Charles grins. "Deal. But you won't. Because the moment you start believing in yourself, the world follows suit." He nudges my shoulder. "And you have no idea how much I'm looking forward to watching you flourish, Frankie. The world has no clue what's coming."

I exhale, watching the last sliver of sun slip beneath the water.

What if he's right?

Chapter Nineteen

Embrace the Chaos

Frankie

Our second evening on board, and I'm halfway through my first glass of wine, watching the sky melt into soft purples and pinks over the harbor, when I hear footsteps on the deck behind me. I assume it's Charles, or maybe a member of the crew. But when I turn, I don't see Charles.

I see Hayes.

I blink, convinced the wine is playing tricks on me. But no, it's definitely him, standing on the deck of this ridiculous yacht like he *belongs* here. Which, of course, he does. He's probably been sailing on superyachts since birth, while I only recently learned that they don't have hatches to batten.

Hayes takes a slow glance around, his expression unreadable. He looks irritatingly good—pressed linen shirt, sleeves rolled up just enough to show his strong forearms, hair perfectly tousled like the sea breeze personally styled it for him. Meanwhile, I'm barefoot, slightly tipsy, and still trying to comprehend why he's here.

"You've got to be kidding me," I mutter, setting my wine down before I accidentally spill it all over the very expensive teak deck.

Hayes's eyes flick to me. "Nice to see you, too, Francesca."

I cross my arms. "Not that I'm not *thrilled* to see you, but why are you here?"

Charles, who has suddenly materialized beside me, answers for him. "I invited him."

I snap my head toward Charles. "You *what*?"

Charles sighs like I'm being unreasonable. "Hayes was in Nice for business, and I thought, why not extend an invitation? I assumed you wouldn't mind."

I turn back to Hayes. "And you *accepted*?"

Hayes shrugs. "Free dinner."

I narrow my eyes. "You're a billionaire."

He smirks. "Doesn't mean I turn down a good meal."

I groan and rub my temples. "Of course not."

Charles pats my shoulder in an infuriatingly paternal way. "Be nice, Frankie." Then he turns to Hayes. "We're having dinner on the aft deck. You'll love it."

Hayes nods like this is all perfectly normal, like we were all *expecting* him, and I'm the only one who finds this turn of events completely *insane*.

I exhale sharply, grab my wine, and take a long sip. It's going to be a *very* long dinner.

Charles shows Hayes around, and together they geek out over some smart control panel. He must sense my mood, because he leans close and whispers near my ear, "Don't worry, I'm not staying, I just came to see you off since I was in the area."

He just happened to be in France? I don't pry, but that seems unlikely. The truce we called in Hawaii seems a million miles ago, and all I feel now is that he's checking up on me again—here to make sure I don't screw up.

Captain Laurent emerges and shakes Hayes's hand, and they exchange pleasantries before launching into a long conversation on the benefits of a twin-turbine engine vs. an inboard diesel.

I focus on my wine.

The sun has dipped below the horizon, casting a soft golden glow over the marina as we settle in for dinner on the aft deck. The table is set with flickering candles and polished silverware, the kind of setting that makes me feel like I should sit up straighter and pretend I know which wine pairs best with fish.

Hayes sits across from me, looking completely at ease, like dining on a yacht in the South of France is as routine as grabbing takeout. Charles, of course, is perfectly in his element. Meanwhile, I'm just hoping I don't accidentally knock over a crystal glass or burp or something.

The chef, a tall, wiry Frenchman named Luc, steps onto the deck with a serious expression, clasping his hands together like he's about to announce a royal decree.

"Çe soir," he begins, accent thick, "we start with seared scallops in saffron sauce, followed by wagyu steak sous vide with foie gras and truffles, and we finish with a dark chocolate tarte with raspberry coulis. Bon appétit." Our plates are set before us, and he waltzes away.

One bite, and I let out a long moan.

"I don't even know like half the words he just said, but one thing is for certain—I need to marry a chef."

Charles smiles, watching me with a look of amusement.

"How are you settling into the boat?" Hayes asks, directing the question to me.

"Good, I guess. It's just that they have all this staff here, what do they possibly need me for?"

He meets my eyes. "That staff takes care of the boat. You are there to take care of him." He looks at his uncle.

Right.

Duh.

"Noted," I say, nodding once and hoping my smile conveys a sense of confidence.

While we eat, the conversation flows easily—Charles steers discussions toward business, art, and a bunch of other things that make me wish I'd paid more attention in school.

We've talked a lot over the past few weeks, just the two of us, and I usually keep up pretty well. But tonight the topics—business, art, global whatever—start to blend into background noise.

Maybe I'm tired. Maybe I'm just distracted.

I poke at my food, half listening, until something shifts in the tone of Hayes's voice. It's quieter now, more thoughtful—like he's letting something slip he didn't mean to share.

"I just . . . I don't know what to do. I hate feeling helpless," he says, and I can hear the raw edge in his tone. He pushes his wineglass aside, his fingers gripping the stem.

I pause, staring at him. I lean forward a bit, unsure where this conversation is headed.

"About what?" Charles asks, frowning.

"It's my assistant, Greta. She's a single mom."

I remember meeting Greta when I went in for my interview. She was sweet and tried her best to make me feel at ease.

"She was just diagnosed with leukemia." His jaw tightens, and he pauses.

Wait. What's this? There's a vulnerable side to the one-dimensional Hayes?

He's still talking, though, his brows knitted together in concern. "I've already told her to take as much time off as she needs, but it's hard. She's not great at accepting help. I've promised her she'll always have her job, and I'm covering her medical bills." He pauses, cutting into his steak. His voice is steady, but his grip on the knife is a little tighter than necessary. "I just don't know what else to do."

I blink, feeling a rush of warmth. Hayes, the guy I've been annoyed with for weeks, the guy I've always pegged as self-absorbed, is plagued with concern, helplessness, and fear of not being able to do more. I'm caught off guard.

"That's . . . a lot," I say, almost stumbling over my words. "It's a kind offer."

"I don't want her to go through this alone," he interrupts, and there's a fierceness in his voice that surprises me. "She's been there for me, and I don't know what I'd do without her. I just wish I could do more."

Something in his voice tugs at me. It's strange, seeing this side of him—the part that isn't completely sure of himself. The part that isn't an unshakable force.

His eyes meet mine, full of an unfamiliar vulnerability.

I stare at him for a beat, unsure of how to respond, because I wasn't prepared for *this* side of him. This man who's been so guarded, so reserved in everything we've talked about. Now, suddenly, I feel like I'm seeing the real person underneath.

"You know," I say, setting down my fork, "for someone who acts like he has all the answers, you're actually just as clueless as the rest of us."

Hayes snorts. "That's supposed to be comforting?"

"A little."

He shakes his head, but there's something almost amused in his expression. Charles watches us like we're an experiment he's observing, sipping his wine in silence.

Then, just as the mood threatens to get too heavy, something *very* unfortunate happens.

Hayes reaches for his glass of water at the exact moment I shift my plate, and in a ridiculous chain reaction, the entire glass tips over—spilling straight into his lap.

For a beat, there's silence.

Then Charles, in the most unhelpful way possible, says, "Well, that's unfortunate."

Hayes jerks back, shaking ice water off his linen pants. "Geez, Frankie."

"I—oh my gosh," I sputter, slapping a napkin against his thigh in pure panic. "I didn't—"

"Stop *helping*," Hayes groans, snatching the napkin from me and dabbing at himself.

Charles, completely unbothered, watches this unfold like it's the best entertainment he's had all week. "This is wonderful. I'm so glad I invited you, Hayes."

And just like that, the whole night shifts. I start laughing—actual, *genuine* laughter—and before I know it, Charles joins in, and then, after a moment of reluctant defeat, Hayes lets out a deep chuckle too.

The three of us sit there, the tension from earlier dissolving into easy laughter, and for the first time all night, I don't feel out of place on this ridiculous yacht.

I just feel . . . like I'm exactly where I'm supposed to be. Which is probably crazy, but it's the truth.

Chapter Twenty

Roll with the Punches

Hayes

In the morning, I'm halfway through with my workout when Francesca wanders onto the sundeck in floral pajama pants. She notices me and stops in her tracks, her forehead creasing.

"I thought you weren't coming with us." Her fingers curl around her coffee mug, and she watches me stretch on the yoga mat.

We departed this morning and are now heading along the coast.

"It's just to Monaco. We'll be there in a little while."

She shrugs, feigning indifference.

I finish the set of push-ups and move on to burpees. "You could join me, you know?"

She snorts. "I pulled a muscle just *watching* you."

She's settled into one of the plush armchairs, and she does seem to be watching me, her eyes lingering over my form.

"How's Greta doing today?" she asks, bringing the coffee to her lips.

"I sent her a text last night. She'll probably see it this morning. I'll let you know."

When I look over again at Francesca, who's been awfully quiet for the remainder of my workout, I see she's got her head in her hands and her skin has a pale-greenish tinge to it.

"Are you okay? You look gross."

"Thanks," she deadpans, shooting me a look.

I hold up both hands. "I'm honest, I'm not blind. Do you normally get seasick?"

She shrugs. "I'm not sure, I've never really been on a boat like this before."

I abandon my cooldown stretches and rise to my feet. "Wait here. I have Dramamine in my toiletry kit."

"What's that?"

"A medication to treat motion sickness."

A few minutes later, I return with the tablets and a cold bottle of water. "Take these, and let's move you to the bow."

She cracks open the water and takes the pills. "The what?"

I roll my eyes. "The front of the boat. It's the best place to be if you start feeling queasy. Come on."

I help her to her feet, and she leans against me as we walk.

We spoke a little at dinner, and I noticed things about her that I hadn't before. Like how funny she was, how bright and witty.

Though to be honest, when she gave me the latest Wi-Fi network, I questioned if she was losing it with her little internet puns—there was nothing funny about Jesus—until I logged on last night and my computer popped up with the notification You are now connected to Jesus.

Well played, Frankie. Well played.

When we reach the bow, she sinks down onto the cushioned bench, and I decide to join her, since she looks miserable. Like comically, pitifully miserable. She has her legs curled up, arms wrapped around herself, looking less like a woman and more like a discarded rag doll that's been through a washing machine one too many times. Her normally sharp mouth has been reduced to a thin, queasy line, and her eyes—usually bright with some kind of argument—are glassy and unfocused.

I lean against the table and cross my arms. "Did you have any breakfast?"

She nods. "Two croissants."

"Two?" I question.

Her head rolls toward me with all the effort of a dying Victorian heroine. "Are you seriously here to mock me while I suffer?"

I consider that. "A little."

She groans, dropping her forehead onto her knees. "You're the worst."

I smirk. "I've been called worse. All I was going to say was that carbohydrates are good for this sort of thing." Then, because I don't actually enjoy watching her turn green, I slide into the seat across from her. "You need a distraction. Tell me something weird about yourself."

She doesn't move, except for a weak hand gesture. "Too sick. No thoughts. Only death."

I chuckle. "Fine, I'll go first. I hate strawberries. They freak me out."

That gets a reaction. She peeks up at me, frowning. "What do you mean *freak you out*?"

"They have *seeds on the outside*. That's unnatural."

She lets out a strangled noise that I *think* is supposed to be a laugh but sounds dangerously close to a dry heave. Her hand flutters toward her stomach. "Oh God. You're making it worse."

I try—*really try*—to keep a straight face, but she just looks so pathetic. All wrapped up in herself, groaning, wincing, fighting her own digestive system like it's a personal enemy. It's almost . . . cute.

The thought blindsides me.

Francesca, *cute*?

I shake it off. Probably just some weird instinctual sympathy thing. Or maybe I just like seeing her too out of it to hurl insults at me.

She rests her head in her hands and closes her eyes. "Just leave me here to die, I don't want to bring you down with me."

"Don't be cute right now. That's not helping."

She cracks one eye open. "Helping what?"

My raging inappropriate crush on you.

"Nothing. Never mind." I reach for a water bottle and shove it in her direction. "Here. Sip."

She does, barely managing two swallows before glaring at me. "If I puke, I'm making sure some of it gets on you."

I smirk, settling back. "Not if I throw you overboard first."

That earns me a weak middle finger before she slumps back down. I roll my eyes, but—God help me—I'm still grinning.

Maybe she *is* a disaster. But for some reason, I don't mind that as much as I used to.

Frankie lifts her head a few minutes later, blinking like she's just woken from a coma. There's still a little pallor to her face, but the sickly green tint is fading. Progress.

She exhales, slumping against the cushion. "Okay. I think I'm past the I'd-rather-die-than-exist phase."

"Shame," I say, smirking. "I was just about to start planning your sea burial."

She glares, but there's no real heat behind it. "You're hilarious." Then, to my surprise, she actually sits up and gives me a look that's almost . . . appreciative. "You're brilliant. Thanks for the meds, they were exactly what I needed."

"You're playing it fast and loose with the b-word, but you're welcome."

"And thanks for the distraction. And for not throwing me overboard. Very chivalrous of you."

I tilt my head. "It was nothing, but since you're officially back among the living, I believe it's your turn."

Her brows knit. "My turn for what?"

I lean forward, resting my forearms on the table. "I told you something weird about me. Now it's your turn to share a fun fact."

She groans. "Ugh. Fine." She thinks for a second, then mutters, "I can't eat gummy bears."

I blink. "What?"

"They're too tragic," she explains. "They have faces. And little stubby arms. I can't bite into them without feeling like a monster."

I stare at her. "That's the dumbest thing I've ever heard."

She shrugs. "Call it what you want, but I refuse to be responsible for the violent deaths of tiny, innocent bears."

I let out a short laugh, shaking my head. "So let me get this straight—you won't eat gummy bears because they have faces, but you'll eat, what, chicken nuggets? Steak?"

She waves a hand. "Those don't have eyes looking back at me, *Hayes*."

It's so ridiculous, so *her*, that I just stare for a second. She's still pale, still slightly wilted, but there's a glimmer of amusement in her eyes. The same quick wit, the same unpredictable spark that's always made her impossible to ignore.

I roll my eyes, but there's no bite behind it. "You're certifiable, you know that?"

She grins. "Yeah, but you just spent the last half hour making sure I didn't die, so what does that say about you?"

I don't have an answer for that. And that realization is the most unsettling part of all.

We sit in what can only be described as a comfortable silence—our first ever—for a few moments, both of us looking out at the horizon. It's going to be a beautiful day, sunny with a light breeze.

"So why are you going to Monaco?" she asks.

"I need to pick up something. I always do a gift for my team each year at our big annual event, and I decided to do custom bottles of rosé. There's this prestigious vineyard in Provence, and they're engraving the bottles for me with their names and a short message. They've sent them on ahead to Monaco for me."

"Wow, that's generous of you."

"It's a splurge, but they deserve it."

"Okay, Daddy Big Bucks." She winks.

Call me Daddy one more time . . .

Chapter Twenty-One

Stay in Your Lane

Frankie

The morning sun warms the air and casts a soft glow over the elegantly set breakfast table. Charles sits across from me, stirring his coffee, his expression mildly amused as I continue my latest deep dive into French history. Hayes is nowhere to be found.

"So, did you know," I say, leaning forward to help myself to another croissant, "that Marie Antoinette never actually said 'Let them eat cake'? It was just propaganda to make her look bad. People wanted a villain, and she was an easy target."

Charles lifts a brow, setting his spoon down. "You don't say."

"I do say!" I gesture, nearly knocking over my orange juice. "She was just a teenager—fourteen years old—when she married King Louis XVI—shipped over from Austria and expected to fit into this crazy, extravagant court life at Versailles. And, okay, maybe she spent too much on dresses and parties, but honestly? Can you blame a girl?"

He makes a noncommittal sound.

I shrug, taking a bite of my croissant. "Do you know how old she was when she was beheaded?"

Charles shakes his head.

"Thirty-seven."

He takes a sip of coffee, studying me over the rim. "And what's got you so interested in French history all of a sudden?"

I grin. "We're in France, Charles. You can't just float around a country like this and not get curious. So I went down a research rabbit hole."

He chuckles, shaking his head. "Well, I can't say I expected to get a history lesson with my breakfast, but it's not the worst way to start the day."

I lean back in my chair, satisfied. "Just wait until I tell you about the Affair of the Diamond Necklace. Now *that's* a scandal."

After breakfast, I change into my swimsuit, grab a paperback, and head to the sundeck.

We're nearing our next stop, and the view from the port side captures my attention. I thought Monaco would be prettier. That's my first reaction. There are an awful lot of orange high-rises perched along a fortified hill. I guess I was expecting more, given how pretty the rest of the Riviera has been.

I'm distracted, so it takes me a moment to notice I'm not alone.

I round the corner near the outdoor shower and freeze mid-step.

Hayes stands under the spray, water streaming over his face and his chest, sliding down the ridges of his obliques and his pale, muscled ass before dripping onto the teak wood beneath his bare feet. And for a second, I forget how to move, how to breathe.

I should turn around. Walk away. But my feet betray me, and instead, I stay rooted in place, my gaze dragging up the length of him like a traitor.

He runs a hand through his wet hair, pushing it back, the muscles in his arm flexing with the motion. He's unaware, unrushed, and I'm mesmerized. My pulse jumps, and for a second, I forget how to do anything but stare.

Then his head tilts slightly, like he senses something, and before I can react, his eyes flick open, locking onto mine.

Shit.

I make a strangled sound—something between a gasp and a cough—and whip around so fast I nearly trip over my own feet.

"Frankie?" His voice is laced with amusement, and I swear I can hear the smirk forming on his lips.

"Nope. Didn't see anything!" I call over my shoulder, already halfway down the deck, my face burning. "Nothing at all."

His chuckle follows me, deep and full of trouble. "Didn't look like nothing."

I don't stop. I don't dare look back.

I'm in so much trouble.

~

I manage to avoid Hayes the rest of the day, which isn't hard to achieve because he heads into town for his errand. Charles sits in the shade while I read in a lounge chair.

"You want anything?" I ask him, dog-earing the corner of my paperback. "I'm going to grab a snack."

He shakes his head.

I'm on my way back from the galley when I hear it—the unmistakable sound of frustration. An irritated grumble followed by the sharp clang of a washing machine door slamming shut.

Curious, I poke my head into the yacht's tiny laundry room and freeze.

Hayes Winters, billionaire, master of the universe, and wearer of crisp, undoubtedly dry-cleaned shirts, is standing in front of the washing machine in a faded T-shirt with his arms crossed, scowling at it like it personally insulted him.

I lean against the doorframe, arms folded. "You okay there, big guy? You look like you're about to challenge that Whirlpool to a duel."

He startles, then smooths his features into something vaguely aloof. "I'm fine. Just . . . figuring this out."

My eyes drift to the laundry detergent sitting, still capped, on top of the machine, then to the buttons on the control panel, all of which seem to have been pressed in a desperate attempt to make something happen. The machine sits silent, unbothered.

"You've never done your own laundry before, have you?" I ask, biting back a smile.

He lifts his chin. "Of course I have."

I raise an eyebrow.

". . . Maybe once." He frowns in concentration.

The laugh I've been holding in escapes before I can stop it. "Oh, this is rich. What happened? Butler on vacation?"

His glare is half hearted at best. "If you're just here to gloat, you can leave."

"Oh no," I say, stepping in and nudging him aside. "This is too good. I *have* to help now."

He gives me a helpless look. "The truth is, I never learned. I went to two different boarding schools. Laundry would disappear and come back two days later clean, folded, and perfectly pressed, so yeah, laundry machines scare me."

"Well, nothing to be afraid of." I peer into the open machine. "At least you sorted your colors."

He hesitates. "Should I have?"

I whip my head around. "You *didn't*?"

His smirk is back. "Relax, I'm not a total lost cause."

I shake my head, grabbing the detergent. "Okay, first, you don't need half the bottle." I pour in a reasonable amount before showing him the settings. "And you want cold water for darks, hot for whites—"

"Why?"

I blink at him. "Why . . . what?"

"Why cold for darks and hot for whites?"

I open my mouth, then close it. ". . . Because that's the rule."

He smirks again, like he's caught me in some kind of trap. "So you don't actually know."

I shove his arm playfully. "Shut up and push the button."

He obliges, pressing Start. The machine rumbles to life, and he leans against the counter, watching me with something new in his eyes. Something warm.

"Thanks," he says, his voice lower, quieter.

It sends a flicker of heat up my spine. This is . . . different. We're different.

I roll my eyes, desperate to steer us back into familiar waters. "You're welcome, Your Highness. Next time, I'll teach you about dishwashers."

His gaze flicks to my mouth, just for a second. "Looking forward to it."

And *that* is when I decide I need to leave this tiny, too-close space before I start thinking about how cute he looks all ruffled and helpless.

Because that would be dangerous. And very stupid.

Charles and I spend the day on the sundeck enjoying the fresh air and gorgeous views of the blue Mediterranean Sea that stretch on forever. We play *Wordle*, swap stories about our most cringeworthy dates.

Mine was a tie—first there was the guy who brought his mom, and then another time, I got food poisoning mid-dinner. Charles, on the other hand, once had a date that was too *perfect*—planned down to the last second—and it completely freaked him out. I could see that. He'd been on his own for so long; having someone new dictate every minute would be a challenge for him. Then we ate an early dinner and watched *Jeopardy!*

All in all, it was a pretty great day. As I sit here, watching his eyelids grow heavy, I can't help but wonder.

Is this what it would have been like to have a dad? Someone to eat dinner with and bicker over meaningless trivia? Someone to play Scrabble with? Who would fall asleep in his armchair by roughly 7:34 each night?

I don't hate it.

There's something predictable and kind of soothing about it.

Later, when I head below deck to do my own laundry, I find a pair of black boxer briefs that appear to have been left behind. I grab them and freeze, running my fingers over the silky material. Whoa. What even is this material? I've never felt anything as soft and buttery before. Is this modal? I never knew what modal was. Maybe this is it.

"Can I help you?" Hayes asks from behind me.

I turn, still clutching his underwear in my hands. I thrust them at him. "I found these in the dryer."

"Thanks."

I blush like crazy but muster a smile. *Act normal.* Hard to do when I saw him naked earlier and now fondled his underwear. Classic, Frankie! "You want to join me for a glass of wine in the main salon?" I blurt. I'm nothing if not smooth.

He looks almost bashful, and I'm confused for a second before he admits, "I actually have a date tonight."

A date?

We arrived in Monaco all of two hours ago. Of course he does.

"Okay," I say, keeping my voice neutral. "Have fun."

~

I should be asleep.

It's late—so late that even the gentle rocking of the yacht has settled into a slow, steady rhythm, lulling the world into quiet. But sleep won't come. Instead, I'm stretched out on the couch in the main salon, aimlessly scrolling on my phone, pretending I'm not waiting for something.

And then I hear it—the low murmur of voices, the distinct sound of bare feet padding along the teak decking. A second later, the door swings open, and in walks Hayes.

With a date.

She's blond, stunning, and barely old enough to order the drink she's currently giggling over. She clings to his arm like he's the last lifeboat on the *Titanic*, her other hand pressing against his chest as she murmurs something in a breathy voice.

I go rigid as a sharp and completely unreasonable wave of irritation slams through me.

"Oops, is this the lobby?" she asks, blinking at me as if surprised to find another human on board.

"Nope," I deadpan, crossing my arms. "Just me. Living here. Existing."

She giggles—an airy, tipsy sound that makes my jaw clench. Hayes, on the other hand, looks . . . tired. Not guilty, not smug, just vaguely exasperated, like a man who accidentally picked the slowest checkout line at the store but is too polite to abandon it now.

"Francesca," he greets me, his voice low and even, as if this is the most normal situation in the world.

"Hayes." I give him a tight, saccharine smile. "Nice night?"

The model—because let's be real, she *has* to be a model—tilts her head up at him. "You didn't tell me there was a *roommate* situation," she purrs.

Oh, for the love of—

I glare at Hayes, waiting for him to correct her. To clarify that I am absolutely *not* his roommate but rather the unfortunate witness to his questionable life choices. But he just exhales through his nose, a small, concerned look on his stern features, and steers her gently toward the hallway leading to his room.

"Good night, Francesca," he says, and before I can even formulate a cutting response, he disappears below deck with his . . . companion.

I stare after them, my blood simmering.

Unbelievable.

I am not mad. That would be ridiculous. He can do whatever he wants. Sleep with whoever he wants. Date whatever human embodiment of an Instagram filter he wants.

Nope. Not mad at all.

I shove my phone under a pillow, yank a blanket over my head, and pretend I don't care.

Badly.

Chapter Twenty-Two

Don't Rock the Boat

Frankie

The morning sun glints off the still water of the marina, the air crisp and carrying the faintest scent of salt. It would be a perfect morning—if not for the fact that I'm currently trapped at a breakfast table with *him*.

Hayes looks obnoxiously well rested and freshly showered, his dark hair slightly tousled in a way that probably costs a fortune at some fancy salon but just happens naturally for him. He sips his espresso, flipping through something on his phone like he *didn't* waltz in with a baby-faced supermodel last night.

I've noticed a pattern. The idea of having a "type" is that you're attracted to something familiar. So being wealthy and thin and emotionally immature is somehow comforting and familiar to him. I guess in the same way that my type is bad boys or jerks because I never knew my father and probably stored up buried anger over that fact.

Clearly neither of us knew jack squat about picking an appropriate partner—something we had in common.

Charles, blissfully unaware, takes a bite of his omelet and glances between us. "You look upset," he says to me. "Did something happen?"

I stab my fork into a piece of fruit, leveling my gaze at Hayes. "Oh, nothing," I say airily. "Just a lot of *movement* last night. Did you feel the boat rocking?"

Charles frowns, thoughtful. "No, actually. It was pretty still—" His expression shifts to realization. "Oh. Ohhh." He sighs, rubbing his temples. "Hayes, for God's sake, did you really—"

"Relax," Hayes drawls, annoyed. "Nothing happened."

I snort. "Right. Because men frequently bring drunk models back to their rooms just for a deep, intellectual discussion on the state of the world."

Hayes sets his espresso cup down and leans back in his chair, his gaze lazily sweeping over me. "Maybe we debated the merits of modern art," he says, lips twitching. "Maybe we discussed philosophy and the fleeting nature of human connection."

I roll my eyes so hard I practically see my brain. "Sure. And maybe I moonlight as a NASA engineer in my free time."

"Do you?" He cocks a brow. "Because that would explain your ability to launch into orbit over something that's absolutely none of your business."

My mouth falls open. "I am *not*—" I snap my jaw shut, because okay, maybe I *was* being a little dramatic. But that's beside the point.

Charles sighs again. "Frankie, please don't take the bait. I just woke up. I don't have the energy for your feud right now."

Hayes smirks at me like he's already won. I glare back at him, but my irritation is cracking under the weight of Charles's stony look.

Then, as if on cue, Hayes reaches for the croissant basket at the same time I do, and our fingers brush. I snatch my hand back like I've been electrocuted.

Hayes lifts the basket and offers me the last croissant. "Truce?"

I exhale sharply, shaking my head. "I hate you."

"And yet," he muses, taking a bite, "you keep ending up at my breakfast table."

I narrow my eyes at him, then grab my coffee and take a long, slow sip. "I'm just waiting for you to choke on that."

He chuckles, and damn it, so do I.

"Well, if you excuse me, I have an errand to run in Monaco today," Hayes says, rising to his feet.

I remember the case of fancy wine he told me he was picking up.

I ball up my napkin and toss it onto the table.

Charles frowns at me once Hayes is gone. "Are you sure you're not mad that he's dating this girl?"

A short, irritated laugh escapes me. "They're not dating, believe me. They're sleeping together. And no, I'm not mad. Why would I be mad about that?"

He shrugs. "That's what I was trying to figure out."

~

When Hayes returns several hours later, I'm stretched out on one of the lounge chairs on the aft deck, flipping through a book I'm barely reading. He strolls up like he owns the place—which, technically, he does.

He's freshly showered, wearing a crisp white button-down with the sleeves pushed up, the top two buttons undone like some kind of Monaco playboy starter pack.

"Get up," he says, nudging the lounge chair with his foot.

I peer at him. "Wow, charming. That line usually work?"

His lips twitch. "We're going out."

I blink. "We?"

"Me. You. Some of the deck crew. Try to keep up. We're going to Monte Carlo for drinks and dancing."

I lower my book fully, trying to gauge if he's messing with me. "Since when do you invite *me* to things?"

He exhales dramatically. "Since I decided you could use a break from . . . whatever it is you do all day." He gestures vaguely at my book. "Reading *War and Peace* or whatever."

I flip the book around and pretend to read the title. "*A Beginner's Guide to Not Murdering Your Annoying Yacht Mate.*"

His mouth twitches, like he's trying not to laugh. "Catchy."

"And what makes you think I'd want to go *anywhere* with you?"

He grins, like he was hoping I'd say that. "Because you've been in France for days and have yet to experience anything but the inside of this yacht."

I cross my arms. "That's not true. I went into town yesterday."

"You bought sunscreen and then came right back."

Damn it. He *notices* things.

"Come on," he continues, his voice taking on that smooth, coaxing quality that probably makes business deals—and women—fall right into his hands. "We'll drink, we'll dance, we'll pretend to like each other for an evening. It shouldn't be too challenging, should it?"

His dark eyes glimmer with hidden thoughts I'm sure he'll never reveal.

Colette emerges from below deck, overhearing just enough to perk up. "Did you say clubbing?"

Hayes nods. "VIP table."

She gasps. "Oh, *hell yes.*" Then she frowns. "Wait—what's the dress code?"

Hayes shrugs. "Expensive."

I roll my eyes. "Of course."

Jack, one of the deckhands, strolls past and catches wind of the conversation. "We're going out?"

Hayes jerks his chin in confirmation. "Better bring your best shirt, mate."

Jack grins and fist pumps before jogging off, presumably to alert the rest of the crew.

Kira, one of the deckhands, appears from the galley, looking effortlessly cool in a slinky black dress. "You coming, Frankie?"

I glance between them, considering my options. I hesitate. It's not that I *don't* want to go—but Monaco nightlife? That's an entirely different universe.

Hayes watches me, head tilting slightly. "What, scared you won't be able to keep up?"

And *that* is all it takes.

I snap my book shut and push to my feet. "Give me ten minutes."

Hayes grins, stepping back to let me pass. "Take your time."

I brush past him with a huff, already mentally sifting through my suitcase for the kind of dress that says *I belong in Monte Carlo*, even if I absolutely don't.

By the time I come back up, everyone is already gathered at the gangway. Charles is sitting this one out, of course—someone has to be the responsible adult—but the rest of us? We're about to step into a world of flashing lights, overpriced champagne, and more bad decisions than I care to count.

I smooth my dress, suddenly feeling self-conscious under the weight of Hayes's gaze. He leans casually against the railing, but there's something different in the way he's looking at me.

"You look beautiful tonight," he says, voice low.

It throws me for a second—long enough for my stomach to flip before my brain reminds me *this is Hayes*. Annoying, smug, disaster-waiting-to-happen Hayes.

I roll my eyes, covering whatever just sparked in my chest with a bored look. "Don't sound so surprised."

He pushes off the railing, still watching me. "Oh, I'm not."

And just like that, I have a feeling Hayes Winters will be right at the center of every bad decision I make tonight.

I hug Charles goodbye and follow the group. Perched above us, the lights of Monaco twinkle in the distance. Kira and Jack lead the way, sharing a bottle of wine between them and talking loudly. Colette and Sebastian are next, then me, followed by Hayes, who's looking at me funny as I navigate the stairs in heels.

"What's wrong with you?"

I release a sigh. "I'm wearing a thong." Which has migrated practically inside me.

"Oh—kay?" He sounds confused.

"I'm normally a granny panty type of girl," I say by way of explanation.

The crease in between Hayes's eyebrows only deepens.

"Never mind," I settle on.

Tessa would understand. She often makes fun of my underwear choice and would get what a monumental occasion this is. One that is never going to happen again, by the way, because these things are terrible. I'd rather have a root canal while being run over by a car than shove dental floss up my ass ever again.

"You're sure not like the other girls, are you?" he says, shaking his head. I can't tell based on his tone if he finds it oddly refreshing or just odd.

I shrug and keep walking, moving past him while trying not to notice how good he smells. *Dear God . . .*

Chapter Twenty-Three

When Walls Come Down

Hayes

The bass thrums through my chest, an unrelenting pulse that matches the headache brewing behind my eyes. Monaco's nightlife is exactly what I expected—too loud, too flashy, too many desperate men looking for an easy way to impress women. And right now, they're all looking at Francesca.

I lean against the bar, watching as some guy in a too-tight button-down leans in closer to her, flashing what I'm sure he thinks is a charming grin. Frankie laughs, tossing her hair over her shoulder, and something sharp twists in my chest.

Where the hell are our drinks?

The bartender slides a cocktail her way first—of course—while I'm left waiting, jaw tightening as I watch the guy introduce himself. His hand hovers near Frankie's arm, testing the boundaries of contact, and I catch myself scowling.

I'm not jealous. That would be ridiculous.

But I am irritated. Annoyed. Mildly homicidal, maybe.

I'm not sure what's come over me.

Frankie's still laughing, oblivious to my mood, but when she finally turns, her eyes catch mine. Something in my expression must tip her off, because her smile falters for just a second before she smirks.

"Why do you look like you're plotting a murder?" she teases, raising her glass.

"Just enjoying the show," I say flatly, finally grabbing my drink. "Didn't realize you had such a fan club."

She rolls her eyes. "Oh, please. He was just being friendly."

I take a slow sip of my whiskey, letting the burn settle. "Yeah? He gets much friendlier, and I might have to remind him you didn't come here alone."

Frankie snorts. "What, you planning to fight him?"

I arch a brow. "You think I'd lose?"

She hums, pretending to consider. "Hard to say. He looks scrappy."

I glance back at the guy, unimpressed. "He looks like he moisturizes more than he works out."

Frankie's laugh is sudden and real, and for some reason, that sound takes the edge off. Maybe I'm being ridiculous. Maybe it doesn't matter if men look at her, talk to her, want her attention.

But the thought of someone actually *getting* it?

That doesn't sit right with me at all.

"I'm glad you talked me into coming out," she says, taking a sip of her sugary cocktail.

"Yeah? Why's that?"

She lifts one bare shoulder. "Because I wouldn't have otherwise, and while this isn't my scene, it's fun to mix it up once in a while."

A guy with slicked-back hair and bad veneers approaches from behind her, placing a hand on her lower back. "Hello, future wife."

Frankie laughs, light and unbothered. "Well, that's ambitious."

His pickup line annoys me—*greatly*—but I stay where I am, pretending not to care while every muscle in my jaw disagrees. As I watch them make small talk, something clicks into place.

Frankie *is* wife material.

Even if this idiot is only seeing her for her curves and that knockout smile, there's more—so much more.

It's in the way she listens when someone speaks, the way she holds her own without needing to raise her voice. The way she lights up when she's proud of something. She's funny. Smart. Kind without being naive. Sharp without being cruel.

Someone's going to be lucky as hell to stand across from her one day and hear her say I do.

Just not this guy.

Not that I care about things like marriage.

My parents' disaster of a situationship cured me of that particular delusion a long time ago.

Still . . .

It's getting harder to pretend I don't care who gets to stand beside her.

"Come dance with me and Kira," Colette says, grabbing her elbow and interrupting her conversation with the guy vying for her attention.

"Sure." She smiles. "Hold my purse?" she asks me sweetly, setting the miniature handbag in my lap.

I grumble something that must sound like consent and watch as she saunters away, moving her hips to the pulse of the beat. I'm transfixed, unable to look away, even for a second. Which is . . . insane. This is *Frankie.*

~

The light streaming through the salon windows is more painful than helpful. My head throbs as I sip on the coffee in my hand, hoping it will work its magic.

Charles is sitting across from me, looking perfectly fine—because he didn't go out clubbing with us last night. He's a picture of health and normalcy, but I can tell by the look on his face that he's enjoying my suffering.

"Good morning," I mutter, my voice rough from last night's abuse.

Charles raises an eyebrow. "You look . . . well, like you had a good time." He's practically holding back a laugh.

"Don't say it," I warn.

He sips his coffee, eyes glinting with amusement. "I'm just saying, I'm glad someone had fun. Can't say I'm envious of the hangover you've got going."

Before I can throw something at him, the door opens and Frankie walks in, looking like she's struggling just as much as I am. She stops when she sees us, putting a hand to her head. "Ugh, good morning to everyone except for me."

I snort, relieved to see I'm not the only one feeling like death. I offer her a cup of coffee. "But maybe this will help."

She raises an eyebrow at the mug. "This looks like something that could wake the dead."

"It's strong. Trust me, it's the only way to survive this," I tell her, raising my own mug in a mock toast.

She sits down next to us with a heavy sigh. "I feel like I'm going to die."

The sound of the doorbell ringing cuts through the conversation, and I stand up, stretching my sore muscles. "IV's here."

Frankie's face falls a little, and she shoots Charles a look. "Did he just say IV?"

I nod, walking toward the door. "Trust me, you'll thank me later."

I return with the nurse, who's already setting up the equipment—a silver pole where various bags of saline filled with vitamins and minerals hang, as well as latex gloves and packets of IV needles. As soon as Frankie sees the needles, her face goes pale, and I'm taken aback. "What's wrong?"

She forces a smile. "I'm fine, just . . . not great with needles." Her voice is barely above a whisper, and I'm surprised at how vulnerable she looks.

I raise an eyebrow, walking over to her. "You're serious?"

She nods, avoiding my gaze. "Yeah, I've never been good with them. I pass out every time."

I stare at her for a moment, not sure what to say. Compassion for others isn't exactly my strong suit. But for her, I feel more than I probably should. "First, you don't have to do anything you don't want to." My tone is gentle but firm.

"That's possibly the sexiest sentence a man's ever said to me," she murmurs, eyes meeting mine.

I kneel beside her, putting a hand on her shoulder. "Well, I'm serious. You don't have to do this, the choice is entirely yours, but if you want to try it, I promise it will make you feel better."

She hesitates, biting her lip. "You've done it?"

"A couple times. Either when I was sick and recovering from the flu, and a couple of times after bachelor parties and things like that. You'll feel great in an hour. But I'm serious, only do it if *you* want to."

She thinks it over and finally nods. "Okay, I'll do it. But don't . . . don't laugh at me when I pass out."

"I won't," I promise, even though I can't help the slight grin pulling at my lips. "I've got you."

The nurse starts setting up, and Frankie's face turns an even paler shade. I sit down beside her, just trying to be there without adding to her nerves. When the needle finally goes in, she inhales sharply, and I feel her tense against me. Then, her eyes flutter shut and—just like that—she's out cold, slumping to the side.

I catch her before she can hit the armrest, my heart racing a little.

"Hey, Frankie?" I say softly, worried. "Come on, wake up."

The nurse steps back, nodding. "She'll be fine, just give her a minute."

I continue holding her steady, my fingers brushing the back of her neck as I keep her head from tilting. I don't even realize I'm holding my breath until she stirs again, slowly blinking her eyes open.

"I told you I'd pass out," she mumbles, barely able to keep her eyes open.

"You did," I say, my voice quiet. "But you're okay now. See?"

She smiles weakly. "I owe you one."

I chuckle softly, reaching for a soda from the table and then offering it to her. "It's nothing. Just trying to keep you alive over here."

She weakly takes a sip, her fingers brushing against mine. "You're way better at this than I expected."

"Well, I do what I can," I reply, feeling oddly protective of her in that moment.

I can't help but notice how close we are. How . . . easy this feels. It's a side of me I'm not used to, but it's hard to ignore when she looks at me like that. A little more vulnerable, a little more . . . real. And for once, I'm not in any rush to back away.

As predicted, a few hours later both Francesca and I are feeling better. She spent the day with Charles, mostly sunbathing, and I made myself scarce. We've just returned from an early dinner in town with Charles—they wanted to be back in time for *Jeopardy!* While the two of them disappeared to the main salon, I venture to my suite to call Maddie. It's early afternoon in New York, and she should be getting out of school. Since I didn't expect to stay here—it's already been several days longer than I told her—I figure I should update her on my whereabouts.

I sink onto the end of my bed and FaceTime her.

Maddie answers with a wave and a smile.

"You lost a tooth," I say, smiling back at her.

She shows off the blank spot where her front tooth used to be, her tongue poking into the space. "Yup. Got four dollars for it too."

"What else is new?"

"Nothing really. When are you coming back?"

I explain to her about the trip so far, basically stalling for time, because I'm not sure, honestly. "Someone's gotta keep an eye on the old man," I settle on.

"Nuh-uh, my mom told me he hired some lady to go with him."

I chuckle. "Francesca is more than just *some lady*."

Maddie's mouth slowly curls up in a smile. "What, is she your *girl . . . friend*?" she draws out the word.

"Not hardly. People my age don't have girlfriends."

"Exactly. People your age have wives . . . and when are you going to get one of those?"

"Hmm, let me think . . ." I tap my chin. *"Never."*

Maddie laughs.

"I gotta go, kid. Be good, okay?"

"I'm always good," she says, smiling.

She is too. Maddie's a great kid. Even if my dad messed up royally, having Maddie in my life has been a nice consolation prize. I'm not sure my mother would agree with that statement, but it is what it is.

After my phone call, I head back out to find Charles and Francesca. They're where I left them in the main salon, but it appears they've changed into pajamas.

Frankie has a huge bowl of popcorn in her lap, and both she and Charles are engaged in some type of self-care ritual, complete with lavender-colored eye masks.

I catch sight of Charles and do a double take, realizing he's also wearing fuzzy pink socks, Frankie's no doubt.

"That's a new look for you," I say.

Frankie shushes me. "His feet were cold."

"And the . . ." I gesture to her face.

"For your information, these are gel eye masks. They increase hydration and reduce puffiness and undereye circles."

"Of course they do." I nod, trying not to smile.

"We're just about to start a movie. Join us," my uncle says, touching one finger to his undereye mask.

I made plans already . . . apparently last night I promised Jack and Sebastian we'd go to the casino tonight.

"I have extra eye masks. But you need to put on pajama pants if you're joining us."

"I don't own pajama pants."

"Then what do you sleep in?" She looks genuinely perplexed.

I cock an eyebrow. "Do you really want me to answer that?"

She holds up both hands. "Nope. Never mind."

The blush on her cheeks tells me she's remembering the time she interrupted my shower.

"Give me five minutes, and I'll join you." Right after I break the news to the deck crew that they should go along without me.

"Do you want popcorn?" Frankie calls after me.

"Obviously," I call back.

I change into something more comfortable and join them again, sinking down on the sofa across from Francesca. Charles has commandeered the leather BarcaLounger in front of the TV. There's a fresh bowl of popcorn waiting for me on the coffee table, and I help myself to a handful.

"What are we watching?" I ask, munching on the popcorn.

My uncle selects a history documentary about World War I and falls asleep after the first fifteen minutes.

"Oh thank God," Frankie says, getting up to grab the remote once we're sure he's out.

I chuckle, watching her. I'm not sure why or even how, but each small thing she does seems to delight me. I wonder why neither of us questioned his selecting this movie, but now I see she was merely biding her time until he fell asleep.

After she changes the channel to a real estate reality show, she peels the sticky eye mask from Charles's face and gingerly covers him with a blanket, and something shifts in my chest.

"I was wrong about you."

"Huh?" she asks, settling back in beside me.

"You're good for him." I tip my chin toward my uncle.

"Well, I'm enjoying his company. Who else can you go to dinner with so early that you're in pajamas by seven o'clock?"

"That's an excellent point." I hesitate, my gaze moving between her and the TV. "I'm not sure if you were serious about never drinking again . . . but what do you think about a glass of wine out on the sky deck?"

"I say let's do it."

She turns the TV off and lowers the lights, leaving Charles asleep in the recliner—at least for now.

Frankie grabs a throw blanket and wraps herself in it while I work the cork out of a bottle of red and pour us each a glass. We navigate the steps and find a spot on the sun loungers. It's dark and breezy, but the stars are out in full force, giving everything a pale glow. The nightlife in Monaco seems a million miles away.

I take a slow sip of my wine, letting the taste settle on my tongue before swallowing. Across from me, Frankie is curled up in one of the lounge chairs, her legs tucked beneath her, her own glass of wine balanced loosely in one hand. Her hair is a little wild from the wind, and the glow from the deck lights makes her skin look soft, golden.

She takes a sip, eyeing me over the rim of her glass. "You know, for a guy who's usually surrounded by models and millionaires, I'm surprised you're slumming it with me tonight."

I smirk, swirling the wine in my glass. "Trust me, I'd rather be here than trapped in some overpriced club, listening to bad remixes and pretending to care about someone's father's hedge fund."

She gasps in mock surprise. "Did I hear you say you enjoy my company? Somebody write this down."

I huff a quiet laugh and shake my head. "I said no such thing."

"Oh, but you implied it," she teases, wiggling her eyebrows. "I think I'm starting to grow on you."

I scoff, taking another sip of my wine. "Let's not get carried away."

She leans forward, resting her elbow on the arm of the chair, watching me like she's enjoying this way too much. "Just admit it," she goads. "I'm charming. Delightful. A ray of freaking sunshine in your otherwise jaded existence."

I exhale slowly like I'm irritated, tilting my head back to look up at the stars. "You are . . . tolerable."

She presses a hand to her chest in exaggerated offense. "Tolerable?"

I fight back a smirk. "Fine. You're . . . slightly better than tolerable."

She lets out a loud, dramatic sigh. "Wow. That's practically a love confession, coming from you."

I shake my head, unable to stop the amused grin that tugs at my lips. "Yeah, yeah. Don't let it go to your head."

She clinks her glass against mine, her eyes twinkling with mischief. "Too late."

I watch her for a moment, feeling something shift—something subtle but undeniable. She's working her way under my skin, and worse, I don't entirely mind it.

The breeze chooses that moment to pick up, blowing her hair into her face. She hands me her glass of wine so she can gather it all up in a neat bun on the top of her head. I'm mesmerized.

"How'd you do that?" I ask, handing her back her glass not even four seconds later.

"Hmm? Oh, girl magic." She smiles and takes a sip of her wine. She looks at me over the rim of her glass. "All right, Mr. Perfect, tell me something humiliating. There's no way you've made it through life without at least one mortifying moment."

"My most embarrassing moment?"

She nods.

"I promise you can't handle it."

"Try me."

I sigh, leaning back. "I once officiated a wedding for my friends after becoming ordained online."

"That's cool."

"Yeah, it was, until the end of the ceremony when I said *You may now* kill *the bride*."

Francesca bursts into easy laughter. "That's actually amazing."

"Is it, though?" The wedding was very fancy—at a country club just outside DC. The hard stares I got from the bridal party were brutal. I'd never put my foot in my mouth like that. Until I did.

She waves me off. "I promise that's nothing. That's like a Tuesday for me."

I chuckle and shake my head.

"Are a lot of your friends married?"

I take another sip of my wine, enjoying this moment with her more than I thought I would. "Some, yes."

"What about you? Ever have the urge?"

I'm contemplative for a moment, no doubt surprising Frankie, who watches me with a stunned expression. Maybe she expected me to scoff at the idea of marriage. "I got close once," I say softly. "Someone my parents thought would be suitable since her family runs in the same circles as mine. I guess we made sense on paper."

"What, like an arranged marriage?"

I scowl. "More like a civilized arrangement—I guess they thought she was the kind of woman men like me end up with. They know the score—ironclad prenup and the like."

"That sounds so romantic."

"Yeah, well, I got cold feet and pulled away. I couldn't really picture myself tied down with one woman. And I was too young at the time."

I wasn't used to feeling this exposed. Around her, it's like my defenses don't work and every word, every look, feels like I'm giving away pieces of myself.

"And now?" she asks, gazing at me like she's genuinely curious.

"And now . . . I'm not sure." I physically shudder at the thought. "My parents are a disaster, and I guess that's left its mark on me."

Francesca nods. Who knows, maybe she can relate to me in some strange way. We're both figuring out our place in the world and what we want out of life. Maybe we have more in common than I ever realized.

That's a weird thought.

"You always assume people with money are just having an easier go of it," she says, swirling the ruby-colored wine in her glass.

"In some ways, sure. They don't have to worry about paying the mortgage, but there are lots of other issues. Trust me. If money buys happiness, why are my parents the most miserable people I know?"

She doesn't have any answers for me, not that I expected her to. But for now, her quiet understanding is enough.

"Thanks for . . ." I pause, searching for the right words.

"For what?" she asks, turning to meet my eyes.

"For listening. Being my friend."

"Are we friends?"

"If we're not, I don't think I have any."

Chapter Twenty-Four

Take It One Day at a Time

Frankie

Talking with Hayes last night was a revelation. He opened up in ways I hadn't expected. Each new side of him surprised me and left me wanting more. He's slowly but surely growing on me—like an unwanted mole. If I'm not careful, I can see myself developing a soft spot for him just like I have for Charles.

The following day, I finally catch up with Tessa via a much-needed FaceTime.

"Don't make a big deal about it, but I just broke up with Big D," she says when I answer.

"Okay . . . Do we need to talk about this?"

She shrugs and messes with her bangs. "Not really. I wasn't feeling it, and there's too many fish in the sea to stress about it. What's new over there?"

I fill her in on the latest and greatest aboard the *Elysium*—basically that we're cruising the French Riviera and it's all *very* bougie.

"How's the yachting life treating you? Not getting seasick or anything like that?"

Aside from that first day, when Hayes gave me medication and distracted me, I hadn't experienced any more queasiness on board. I learned later that that day was particularly windy and we left when we did to avoid an incoming storm, so it appeared it was a one-off situation related to the weather and not my body's reaction to life on the water.

"It's honestly been great. I've never slept better, I can tell you that."

When I mentioned that to Charles yesterday, he pointed out that it was likely due to the lulling sound of the sea. The *shh* sound a mother makes to calm a baby is a universal sound across cultures—it was as though the ocean was *shh*ing me to sleep every night. And I kind of liked that idea.

"What else is new? You've gotta give me something."

I draw a breath, hesitating. "Okay so don't hate me . . . but Hayes is growing on me."

"Um, I'm going to need more information." She sounds skeptical, and rightly so. I spent *a lot* of time complaining about him. A lot of time fixating on how awful he was.

When I didn't know much about Hayes, but assumed I had him all figured out, I thought his life's mission was burning through money, making my life a living hell, and worrying exclusively about himself. (In that order.) Now that I've peeled back the onion, so to speak, I realize I may have been a little judgmental. Now I see him as someone who cares deeply for others—even in his limited capacity. He feels a lot for Charles and Maddie and especially his assistant, Greta. He looks out for them, worries for them—possibly more than he does for himself. The level of care he set up for Greta floored me.

Instead of looking at him and seeing only a perfectly manicured life, I'm starting to see the cracks and bruises too.

I picture him just yesterday . . . hunched over a tattered paperback at the breakfast table with his hair flopped over his forehead. Something in me softened. Maybe it's not him that's changed . . . maybe it's me. I don't know how to explain all of that to Tessa.

It's been a slow, gradual process, like the changing of the seasons. One thing has blended into another until it's almost unrecognizably different.

"Okay, yeah, he's grumpy and judgy and impossible—but he also listens. Not just nods-and-smiles fake listening. Like, actually remembers things I say. He smells stupidly good too. Like woodsy aftershave and mint. It's honestly distracting."

"You seem to be talking an awful lot about Hayes. How's Charles, by the way?"

"Charles? Oh, Charles is great."

I launch into a story about our latest obsession—RummiKub and how he beat me last night.

"What if I just slept with him?"

"Charles?!" she screeches. "He's like ninety!"

"No!" I sputter, nearly choking. "Hayes!"

"Oh, I'm sure that will end well. You finally have a job you love, and you're all going to be stuck together out at sea. Classic Frankie—might as well ruin it by sleeping with the boss's jerk-nephew."

I roll my eyes. She might be right, but I'm unable to completely abandon the idea. Maybe the salty ocean air has gotten to my head—messed with my brain somehow.

"Be sensible!" Tessa says, her tone sharp.

"Sensible who? Don't know her." I stick out my tongue and wave goodbye before pressing the button to end our call.

~

"What if we skipped our next port?" Charles says over breakfast the next morning.

"What does that mean?"

He shrugs. "It means, where's your sense of adventure? Let's stay out at sea, skip the whole stopping at every fancy port along with every other megayacht in the Med, and cruise around to Spain."

"What would that entail?"

"A longer trip, I'd guess. We'd probably have to stop for provisions in Marseille."

My brain jumps into overdrive. Before I can even process what this extended jaunt would mean for Hayes's time on board, I'm busy thinking about Charles. Why the sudden change in plans? Is he doing okay?

I don't love that he occasionally needs help getting up out of his chair and suddenly can't seem to remember to take his pills without me reminding him. But he seems happy and in good spirits, and he loves being on the water just as much as I do. Life is good, at least for now, but that doesn't mean it's time to get complacent.

"When's the last time you had a physical?" I ask him.

His mouth slips into a wry grin. "Why? Are you worried about me?"

"Maybe. We'll be at sea for a couple of weeks. If something happened, we'd be far from a hospital. What if you just humor me by having a checkup before we go?"

"Whatever will make you happy."

I arrange for a concierge doctor to visit the boat the next day when we stop in Marseille—just for my own peace of mind.

~

I knock softly on the door before pushing it open, then stepping into Charles's cabin, where he sits on the edge of his bed, his posture rigid, his expression unreadable. Dr. Fournier stands near the small desk, flipping through a leather-bound notebook, his brows drawn together in a way that makes my stomach tighten.

"Everything okay?" I ask, my voice careful, controlled.

Dr. Fournier looks up, offering a small, practiced smile. "Frankie. I was just going over Charles's exam results." He hesitates for a fraction of a second before continuing. "There are some concerns."

Charles lets out an exaggerated sigh. "They always have concerns," he mutters. "A doctor's job is to be worried about things I have no time to worry about."

Dr. Fournier doesn't take the bait. He flips the notebook closed and tucks it under his arm. "His blood pressure is higher than I'd like. There are also some irregularities in his heart rate. Nothing immediately dangerous, but at his age, these are things we have to monitor closely."

I swallow hard, shifting my gaze to Charles. He's staring out the porthole, his jaw tight. I know him well enough to recognize the frustration in his silence. He hates this—hates being reminded that he's anything other than invincible.

"What can we do?" I ask.

"I'd like to run further tests," Dr. Fournier says, his voice calm but firm. "I can arrange for them at our next port. But beyond that, he needs rest. Less stress, better hydration. And, if I had my way, less red meat."

Charles snorts. "Now that's asking a lot."

I shoot him a look, but he ignores it, still fixated on the ocean beyond the window. The light reflects in his silver hair, making him look older than I want to admit.

"Charles," I say softly. "We need to take this seriously."

His shoulders lift in a shrug, but the movement is slow, heavier than usual. "I hear you."

Dr. Fournier exhales, sensing that the pushback isn't worth more arguing. "Check in with me anytime."

Charles waves him off with a flick of his fingers, and Dr. Fournier gives me a look on his way out, one that silently passes the responsibility over to me.

When the door clicks shut, I cross my arms. "Are you going to listen to him?"

Charles finally looks at me, his lips twitching into something that isn't quite a smile. "I'm eighty-two years old, kid. I listen when it matters."

I hold his gaze. "This matters."

A beat passes, and then he sighs, running a hand through his thinning hair. "I know."

It wasn't a promise. But it was something.

After dinner, I find Charles on the aft deck, a tumbler of whiskey in hand, watching the sun dip toward the horizon. He looks small against the vast stretch of ocean, though I know better than to say that out loud. In my mind, he's grown to this larger-than-life character, someone steady—as dependable as a Swiss timepiece. Someone fatherly, brilliant, and almost all-knowing. But as I look at him now, the silhouette of his shoulders against the inky sky, he looks far less imposing than I've built him up in my mind. Almost slender. Frail. A nervous lurch rises in me.

I clear my throat. "Mind some company?"

He glances over, one brow lifting. "If it's not to scold me about the drink, then sure."

Smiling, I lower myself into the chair beside him, the wood warm from the day's heat. The view is spectacular, but I can't even appreciate it.

Steeling my nerves, I ask the question that's been rambling around in my brain all afternoon—probably with far less tact than I should. "Are you dying?"

He sighs and sets the tumbler down on the railing. "We're all dying, Frankie."

It feels like maybe we should have had this conversation before now. Like back when I was interviewing for the job. But the me back in that coffee shop didn't know what she didn't know and was mostly curious—I'd never even heard of a travel companion. And I was enamored with the idea of running away from my problems, if I'm being totally honest.

"Charles?" I manage, my voice soft.

"Just like any of us, I have no idea how much time I have left, and neither does that doctor."

I frown, watching the way his fingers tremble slightly around the glass. "Is this some bucket list thing for you? This trip? One last hurrah . . ."

He doesn't answer me, not with words anyway. He takes another sip of his drink and stares blankly out at the choppy water as it swirls and crests. The unease in my chest grows.

Chapter Twenty-Five

Live While You Can

Hayes

I expected Charles and Frankie to be playing some board game or watching TV together in the main salon, but I find Charles alone on the aft deck. The sun has just set, casting everything in a dim glow.

"No *Jeopardy!* tonight?" I ask, coming to a stop at the balcony railing beside him.

"Not tonight. I think Frankie's tired."

She's not tired, she's upset, but I don't correct him. Dinner was a little tense, and I could sense her concern following my uncle's physical. I don't like seeing her upset, and the news from his doctor—while not surprising—obviously upset her.

"You could join me." He tips his chin to the table behind us, which contains a bottle of Macallan.

"I'm good. Better than you, it seems."

He lets out a long-suffering sigh. "Not you too."

"I've been doing some research. There's a hospital with a well-renowned cardiac unit where you could get that testing done. We'd have to circle back to Nice, but . . ."

He waves me off. "I'm not bothering with all that here. I'll make an appointment when we get back to the States."

I figured it's what he'd say, but I'm no less annoyed by it.

"Charles," I say firmly, turning to face him, "if it was *my* heart that needed looking at, you'd turn this boat around immediately."

He takes a sip of his drink. "Doctors get paid to worry. It keeps them employed."

"And what if this isn't just worrying?" My voice is sharper than I intend, but I can't help it. "What if it's real? What if one of these days, you don't just bounce back?"

"I've been alive longer than you've been a thought in this world. I know my body. It's not as quick as it used to be, but it's mine. And I'll decide how I go out, not some doctor with a clipboard."

Something tight coils in my chest. "Do you even hear yourself? You talk like it's inevitable. Like you're just waiting for it to happen."

His gaze softens—just barely—but it's enough to make my throat burn. "We all go sometime, kid. That's just life."

I press my fingers against my forehead, trying to keep my frustration in check. "Fine," I say, forcing the word out. "But if you won't take care of yourself for your own sake, maybe do it for the people who actually give a damn about you. Frankie's worried."

His expression flickers, a split-second crack in his armor. "Yeah, well, maybe she worries too much."

"She cares," I snap. "All she does is try to make everything perfect for you. We both know that she's been great for you. Which is why I need to ask you something."

Charles turns his head, giving me a knowing look. "Let me guess. You want to steal her away for the day."

I nod, swallowing against the knot in my throat. "Just a few hours. I want to take her off the yacht for a while. Give her a break."

He exhales slowly, rubbing a hand over his jaw. "She'd never ask for time off herself, you know."

"I know," I say. "That's why I'm asking for her."

The silence between us is heavy. The waves lap gently against the hull, the hum of the ship a low, steady vibration beneath us. Finally, he picks up his drink, tilting it slightly in my direction.

"You have her back before dinner," he says gruffly. "And make it worth her while."

A breath I didn't realize I was holding shudders out of me. "Yes, sir."

Charles shakes his head. "God help me." But his voice is quieter now. Maybe even a little fond.

And for now, that's enough.

Chapter Twenty-Six

The Best Is Yet to Come

Frankie

I'm not sure how long I've been sitting on the floor, my back against the cool metal wall of the hallway near the engine room. It's warm here, the hum of machinery vibrating through the floor beneath me. It offers a strange kind of comfort, steady and reliable.

I just need a minute to breathe.

I'm not expecting Hayes to show up.

He rounds the corner, his brows pulling together when he sees me. "What are you doing down here?"

I lift a shoulder. "Needed a break. You?"

He holds up a wrench like that answers everything. "Just checking something." Then, instead of walking past me, he surprises me by lowering himself onto the floor across from me, stretching out his long legs.

For a moment, neither of us speaks. The hallway is dim, lit only by the glow of an overhead bulb. It feels removed from everything else on the yacht, like we exist in our own little pocket of time.

I know he's thinking about Charles, too, wondering if he is going to be okay.

"I talked to the chef about keeping red meat off the menu."

Hayes nods.

"My uncle was always there for me growing up. My parents were a mess, but Charles always made time for me."

"He's one of the good ones," I confirm.

Hayes lets his head fall back against the wall. "Growing up, my parents' issues, coupled with their disinterest in me, left me wondering why I could never make them happy." His voice is quiet, the kind of tone that makes me sit up a little straighter, like I am being let in on something real. "They were always too stuck in their own shit to really care."

I swallow. I didn't expect him to say that.

I watch the way his fingers toy with the wrench, spinning it absent-mindedly. He says it so matter-of-factly, but I can hear the weight behind it.

"My uncle Charles never missed a single tennis match of mine. Not once. He joined the athletic booster club, bought all the spirit wear—would show up decked out in crimson and gold and just sit there, smiling."

It's a nice mental picture. A much more vibrant Charles watching, rapt, the tennis match of a young Hayes.

"The second you let your guard down," he continues, his gaze fixed on some invisible point in the distance, "everything around you can topple like a house of cards."

I exhale, my own thoughts pressing in on me. "Yeah," I murmur, staring down at my hands. "I get that."

Hearing his experiences is like peeling back the layers of an onion—I can see why he is the way he is.

I was fortunate to grow up just getting to be a kid. He was saddled with responsibilities and expectations that far outweighed his ability to manage them at such a young age. His parents' messy dynamic, the drama that often accompanied any family function.

Hayes turns his head slightly, watching me. Waiting.

I hesitate, but then the words come out anyway. "I think I've spent most of my life trying to figure out where I fit. Like if I could just be the right version of myself, everything would click into place. But it never really has." I let out a small, self-deprecating laugh. "It's exhausting, honestly."

He studies me, his expression unreadable. "Yeah," he says after a beat. "It is."

It isn't much. Just a few words. But somehow, it feels like understanding. Like maybe I'm not as alone in that feeling as I thought.

The hum of the engine fills the quiet between us, but it isn't uncomfortable. It is something else entirely. Something heavier, unspoken. He shifts, his knee barely brushing against mine. A small touch, fleeting, but I feel it like a spark.

I'm not sure who moves first—him or me. Maybe neither of us do. Maybe we just exist in this strange little in-between space together, where words mean more than they usually do and silence says just as much.

"No one knows me like you do, Francesca."

I love the way he says my name. Not Frankie, even though I told him to call me by my nickname a million times. Francesca. It rolls off his perfect lips like a sacred offering.

"That's because you don't let anyone get close enough," I whisper, winking like it's some big secret.

He meets my eyes. I expect him to laugh—to brush off my remark, but he doesn't. His look is serious. "No, it's because you really see me. Past all the excess and opulence, the name. You see *me*."

His praise feels oddly good, comforting and wholesome.

I can't imagine that a man like Hayes Winters doles out compliments very often, so I decide I better soak in his words. They are like a balm to my soul. All I ever wanted was to be good at something. When I was young, it was math. Later, it was accounting . . . Now, I suppose, it's taking care of an old man on his last jaunt around the world.

"I convinced Charles to give you the day off tomorrow," he says out of the blue.

I blink, turning my head toward him. "What?"

He lifts a shoulder. "Figured you wouldn't ask for one yourself, so I did."

I stare at him, waiting for some kind of punch line, but he just watches me, his expression unreadable.

"Why?" I ask, my voice quieter than I intend.

His fingers stop playing with the wrench. "Because you deserve a break. And because I want to take you out."

My stomach flips. "Take me out?"

"Yeah." He turns to face me fully, his knee knocking against mine. "Off the yacht. Away from all of this for a few hours. Just you and me."

I don't know what to say. My pulse thrums in my ears, and I suddenly feel hyperaware of everything—the warmth of his leg brushing against mine, the way his gaze lingers, steady and sure.

"Unless you don't want to," he adds, his voice softer now.

I should say something. I should form words, but my brain is lagging, stuck somewhere between disbelief and something dangerously close to anticipation.

"I—" I clear my throat. "I just wasn't expecting that."

He smirks, but there's something nervous about it. Like he's not as sure of himself as he wants me to think. "That a yes?"

I let out a breath, my lips curving despite myself. "Yeah. That's a yes."

His smirk turns into a full smile, and I feel it like a spark in my chest.

Maybe stepping off this yacht with Hayes is a bad idea. Or maybe it's exactly what I need.

Chapter Twenty-Seven

When You Least Expect It

Frankie

I smooth down the flowy white sundress I changed into, the light fabric swishing around my legs as I step onto the deck, where Hayes is waiting. He looks effortlessly put together in a crisp navy button-down with the sleeves rolled up, paired with khaki shorts that *probably* cost more than my entire wardrobe. Sunglasses hang from the collar of his shirt, and his hair is still slightly tousled from the breeze, making him look unfairly good.

Charles stands nearby, watching us with the same mild amusement he always carries, but today, there's something softer in his expression.

"You two look decent enough," he says, taking a slow sip of his coffee. "Try not to embarrass the yacht."

Hayes shrugs, a grin tugging at the corner of his mouth. "No promises."

I roll my eyes but smile, stepping closer to Charles. "You sure you'll be okay without me for a few hours?"

He scoffs. "I think I'll survive. Go. Enjoy yourselves. And don't let this one"—he gestures at Hayes—"get you into too much trouble."

Hayes places a hand over his heart. "I would never."

Charles snorts, shaking his head as he waves us off. "Go on, before I change my mind."

As we step onto the dock, Hayes glances over at me, a small smile tugging at his lips. "Ready?"

I take a breath, strangely nervous, and nod. "Yeah. Let's go."

A sleek silver car waits for us at the curb, parked like it belongs in a Bond movie.

Hayes opens my door before sliding into the driver's seat. As with most things in his life, I'm sure, things just appear where and when he needs them to.

We pull away from the port, tires humming against cobblestone before the road smooths into narrow, winding lanes that cut through hillsides dotted with olive trees.

I bask in the warmth of the sun as it spills through the window and dances across my bare arms.

"You're awfully quiet over there," he muses, shooting me a quick glance. "Regretting your decision to get in a car with me?"

I smirk. "I'm good. Just wondering if you have a plan or if we're *winging* it today."

"Of course I have a plan," he says, slipping on his sunglasses. "We're going on a picnic."

"A picnic?"

For a man with all the money, all the connections, and everything at his disposal . . . he's going to throw a blanket down in the grass and call it good? I'm not sure whether to laugh or be disappointed.

He scoffs, feigning offense. "I'll have you know, I take my picnicking very seriously. Blanket? Check. Food? Check. Extremely charming company?" He gestures to himself. "Check."

I shake my head, laughing. "Wow. The humility is astounding."

"I try." He grins, tapping a few fingers on the steering wheel. "And what about you? What's your picnic contribution?"

I pretend to think. "Well, I brought my sparkling personality, which, let's be honest, is carrying this entire outing."

Hayes laughs, deep and warm, and it settles something in my chest. "You're going to love the lavender fields. You'll see."

While I gaze out the window, taking in the breathtaking scenery, Hayes hums along to the soft music playing from the car's speakers, one hand on the wheel, the other draped casually over the back of my seat.

A little while later, Hayes makes good on his promise. Provence is a dream—rolling hills, charming villages, and the golden glow of the late afternoon sun spilling over endless fields of lavender that sway in the breeze.

He parks along a gravel country road, and we climb out. I gaze out at the field stretching before us—vibrant purple against green hills. It looks like something out of a watercolor painting. The fragrant scent of lavender surrounds us, warm and intoxicating in the June breeze.

"Wow," I whisper, turning to take it all in. "This is unreal."

I hadn't realized how much I needed this. To be off the yacht—to feel the ground beneath my feet.

He grabs a picnic basket from the back seat and grins. "Not bad, huh?"

We find a perfect spot among the lavender and lay out a blanket under the open sky. Bees hum lazily nearby, uninterested in us, and the sun casts everything in a soft, honey-colored glow. Hayes unpacks our picnic—fresh baguettes, creamy cheeses, ripe summer fruit, and a chilled bottle of Provençal rosé.

"Very civilized," I murmur as he pours the blush-pink wine into two glasses.

He hands one to me, his fingers brushing mine for just a second too long. "Only the best," he says, eyes catching mine as he takes a sip. "Santé."

I accept the wine and clink my glass to his. "Santé."

The wine is delicious. Crisp and buttery with soft floral notes. I help myself to all the goodies, not even minding that these snacks are more gourmet and less grocery store grab-and-go.

"I can't get over how beautiful this is," I say, gesturing to the purple flowers.

"Agree. But the color's more of a wisteria than a lavender."

I eye him. "Where'd you get that?"

"Crayola." He shrugs.

I laugh until I realize he's being serious. He tells me a story about coloring with his sister, Maddie, and how one of his favorite parts is listening to her theories on color names being a conspiracy.

It's surprisingly easy, being here with Hayes—natural, even. The conversation flows, and we snack and laugh together.

The soft rustle of the breeze through the flowers. The *absolutely gorgeous* man lounging beside me.

I'm not sure how it's happened, but this feels almost . . . normal.

As we continue to chat, a lull falls over us, and for a moment, we just sit there, drinking in the stillness of the lavender fields. But then, Hayes breaks the silence.

"Do you think life gets any better than this?" he asks, gazing out at the horizon.

I hesitate, biting my lip. "I should think so, yes."

He looks at me curiously. "How do you figure?"

I shake my head. "Never mind."

"Tell me. I genuinely want to know."

I sigh and look at him, my thoughts shifting. "I would trade all of this for a cozy house, the smell of chocolate chip cookies baking, and a big ol' Christmas tree. Wrangling chubby little limbs into pajamas. Homemade Halloween costumes. Homework. Saturday morning soccer games. I want a family."

I feel vulnerable saying it, but it's the truth.

Being thousands of miles away from home has only deepened that longing.

He goes quiet for a moment, his eyes scanning my face. I know he's trying to find the right words, but they don't come.

He finally speaks. "You make it sound so easy."

I glance over at him. "It wasn't easy for me. I didn't have that growing up, and I know what it feels like to long for it. To want to create something different. That's why it feels like the most extravagant thing to wish for."

He's silent for a moment, his expression unreadable. I don't know if he understands.

After a beat, Hayes speaks, his voice low. "That's not the childhood I had. It was piano lessons, pressure, constant criticism, rehab stints for my parents, and family drama."

I glance at him, eyebrow raised. "Sounds like a blast."

He chuckles, rolls his eyes.

I take a sip of my wine, trying to act like this is no big deal. But there's something in his eyes that's different. Instead of our usual bickering banter, we're opening up. I think I like it.

This time, when I meet his eyes, my tone softens. "Family's complicated. I get it."

He gives me a half smile. "So, what about you?" he asks, turning the question on me. "What did your childhood look like?"

I sip my wine again, not meeting his eyes. "It wasn't . . . conventional. No huge holiday dinners, no piles of presents. I didn't really have a traditional family." I pause, letting the words hang. "So I guess that's why I want something different now."

He's quiet for a second, and then he says, "For what it's worth, I think you'd be a great mom. Fun and real and just . . . accepting."

I wonder if that's what he never had—someone to just accept him for who he is—not who he was supposed to be.

I never talk about these things—not even with Tessa. My dating life has always been a disaster—and if I couldn't hold down a boyfriend, how was I supposed to become a wife . . . a mother?

I look away from him, staring out over the lavender, feeling a little too exposed now. "I guess that's the kind of life I always wanted. The one that's not perfect, but it's mine." I finish my wine and glance back at him. "I know, it's a lot. But . . . what about you, Hayes? What do you want?"

There's a beat. Then he shakes his head. "I don't even know anymore. I've got all the things people say are supposed to make you happy—money, connections, nice suits, an amazing house. But when you have it all, you start wondering if it's really what you wanted. I mean, look at me," he says with a dry chuckle. "I've got everything I could possibly need, and sometimes I think about what it would be like to just . . . walk away from it all."

He meets my eyes, and I get the feeling he's not just talking about his job. "Maybe I need to stop trying to control everything."

I stare at him for a second, almost as though I'm seeing him for the first time. "You think you can do that?"

He shrugs, his gaze distant. "Not sure yet. But I'm starting to think maybe I need to figure out what really matters . . . without all the bullshit."

I smile a little, the wine buzzing in my system, but it's not just the wine. There's something about this moment that feels different. More honest. Like we're both not quite sure where we're headed.

"You're not as much of a grump as I thought," I tease, trying to lighten the moment.

He smirks, but there's something behind it. "Only for you, Frankie."

The conversation falls into a quiet space, and I can't help but wonder how we got here. Two people who couldn't be more different, yet somehow, we're here talking about life and sharing our insecurities.

After eating, we wander through the fields, my fingers grazing the lavender as we walk. The lavender-scented air wraps around us.

Hayes pulls out his phone and snaps a picture of me just as I turn, laughing.

"What?" I ask, narrowing my eyes.

He glances at the screen, then back at me. "You look . . . perfect. I had to capture it."

I raise an eyebrow, but I can't help but smile. "Okay, now I know you're just trying to flatter me."

His mouth lifts in a grin. "I have to admit, you're different than I imagined . . ."

He smirks, looking so effortlessly smug, and I catch myself glancing at the way the sunlight hits his face. His jawline's perfect, and his eyes—those damn eyes. They're warm, like melted caramel, and they *definitely* do things to me that I can't ignore.

But it's not just his face. I can't help but notice the way his body moves. It's . . . well, distracting.

And then my mouth opens—and to my horror—words start coming out.

"I've decided that it's weird that I've seen you naked twice . . ."

"Twice?" He blinks.

Or maybe once. I possibly imagined the second time, not that I'll admit that to him.

"And we haven't kissed . . ."

"You want to kiss me." It's not a question, and he doesn't phrase it like one.

"No." I hesitate. "Well, yes."

His lips lift in a teasing half grin that makes my stomach tighten. But he doesn't kiss me. He just keeps walking, slowly, leisurely beside me.

As the sun dips lower, we pack up and make a quick stop in a nearby village, browsing through market stalls filled with handmade soaps and lavender honey. Hayes buys me a small satchel of dried lavender, slipping it into my bag with a satisfied smile.

"Something to remember the day by," he says.

Back at the yacht, Charles greets us with a knowing glance over his evening tea. "I take it you two managed not to burn down Provence?"

I laugh, dropping into a chair beside him. "Barely."

Hayes moves across from us with a purposeful stride, his gaze lingering on me for a moment longer than necessary. As he takes a seat, his eyes flicker to mine, and there's a charged silence between us, something deeper than the usual teasing.

"Might have to go back just to double-check," he says, but a smile tugs at the corners of his mouth. It's the kind of look that makes me feel like he's thinking about something else entirely.

Charles hums, clearly amused. "I'm sure you will."

It's been a few hours since we got back, and Charles is half asleep in his chair, eyes glazed over as he watches C-SPAN. I'm pretty sure he's not even really watching it—just the white noise of politics keeping him company while the world passes by.

I yawn, stretching my arms above my head. The day's been . . . a lot. But in a good way. It's hard to put into words, but I feel something different. Something lighter. Something I didn't expect.

"I think I'm going to turn in," I announce, glancing over at Charles. He barely stirs, just grunts in acknowledgment.

I make my way to my room, running a hand through my hair, but just as I'm about to close the door, I hear it—a soft knock.

My heart skips a beat.

"Frankie?" Hayes's voice, low and unmistakable, says from the other side.

I open the door, leaning against the frame. "Yeah?"

Without another word, he steps inside. The air around us shifts immediately, charged in a way that leaves me breathless before he even gets close.

He shuts the door and moves.

Before I can say anything else, his hand is on my waist, pulling me gently toward him. His mouth crashes into mine, hungry, insistent. I barely have time to register what's happening before my back hits the door and Hayes is kissing me like he's been waiting for this moment all day.

His lips are firm, but there's something soft about it, too—something that makes my body go still for just a second before my mind catches up. It's like the tension that's been building between for months has just burst—an explosion I wasn't prepared for but can't pull away from.

I feel the heat of his body against mine, the pressure of his kiss, and suddenly, everything else in the world disappears. It all fades until it's just Hayes and me, tangled in what I can confidently say is the best kiss I've ever had.

When he finally pulls back, I'm breathless, my heart pounding against my ribs. I blink, trying to get my bearings.

"So that was . . . fine. Totally normal. Nothing to overanalyze at all."

His mouth quirks, clearly amused. "Everything okay?"

"Yeah," I say, nodding too quickly. "Just needed to make sure I still have bones in my legs."

He's still standing too close—*way* too close—his breath warm against my skin.

"That's how I've been feeling all day," he murmurs, his voice low. Like a confession meant only for me.

I glance up at him, searching his face for any sign of doubt or hesitation. There's none. Just that same intensity, the same thing I saw earlier, that I've been trying to ignore since we met.

"Well," I say, trying to shake off the haze of the kiss, "what are we supposed to do about that now?"

His fingers trace lightly down my arm, a grin tugging at his lips. "I don't know. But I'm sure I can think of a thing or two."

A low pulse of desire races through me.

"Frankie!" I hear Charles call from the other room.

Hayes lifts one eyebrow.

"Gotta go," I say, still breathless.

~

Later that night, I slip into bed, the sheets cool against my skin, but my mind is anything but cool. I stare up at the ceiling, trying to make sense of the mess in my head. What the hell happened today?

Hayes happened.

The guy I thought was an arrogant, entitled ass—who couldn't be bothered to give anyone the time of day without it being in his best interest. The guy who made me want to slap him one minute and throw him in the ocean the next. That guy.

And yet, somehow, he's been . . . different. More than I expected.

It's weird, honestly. He's not the guy I imagined. At first, I thought he'd be the kind of guy who walks around with his nose in the air, thinking the world revolves around him. But today, he was . . . well, different. He arranged for me to have a day off. Took me off the boat. He was *charming*. He actually listened when I talked. He even seemed to care when I said something, instead of brushing me off like I was an inconvenience.

And the way he looked at me earlier . . .

The way he kissed me . . .

I roll onto my side, burying my face in the pillow. What the hell is wrong with me?

I *shouldn't* be thinking about him this way.

It's not that I'm attracted to him—well, okay, I'm definitely attracted to him. That's a given. He's not my type, but then again, my type has never worked for me anyway. But that's not what's messing with me.

What's messing with me is how he's . . . *surprising* me.

The way he wasn't as full of himself as I thought. The way he actually made me laugh today. Several times, in fact. Hell, even the way he stared at me, like I was a puzzle he was dying to figure out. I thought I'd be irritated with him by now, but instead, I'm intrigued.

And then there's that kiss . . .

I exhale sharply, remembering the strange zip of electricity between us when he grabbed my waist and hauled me in. How his lips felt, the warmth of his body pressing to mine. I hadn't been expecting it, not at all. But now that it's happened, I can't stop thinking about it.

What does it all mean?

I let out a frustrated sigh and pull the blanket over my head. I remember confiding in Tessa about my growing attraction. She warned me not to do something rash—like sleep with him. He's my boss's nephew . . . we're stuck together in the middle of the ocean. If it was weird, or bad . . . it would make things terribly awkward for me.

But there's something different about him. Something that's pulling me in. And that, more than anything, is what scares the hell out of me.

I take a deep breath, trying to calm the storm of thoughts. One thing's for sure: tomorrow, I'm going to need to put a little more space between myself and the ever-surprising Hayes Winters. Because if I keep going down this rabbit hole, I might find myself lost—and I don't know if I'm ready for that.

Chapter Twenty-Eight

Let Your Guard Down

Hayes

I try not to stare. I really do. But there's something about her today that's making it impossible.

Frankie's sprawled out on the sundeck in her bathing suit—something simple, black, with a hint of edge that makes me think it's the only thing she could've picked in five minutes, but she somehow makes it look like it was tailored just for her. Her hair is wet from the pool, and it falls in damp waves around her shoulders.

She's talking to Charles, who's seated in the lounge chair next to her, his wrinkled hand holding a book that he's barely reading. His attention is mostly on her, and I can't blame him. Frankie has this way of making even the most ordinary moments feel . . . different.

Her laugh drifts across the deck, light and genuine, and I find myself smiling without meaning to. She's telling Charles some story about a disaster she had in college—something involving a bouncy castle, a broken arm, and a very confused police officer. The way she tells it, with all her exaggerated hand gestures and that self-deprecating humor, has Charles chuckling like he's heard the joke a thousand times, even though it's obvious he's never heard it before.

The contrast between them is striking—Charles, with his years of experience, a calm demeanor, and that kind of gruff warmth that only old men can pull off, and Frankie, with her unfiltered, unapologetic energy. It's like they've known each other for years.

And then there's the way she's just so . . . kind.

I'm used to people being polite to Charles, but Frankie? She's real with him. She doesn't just listen; she engages, asks questions, makes sure he's included. She even pokes fun at his odd obsessions, like C-SPAN, which is something I'd never dare to do. He loves it. You can see it in the way his old eyes twinkle with amusement. She's cracking him open like a walnut—in a way that no one else has quite managed to.

He knew what he was doing, hiring her. I thought it was odd at the time—thought the old man was really losing it. Now I see how perfect she's been for this job.

Her voice rises in the air again, teasing Charles about his collection of golf hats. "Come on, Charles," she says, giving him a playful nudge. "Isn't it time to throw out that one from the eighties? It's practically vintage!"

Charles grumbles good-naturedly but lets her win, chuckling as he adjusts the hat she's teasing him about. I've spent so much time in the circle of people who only care about the right brands, the right image. And here's Frankie—no filter, no pretensions—just real. And it's . . . pretty damn refreshing.

I glance over at her again, only to find her catching my eye. She grins at me like she knows exactly what I'm thinking—like she's somehow cracked the code that's always kept me at arm's length.

Her smile is crooked, a little mischievous, and I'm hit with a wave of something I can't quite place. My chest tightens. It's more than just attraction—it's the way she makes me feel . . . like I can *breathe*.

When she's around, everything else fades. The pressure, the expectations—none of it matters when she's talking, laughing, or even just sitting there, her bare feet dangling off the edge of the deck, kicking the water with a little splash. She doesn't care. She's not trying to impress anyone. And that's . . . rare.

She turns back to Charles, asking him if he needs help getting into the pool, and I see her kindness once more, that little spark in her that's so easy to miss if you're not paying attention.

The truth is, I should be the one helping him.

But she just . . . does it. No hesitation. No show.

I don't know why, but it hits me harder today. Maybe it's because of what we shared yesterday. I can't stop thinking about that kiss. The way her lips felt under mine, soft but urgent, the way her fingers felt, threaded in my hair. When her mouth met mine, it was like everything else faded away. Nothing mattered but her.

We're so different, and she's employed by my uncle. Which means she's the *last* person I should be letting get under my skin. But she's pulling me apart, bit by bit. I can feel it—like she's carefully loosening a tie that has been tied too tight.

"She's something else," Charles mutters, catching me looking. He's got that knowing smile on his face, the one he always gets when he sees me slipping up in my self-imposed walls.

I don't respond, just lean back in my chair, crossing my arms. "I don't know what you're talking about."

Charles just chuckles to himself, shaking his head.

But I know he's right. Frankie's got me more off-balance than I've ever been in my life—and it's making me feel things I didn't know I was capable of.

She glances at me again, catching my gaze for a split second. This time, there's something different in her eyes, too—something more knowing. I can't put my finger on it, but she's not looking at me the same way she did before. There's a softness there now. Maybe even a little curiosity.

And that's when I realize—I've been letting myself look at her differently too. The change is subtle, but it's there. And I can't tell if that's a good thing or not.

Chapter Twenty-Nine

When the Walls Start to Fall

Frankie

The soft hum of the yacht's engines is the only sound as we sit in the lounge, Hayes and I nursing the last of our drinks. The evening was . . . unexpected. We'd laughed, swapped stories about the most ridiculous things that had happened to us in our lives, and for once, I didn't feel like I was walking around on eggshells, trying not to screw something up. Charles and now even Hayes seem to get me, to accept me.

"I think you're the first person who's ever made me laugh this much," he says, swirling the last of his wine. Hayes is leaning back on the couch, his arm stretched across the backrest, looking at me like he's trying to figure me out. The kind of look that usually makes me want to squirm.

"Is that a compliment?" I ask.

"Of course it is," he says, voice low.

I roll my eyes, trying to play it off. "I guess you *can* be tolerable, too, for a billionaire."

"Wow," he says, feigning offense. "I'm hurt."

I can't help but laugh. His teasing is starting to feel . . . comfortable. Maybe it's the way his eyes light up when I make him laugh, or how he actually listens when I talk about all the stupid things that have gone wrong in my life.

The silence stretches between us, but it's not awkward. Just comfortable. And something shifts. Maybe it's the way he's looking at me now, like he's seeing me for the first time without all the walls up.

I glance away, trying to shake the sudden heat spreading through me. It's ridiculous. Hayes is . . . *well, Hayes.* He's all wrong for me, and not to mention probably leaving soon. But I can't stop replaying that kiss . . .

"Why do you do that?" he asks suddenly, breaking the silence.

"Do what?"

"Hide. Whenever things get too real, you shut down."

I freeze, caught off guard. "What are you talking about?"

He reaches over, brushing the hair from my face, and touches my cheek.

He looks at me like he sees through all the things I worry about. My finances, my anxiety, my weight. He looks at me like none of it matters—and maybe it doesn't. In his presence, I feel weightless, like the world is my oyster. But I know none of this is real. My time with Charles will eventually end, the bubble will burst, and I'll be back to sharing a crappy apartment in Jersey—alone and lonely. And Hayes will probably move on to some supermodel or actress.

"You're good at pretending like nothing gets to you. Like you don't care about the things that matter," he says softly, his voice uncharacteristically serious. "But you do. I can see it."

I blink, unsure of how to respond. Is it that obvious? I thought I'd been hiding it better. But Hayes—he's always paying attention, isn't he?

I sigh, setting my glass down. "I don't know. I guess it's easier than showing anyone the stuff that really gets to me. The things that make me . . . vulnerable."

There's a long pause. Then he leans forward, his voice low. "I get it. More than you think."

I look up, and for a second, the world outside this room fades. It's just him and me. No more pretending. The tension between us is undeniable, and for the first time, I don't want to run from it.

Then he does something unexpected. He reaches out, lightly brushing his fingers over mine. It's such a small gesture, but it sends a spark through my entire body. He notices the way I freeze, but instead of pulling away, he holds my hand gently, as though waiting for me to make the next move.

"I'm not going to bite," he says softly, his voice low. "You're safe."

I swallow hard. "I'm not so sure about that."

His thumb moves slowly over my hand, and I'm so aware of the way it feels—his touch is both comforting and electrifying. I should pull away, distance myself, but the truth is . . . I don't want to.

"Why do I feel like you're trying to push me away?" he murmurs, his gaze on mine so intense it makes it hard to breathe.

I open my mouth to say something, but the words don't come. Instead, I just stare at him. And then, without thinking, I pull my hand free, moving a little closer, my breath catching in my throat.

"You're remembering that kiss, aren't you?" he whispers, his lips barely an inch from mine now.

I close my eyes for a moment, letting the silence stretch between us. There's so much I could say—but instead, I just nod my head.

And before I can process what's happening, his lips are on mine, gentle but insistent. The kiss is slow at first, as if he's waiting for me to pull away. But I don't. I don't want to.

The kiss deepens, and my heart is racing now. His lips move against mine, slow and deliberate, as if he's waiting for something. Maybe he's waiting for me to fully give in.

But then, the sound of footsteps echoing across the deck breaks through the haze of desire. My eyes snap open just in time to see a crew member walk past, his eyes briefly flicking over us. I feel the moment like a slap in the face—too exposed, too real—and I jerk back, quickly pulling away.

I stare at Hayes, my chest heaving. His eyes are still closed for a second, as if he's in a daze, before he opens them, locking on to mine. There's a flash of something—disappointment, maybe? Or just surprise that I pulled back.

I swallow hard, breaking the silence between us. "I should . . . I should go," I murmur, my legs shaking, like they might give out beneath me.

Before he can say anything, I push to my feet, my heart pounding in my throat. "Good night," I say, my voice a little too shaky. I turn and quickly head toward my cabin, not looking back. I don't want to look back. Because if I do, I might not leave.

The hallway is cool as I slip into my room and close the door behind me. I lean against it, taking deep breaths, trying to steady myself, but I can't. The kiss lingers on my lips. The heat of his touch is still burning through my skin.

I walk over to the bed and sit down, my mind racing, wondering what the hell just happened. This wasn't on my radar at all, me and Hayes, but I feel like I've stepped off a cliff and now I have no idea how to climb back.

Then, just as I'm about to collapse onto the bed, I hear a knock. Soft. Gentle.

My heart skips a beat. I freeze, my breath catching in my chest. I don't want to open the door, but I also don't want to ignore it.

I stand and walk slowly to the door, hesitating for a moment before I turn the handle.

The door opens just a crack, and there he is—Hayes. His expression is different this time, softer, almost . . . tentative.

"Frankie," he says, his voice low. He steps forward, closing the distance between us in a heartbeat. "I didn't mean for things to end that way."

I open my mouth to say something, but he doesn't give me the chance. His hand comes up, cupping my cheek, and he kisses me again.

But this time, there's no hesitation. No space. This time, it's all heat and need, and it's so much more than I can handle.

My legs go weak again as he presses me back against the door, the kiss deepening, his hands moving to the buttons of my shirt. I don't protest. I don't want to protest. His lips trail down my neck, and my head falls back with a soft gasp. He kisses a line down to my collarbone before looking up at me, his eyes dark and intense.

"I want you," he says, his voice barely a whisper, but it's enough to send a thrill through my entire body.

But then, he pulls back slightly, his forehead resting against mine, his breath heaving like he just swam laps.

"Tell me to stop." His voice is low, and his eyes are intense. There's a vulnerability in them that catches me off guard. He's waiting for me, asking if I want this too.

I swallow, my heart racing, and I nod. "Don't stop," I manage to get out, voice trembling with excitement.

He kisses me. Hard. A demanding, *urgent* kiss that seems to stretch on for days. Weeks. Years.

When he finally pulls back, I'm lost—sinking. I can't speak. It seems that neither can Hayes. He just watches me with a stunned expression.

I don't know what's happening, but I do know it's unlike anything I've ever experienced.

He leans in again, his lips capturing mine in a slow, deliberate kiss, and his hands move with purpose. I can feel every inch of him against me, the heat of his touch making every reason why we shouldn't vanish entirely.

Without another word, he pulls my shirt off, then drops the fabric to the floor. I do the same to him, my fingers shaking as I undo his shirt, exposing the warm skin underneath. His hands are on me again, pulling me closer, as if we're both starving for this. For each other.

His lips find mine, desperate this time, as he advances me toward the bed. I barely have time to react before I'm on the mattress, his weight pressing me down. My breath hitches as he moves to undress me completely, his hands gentle but firm, as if he knows exactly what I need and when.

His lips trail lower, unhurried, leaving warmth in their wake. Every place he touches feels lit from within, a slow burn spreading through me until I can't take much more.

When his mouth finds mine again, it's softer this time—less hunger, more promise. He's steady where I'm trembling, certain where I'm undone.

"Please stop being so good at this," I murmur.

"I'll see what I can do," he says, his lips moving to my neck. He laughs softly against my skin, the sound low and warm, and for a moment, everything else disappears—the hum of the yacht, the weight of the day, the ache I've been carrying for so long.

"Was that okay? You're kind of spacing out," Hayes asks, clearly not getting why I'm suddenly silent.

"Huh? No, that was *not* okay. What just happened?"

I'm still processing the whole thing. The bar has been set so high, I don't know how anything else could ever compare. "I don't know who you are or what kind of sorcery you pulled, but no—*I am not okay.*"

"Come again?"

"Exactly!" I burst out, trying to collect my thoughts.

He chuckles, clearly amused.

"No, seriously, Hayes. That was *intimidating*. I feel like I just went through an intense workout with no warm-up. I don't even know where to go from here."

"Shh." He leans in to kiss me, trying to smooth things over with a dose of charm.

I blink, still stunned. "What am I supposed to do? Pretend it never happened?"

He shrugs, a little too casual, then covers us with the sheet. "Nope. We don't have to pretend anything. Just act normal. I've found it's best to maintain a 'business as usual' policy after these sorts of things."

I squint at him, crossing my arms. "*These sorts of things* as in . . . hooking up with the help?" I raise an eyebrow, giving him a pointed stare.

He waves a hand, nonchalant. "You're not really the help. I'd say you at least qualify as Charles's companion by now."

I huff before turning on my side, snuggling closer—because he's warm, and solid, and well, gorgeous. Even if that was annoying.

"You're something else, Frankie," he says around a deep, satisfied sigh.

"Yeah well, I really think I pulled a muscle."

Hayes laughs.

Chapter Thirty

Hayes Is Bad at Feelings

Hayes

I can't sleep.

I'm lying in bed, staring at the ceiling, the weight of everything that happened tonight practically crushing me.

I might have laughed and let her stroke my ego . . . but alone now in my cabin, I can't lie to myself. Something happened between us. Something that shouldn't have.

Which is why I had to get the hell out of there. The last thing I can afford is to get tangled up with feelings I swore I'd never entertain. As soon as she fell asleep, I crawled from the bed, grabbed my clothes, and shuffled off to my own cabin. Which is where I am now—spiraling.

I force my eyes closed, but it doesn't help. I keep seeing the way she looked at me, gazing at me in wonder. I keep hearing the sound of her soft voice . . . remembering the way her lips tasted. The way her hands . . .

Damn it.

Why did I let myself go there?

This is only going to cause problems. She works for my uncle, and she makes me think about things I swore I never wanted. Talk about a cluster . . .

She challenges me, argues with me over nonsense . . . she makes me feel like I've been sleepwalking my entire life. When she kissed me, something inside me—something that had been dormant for years—woke up. It felt like I was . . . alive again. And it scares the shit out of me.

I shake my head, frustrated.

The morning sun comes too quick, and I force myself out of bed.

I struggle through a sunrise workout and almost quit eight times.

What's wrong with me? Am I sick? Dying?

I replay everything from last night in my head, still stunned by what happened. I don't even know what to *do* with the fact that I'm feeling . . . *something*. I keep trying to shake it off like it's just a weird fluke—maybe the flu? Or some sort of brain fog?

I'm just tired. My body is on edge, maybe from the trip. Hell, maybe I just need a nap. That's it. A nap. I didn't sleep much last night.

I find Charles on the aft deck, alone with a cup of coffee.

"Morning," he says.

"Morning," I grumble.

"You okay?" He's staring at me now.

I scrub a hand down my face. "Didn't sleep well."

He nods, looking thoughtful, then tips his chin toward the cabins. "Did that have anything to do with the fact you spent the night in her cabin?"

"Damn boat's too small," I mutter.

"It's forty meters. And you didn't answer the question."

"Of course not," I mutter. But when I glance over, I see his frown. I really don't want to deal with this right now.

"Hmm," he says, sipping his coffee.

"Everything's fine," I lie.

Charles sees straight through me. "I doubt that's true."

I release a slow, shuddering exhale.

"Maybe I treated Frankie with less kindness than I should have," I say, voice tight. "I may have implied our night together was . . . sort of, you know, run of the mill. And then I left after . . . well, *after*."

Charles raises an eyebrow. "Why'd you do that?"

I rub the back of my neck. The words are so much harder to say than I imagined. "Because there's a chance that I could see myself . . . falling in love with her."

He doesn't react right away. Instead, he watches me with a long, calculating stare. "And that worries you?" he asks.

"No, that doesn't *worry* me," I say quickly. "It terrifies me. I'll mess it up."

I try to swallow the lump in my throat, but it's there, lodged like some kind of foreign object I don't know how to get rid of. I've never been like this, never felt . . . whatever the hell this is.

Charles just stares at me, as if he's waiting for me to catch up with myself. And then finally he speaks again, like he's seen this coming all along. "She's a good girl, you know?"

I nod.

If there's one thing I know, it's that I'll screw it up. I'll ruin everything.

It doesn't matter. What I told her was true—it was a one-time thing.

It has to be.

Chapter Thirty-One

The Morning After Everything Changed

Frankie

I wake up to an empty bed.

I can still smell his cologne on the sheets, but the warmth feels distant now. I sit up slowly, pulling the blanket tighter around me, trying to shake the fog of sleep from my brain.

I replay the last few hours. The way he touched me. The way he kissed me. It felt real. It felt . . . good. *Too good.* Almost perfect.

I hear the soft murmur of voices coming from outside my room. Charles and Hayes are talking, laughing—normal, like nothing's changed. Like I didn't just let him into my life in a way I never intended. Like it wasn't the most vulnerable thing I've done in years.

I push myself out of bed and stand there for a moment, unsure of what to do.

I throw on a robe, tugging the edges tighter to hide the way I feel so damn *exposed*, and step into the hallway. Hayes is in the main salon with Charles, dressed and dapper as always, like nothing's different. Like we didn't share something last night that's suddenly making my chest tighten.

I pause just outside the door, wanting to say something but unsure of what. *What the hell is wrong with me?* It was just like Hayes said—casual and fun, and it meant absolutely nothing.

I clear my throat and walk in, my voice a little too loud, a little too forced. "Hey."

Both men look up. Hayes gives me a quick glance, no more than that, and then turns back to Charles. He doesn't say anything. Not a word. He doesn't even acknowledge what happened. Not even an offhand remark or a casual smile. Just . . . nothing.

My stomach twists, and I feel it: the sudden, sharp pang of hurt. I want to say something—anything—but my mouth feels like it's full of cotton. I *could* ask him if last night meant anything to him, but I already know the answer.

Instead, I force a smile that feels too tight. "I, uh, guess I'll go get some breakfast," I say, the words coming out so flat I can barely recognize my own voice.

Hayes doesn't even look at me. He nods at Charles, then grabs his coffee like I'm nothing more than a blip on his radar. The casualness of it burns more than I expected.

I turn and walk away, my heart pounding in my chest, my head spinning. Did I misread everything? Did I actually think there could be something between us? It was just a hookup. But why did it feel like more? Probably because of that thoughtful date he took me on and all the little things in between . . .

My chest aches as I make my way toward the kitchen, away from the two men who seem so at ease, so *normal*, while I'm here, spiraling.

I reach for the coffee pot, needing something to steady my hands. I pour myself a cup of coffee and head back to the table.

Hayes meets my eyes and frowns before his gaze darts away.

I almost choke on my own spit.

Okay?

No need to be an asshole.

We slept together.

And damn him, he's acting like it's no big deal. Meanwhile, I'm still trying to process that it *was* a big deal. A *huge* deal.

For starters, I'm almost certain I *did* pull a muscle.

He chuckles at something Charles says, totally at ease. Meanwhile, I'm sitting here, acting like someone who just discovered fire for the first time. Like . . . what's even happening?

He stretches a little, looking over his shoulder at me.

And that's when I notice it—the way his gaze lingers on me just a little too long, the way he smiles softly, as if he's memorizing this moment. I feel a flutter in my chest, something warm and new.

From across the table, Charles watches us curiously, his brow furrowing. He looks from Hayes to me and back again, like he's trying to piece something together. I can practically hear the gears turning in his head.

I meet Charles's gaze, giving him an innocent smile and a little shrug. Nope. Nothing to see here.

But Hayes catches the exchange, too, and his frown returns.

I turn my attention back to Charles, who's still giving us a look, and force a casual smile, but something about Hayes's cavalier attitude stings. I didn't often do the casual hookup thing, and last night felt different. Except, apparently not to him.

I stir my coffee like it personally wronged me.

Hayes sits three feet away, scrolling through his phone like last night was just another Tuesday. Like he didn't completely rearrange my understanding of what good sex could be. Like I didn't fall apart in his hands and put myself back together as someone entirely different.

The worst part? He looks *good.* Hair slightly messed up, that post-sex glow that should be illegal on someone who's currently pretending I don't exist.

Charles glances between us again. The man's eighty-two, not blind.

"So," Charles says, setting down his newspaper. "What's the plan for today?"

Hayes doesn't look up from his phone. "I need to fly back to New York this afternoon."

My coffee cup freezes halfway to my lips.

This afternoon?

"Business emergency," he adds, still not making eye contact with me.

Right. Of course. A convenient business emergency exactly twelve hours after we had the most intense sexual experience of my life. What are the odds?

"That's sudden," Charles says, frowning.

Hayes shrugs. "These things happen."

I set my cup down harder than necessary. The clink echoes across the deck.

"Frankie?" Charles asks. "Are you okay?"

"Perfect," I say, voice bright as bleach. "Absolutely fantastic."

Hayes finally looks at me. For exactly two seconds. Then his gaze slides away like I'm made of something that burns.

"I should go pack," he says, standing abruptly.

And just like that, he's gone. Leaving me sitting here with Charles, who's watching me with those sharp eyes that see everything.

"Want to talk about it?" Charles asks.

"Nope." I force a smile. "Nothing to talk about."

But my hands are shaking around my coffee cup, and we both pretend not to notice.

An hour later, I'm stress-cleaning the already spotless galley when I hear the helicopter.

My hands still on the counter I'm scrubbing for the third time.

He's really leaving.

I listen to the sound fade into the distance, taking with it any stupid fantasy I built up about what last night might have meant.

Charles appears in the doorway, looking older than usual.

"He's gone," he says unnecessarily.

"Good." I scrub harder. "More room for the rest of us."

"Frankie."

"What?" I turn, and whatever he sees on my face makes him frown.

"Come here."

I don't want to. I want to keep scrubbing things until my hands are raw and I stop feeling like someone hollowed me out with a spoon.

But Charles has that look—the one that says he's about to dispense grandfatherly wisdom whether I want it or not.

I sink into the chair across from him.

"My nephew," he says carefully, "is an idiot."

Despite everything, I almost smile. "Yeah. I'm starting to figure that out."

"He's also terrified."

"Of what?"

"Of being happy."

The words settle between us like stones.

"His parents screwed him up pretty good," Charles continues. "Made him think love was just another way to get hurt. So he runs when things get real."

"Well, he's good at it," I mutter.

Charles reaches across and pats my hand. "Give him time."

"Time for what? To find another supermodel to bang and abandon?"

The bitterness in my voice surprises even me.

"Time to realize what he's lost."

I pull my hand away. "Charles, I appreciate what you're trying to do, but I'm not going to sit around waiting for some emotionally constipated idiot to figure out his feelings. I have more self-respect than that."

At least, I'm trying to.

Charles nods slowly. "Good. You *should* have more self-respect than that."

Wait. That's not the response I expected.

"But," he continues, "you should also know that I've never seen him look at anyone the way he looks at you."

"Yeah? And how's that?"

"Like he's drowning, and you're the life raft."

That night, I stand on the deck, watching the sunset paint the Mediterranean in shades of pink and gold. It's beautiful. Postcard perfect.

I feel like garbage.

I can't believe I let him in. Can't believe I ended my self-imposed boy ban for him. And for what? To feel like absolute crap about myself now that he cast me aside.

A two-line text message telling me hey thanks, you were good for Charles, but absolutely nothing about how I was good for him too? It's horseshit. I *was* good for Hayes. Whether he saw it or not. I guess Tessa wasn't wrong about me—I do pick the worst guys. I thought Hayes was giving beige flags when in reality they were red, red, red.

My phone buzzes. Text from Tessa.

Tessa: How's life on the love boat?

Frankie: Crashed and burned spectacularly.

Tessa: Details. Now.

Frankie: Can't. Too humiliating.

Tessa: Did you sleep with Hayes?

Ugh, she knows me too well.

Frankie: Maybe.

Tessa: FRANCESCA.

Frankie: Fine. Yes. And it was amazing. And now he's gone.

Tessa: Gone as in . . . ?

Frankie: Gone as in flew back to New York immediately after like I was a prostitute he regretted hiring.

My phone rings thirty seconds later.

"What the actual hell?" Tessa's voice is sharp. "He just *left*?"

"Yep. Had a sudden business emergency." I lean against the railing. "God, I'm so stupid."

"You're not stupid. He's an ass."

"Same difference."

"No, it's not. You took a chance. That takes guts."

"Guts and apparently zero common sense."

"Frankie." Tessa's voice softens. "Did it feel real? When you were together?"

I close my eyes, remembering the way Hayes looked at me in the lavender fields. The way he touched my face like I was precious. The way he held me afterward, like he didn't want to let go.

"Yeah," I whisper. "It felt real."

"Then maybe it was. Maybe he's just scared."

"Since when do you defend the men who hurt me?"

"Since never. But this one . . . I don't know. Something about him seems different."

Different. Yeah. That's the problem.

Hayes Winters isn't like my usual disasters. He's not obviously broken or clearly wrong for me. He's successful, smart, devastatingly handsome, and absolutely incredible in bed.

Which makes it so much worse when he runs.

"I need to forget about him," I tell Tessa.

"Good luck with that."

After we hang up, I stay on the deck until the stars come out. The yacht rocks gently beneath me, and for the first time since I took this job, I feel truly alone.

Charles finds me there an hour later.

"Can't sleep?"

"Something like that."

He settles into the chair beside me with a soft grunt. We sit in comfortable silence for a while, watching the lights of distant boats twinkle on the water.

"You know," he says eventually, "when I met Betsey, I nearly didn't ask her out."

"Why not?"

"I was scared she was too good for me. Too smart, too beautiful, too everything. I figured she'd realize what a mess I was and run."

"But she didn't run."

"No. She saw through all my bullshit to something worth keeping." He pauses. "Sometimes the best things in life come disguised as the scariest."

I know what he's trying to do. And I love him for it.

But I'm not sure I believe in fairy tales anymore.

Chapter Thirty-Two

Distance Makes the Heart Grow Stupid

Hayes

I threw my clothes into the suitcase like the yacht was on fire. Which, metaphorically, it was.

Last night was . . . Damn it. I still can't think about it without my chest doing this weird tight thing. The way she looked at me afterward, all soft and trusting. Like I was someone worth keeping.

That was the problem.

Charles knocked on my door right as I was zipping up my bag. His face when he walked in—disappointed but not surprised. Like he was expecting me to run.

"Running away?" he asked.

"I have work."

"Bullshit."

And when I finally admitted the truth—that I let it mean something—he gave me that look. The one that said I was breaking his heart along with my own.

But I couldn't stay there, not now. Not after . . .

"Hayes." His voice carried that authoritative tone that made him a billionaire. "I'm old, not stupid."

I sank onto the bed, defeated. "I messed up."

"How?"

"I let it mean something."

Charles was quiet for a long moment. Then he asked, "And that's bad because . . . ?"

I told him I didn't have time for a relationship and that I didn't do flings with women who worked for the family.

In my mind, it all made perfect sense.

"She won't work for me forever," he said quietly.

The words hit me like a punch. Right. This job has an end date. She'll go back to New Jersey, find some normal guy who deserves her, and I'll go back to my pristine, empty life.

Perfect.

"Since when has being scared of something ever stopped a Winthrop?" he asked.

Since never. But this felt different. This felt like it could destroy me.

Now, three days later, New York feels like a prison.

I'm back in my penthouse, surrounded by all my expensive things, and I can't shake the feeling that I've made the biggest mistake of my life.

I had my entire life planned to a T.

A crisp *Wall Street Journal* on my desk.

A glass of whiskey in the evenings.

Golf on the weekends.

I knew exactly who I was and what I wanted out of life.

And now?

Now I don't know who I am or what I'm doing.

My phone buzzes. Malachi.

Malachi: Drinks tonight? The usual spot?

I stare at the text. The usual spot. Where we go to pick up women whose names I'll forget by morning. Where I used to feel at home.

Now the thought makes my skin crawl.

Rain check I type back.

Malachi: You okay?

No. I'm the furthest thing from okay.

Hayes: Fine. Just tired.

I toss my phone aside and pour myself a drink I don't want.

The silence in my apartment is deafening. No sound of waves. No Charles reading the newspaper aloud. No Frankie humming off-key while she makes coffee.

God. I miss her humming.

I miss everything about her.

The way she calls me on my shit. The way she makes me laugh without trying. The way she looked at me that last morning like I hung the moon.

Before I ruined everything.

My phone rings. Charles.

I let it go to voicemail.

Then I listen to the message.

"Hayes. I know you're screening my calls. Call me back. We need to talk."

I delete it without calling back.

But an hour later, I'm still thinking about it. About him. About the disappointed look on his face when I said I was leaving.

About the hurt in Frankie's eyes that she tried so hard to hide.

I pour another drink and try to forget.

It doesn't work.

My assistant, Greta, knocks on my office door the next morning. She looks better—the dark circles under her eyes are fading, and she's gained back some weight.

"How are you feeling?" I ask.

"Better every day. The doctors are optimistic." She sets a stack of papers on my desk. "But I'm more worried about you. You look like hell."

"Thanks. That's exactly what every boss wants to hear."

She doesn't laugh at my attempt at humor. "Hayes. What happened in France?"

I lean back in my chair. Greta's known me for five years. She's seen me through breakups, family drama, board meetings that went sideways. She's never seen me like this.

"I screwed up."

"How bad?"

"Nuclear-level bad."

She settles into the chair across from my desk. "Tell me."

So I do. I tell her about Frankie—her laugh, her kindness with Charles, the way she makes me feel like a human instead of a walking trust fund. I tell her about running away like a coward.

When I finish, Greta just stares at me.

"You're an idiot," she says finally.

"I'm aware."

But she deserves better than me. She deserves someone who doesn't run when things get complicated.

Which means it's better this way.

~

I've been back in New York for two weeks, and nothing makes sense anymore. My coffee tastes like ash. My Egyptian cotton sheets feel like sandpaper. Even my view of Central Park—the one that cost me eight million dollars—looks gray and lifeless.

It's like someone sucked all the color out of my world and left me with this black-and-white existence that I used to think was enough.

I'm standing in my kitchen, staring at the espresso machine like it might spontaneously combust, when my phone buzzes.

Mom: Need you at dinner tonight. Bringing someone I want you to meet.

Not this again.

Hayes: Can't. Work.

Mom: 7 PM. Don't be late.

The woman doesn't take no for an answer. Never has.

Two hours later, I'm sitting in Le Bernardin across from Victoria Ashworth-Sterling, who's everything my mother thinks I need. Blond. Beautiful. Trust fund. Harvard MBA.

She's been talking for twenty minutes straight about her charity work, and I haven't heard a single word.

"The thing about philanthropy," she's saying, cutting her fish into perfect little squares, "is that you have to maintain proper boundaries. You can't get too emotionally invested."

My brain stutters. "What?"

"Emotional distance. It's crucial when you're trying to help people. Otherwise you lose objectivity."

I think about Frankie feeding Charles liverwurst at 6:00 a.m. because it made him happy. The way she'd sit with him during *Jeopardy!*, genuinely delighted when he got the answers right.

"Right," I manage. "Boundaries."

Victoria smiles. "Exactly. That's why I prefer board positions to hands-on work. More efficient."

More efficient.

My phone buzzes. Malachi.

Malachi: How's the setup dinner going? Mom find you a wife yet?

I excuse myself to the bathroom and call him back.

"That bad?" he answers on the first ring.

"She just said helping people requires emotional distance."

"Yikes."

"I keep thinking about—" I stop myself.

"About Frankie?"

Her name hits me like a physical blow. "Don't."

"Dude, you've been miserable for two weeks. Maybe it's time to—"

"Time to what?" Fly back to France and beg? "She's better off without me."

I lean against the sink, staring at my reflection in the mirror. I look like hell. Dark circles under my eyes. Stubble because I can't be bothered to shave properly.

"That's not your call to make."

When I get back to the table, Victoria's ordering dessert for both of us. "I hope you don't mind, but I took the liberty. The chocolate soufflé here is divine."

I hate chocolate soufflé. Have since I was a kid.

But I smile and nod, because that's what I do. Smile and nod and pretend everything's fine while my chest feels like someone's sitting on it.

"So," Victoria continues, "any plans this weekend? It might be nice to get away to the Hamptons for the holiday."

Before I can answer, my phone pings. It's the invite for my mother's annual Fourth of July party.

"Sorry, I can't," I tell Victoria, brain already working overtime. Charles always attends my mother's party. And now I'm wondering if Frankie will be joining him.

Chapter Thirty-Three

New Normal

Frankie

The cubicle walls are beige. Not cream, not tan—beige. Like someone took the color of sadness and slapped it on particleboard.

I stare at my computer screen, where spreadsheet cells blur together in neat little rows. Column A: Account numbers. Column B: Transaction dates. Column C: My will to live, slowly draining away.

"Frankie?" My supervisor, Janet, hovers beside my desk, clutching a stack of invoices. "Can you reconcile these by end of day?"

"Sure." I take the papers without looking up. More numbers. More beige.

Janet walks away in her sensible shoes, and I go back to typing. Click, type, click, type. The rhythm that used to soothe me now feels like a metronome counting down to my death.

My phone buzzes with a text from Tessa.

Tessa: How's the dream job?

Frankie: Living the dream. If the dream involves slowly losing your mind in a fluorescent-lit prison.

Tessa: That bad?

Frankie: I just spent twenty minutes entering data about toilet paper purchases for a law firm.

Tessa: Glamorous.

I set my phone down and rub my temples. This is what I wanted, right? Stability. Predictability. A job where the biggest surprise is whether the coffee in the break room is slightly less terrible than usual.

So why does it feel like I'm suffocating?

At lunch, I sit alone in the break room, picking at the turkey sandwich I brought from home while my coworkers discuss their weekend plans. Concerts in the park. Beach houses in the Hamptons. Wine tastings up in Beacon. Normal people doing normal things.

I think about Charles. The way he'd hum off-key while doing the crossword. How he'd get excited about stupid things like finding a good liverwurst sandwich.

How he'd look at me like what I had to say mattered.

"You're new, right?"

I look up. David from HR is standing there with a sad desk salad, smiling hopefully.

"Sort of." I've been here for a week. In cubicle time, it feels like three years.

"Mind if I sit?"

I gesture to the empty chair. David settles in, adjusting his tie. He's nice. Safe. The kind of guy who probably has a 401(k) and sends his mom flowers on Mother's Day.

"How are you liking it so far?"

"It's great," I lie. "Very . . . structured."

"That's what I love about it. You always know what to expect." He takes a bite of lettuce. "I heard you used to travel a lot? For work?"

"Something like that."

"That must have been exhausting. All that uncertainty."

Uncertainty. Like it's a disease.

I think about waking up in Provence, not knowing what Charles would want to do. Maybe we'd explore a market. Maybe we'd sit by the pool all day, reading. Maybe Hayes would show up and turn my world upside down with a single look.

The uncertainty was the best part.

"Yeah," I tell David. "Exhausting."

That night, I'm sprawled on Tessa's couch, still in my work clothes, when she arrives home from her gallery job. She takes one look at me and opens a bottle of wine.

"That good, huh?"

"I'm fine."

"You look like someone ran over your dog."

"I don't have a dog."

"Exactly. You're too sad to even get a dog." She pours two enormous glasses. "Talk to me."

I take a sip. It's the cheap grocery store wine that I've always thought was fine. Now it tastes like cardboard compared to the vintages Hayes used to order. Everything tastes like cardboard now.

"I miss them."

"Charles?"

"Both of them."

Tessa sits beside me, curling her legs under her. "Have you talked to either of them?"

"I've texted Charles. And he calls sometimes. Checks in." I don't mention that I can hear something different in his voice lately. A tiredness that scares me. "Hayes . . . no."

"Do you want to?"

The question hits me like a slap. Do I want to talk to the man who made me feel like I mattered, then treated me like a one-night stand? The man who looked at me like I hung the moon, then couldn't get away fast enough after he got what he wanted?

"It doesn't matter what I want."

"Bullshit."

I turn to stare at her. Tessa doesn't usually call me on my crap this directly. It's a little jarring.

"You're miserable," she continues. "You've been miserable since you got back. Maybe it's time to stop pretending you're fine."

"I am fine."

"You're working a job you hate, living on my couch, and you've been wearing the same bra for three days."

I look down. She's not wrong.

"That's just . . . practical."

"That's depression."

Before I can argue, my phone rings. It's Charles.

I almost don't answer. But it's late for him to be calling, and something about the timing makes my stomach clench.

"Hey, Charlie."

"Frankie." His voice sounds thin. Fragile. "How are you, sweetheart?"

"Good. Great. How are you?"

"I've been better." He pauses, and I hear him breathing carefully. "But I'm okay."

He's lying. I can tell by the way he's choosing his words too carefully.

"Charles."

"I'm fine, Frankie. Really. Just . . . miss having you around."

The words hit me like a punch to the chest. I miss him too. Miss everything about that ridiculous, wonderful routine we built together.

"I miss you too."

"Listen, I want to invite you to a little gathering this weekend. Fourth of July party at my house. Nothing fancy, just family and friends. I'd love it if you came."

That's the Winters Estate. Hayes's parents.

Which means Hayes will be there. One would assume, anyway.

My heart does this stupid fluttering thing that I immediately squash.

"I don't know . . ."

"Please, Frankie. It would mean a lot to me."

There's something in his voice. Something that sounds like he needs this more than he's letting on.

"Okay," I hear myself say. "Yeah. I'll be there."

"Wonderful. I'll text you the details."

After he hangs up, I stare at my phone.

"Well?" Tessa asks.

"I'm going to a party."

"What kind of party?"

I drain the rest of my wine. "The kind where I'll probably make a complete ass of myself."

"Sounds perfect." She grins. "What are you going to wear?"

"A paper bag over my head?"

"Frankie . . ." She chuckles and tosses a throw pillow at me. "I'm thinking blue. Brings out your eyes."

I groan and sink deeper into the couch. In three days, I'll be in the same room as Hayes Winters again. The man who kissed me like I was oxygen and he was drowning, then left like I was nothing.

This is either going to be the best decision I've made in months, or the worst.

Knowing my track record, probably the worst.

But Charles asked. And when Charles asks for something, I can't say no.

Even if it might destroy me.

Chapter Thirty-Four

Fireworks and Pimples

Hayes

The Hamptons estate looks like Martha Stewart threw up red, white, and blue all over my childhood summer home.

Mom's outdone herself this year. White tents dot the manicured lawn like expensive mushrooms. String lights drape between oak trees. The pool sparkles with floating candles shaped like stars.

It's perfect. Tasteful. Everything Mom prides herself on.

I hate every inch of it.

"Hayes, darling." Mom glides over in a white dress that probably cost more than a car. "You look handsome. Where's your date?"

"Don't have one."

Her smile tightens. "Well, that's disappointing."

"I'll mingle," I say, already walking away.

Dad's holding court by the bar, telling some story about his drumming days to a group of politicians who are pretending to be interested. Senator Morrison laughs too loud at whatever punch line Dad just delivered.

I grab a whiskey and find a corner where I can watch without participating. It's my preferred party position—close enough to seem social, far enough away to avoid small talk about the economy or my nonexistent love life.

"You look like you'd rather be getting a root canal," Malachi says, appearing beside me with a beer.

"That's because I would."

"Come on. It's not that bad. Your mom throws a good party."

I take a sip of whiskey and appreciate the way it burns on the way down. "She invited half of Manhattan. Including the Ashworth girl."

"Ah." Malachi grins. "The one with the trust fund and the personality of wet cardboard?"

"That's the one."

"She's over there, by the way. Talking to your mom about her charity work."

I glance over. Victoria's wearing a pink dress and pearls, gesturing animatedly while Mom nods with approval.

"Lucky me."

"You know what your problem is?"

"I'm sure you're going to tell me."

"You're comparing every woman to—"

"Don't." I cut him off with a look.

Malachi holds up his hands. "I'm just saying, maybe it's time to—"

"There she is!" Charles's voice booms across the patio.

I turn toward the French doors, expecting to see some family friend or political donor.

Instead, I see her.

Frankie stands in the doorway, wearing a blue sundress that makes her look like summer decided to take human form. Her hair's shorter now, just brushing her shoulders, and she's clutching a small purse like it's an anchor.

My chest does this stupid thing where it forgets how to expand properly.

She looks incredible. Nervous as hell, but incredible.

"Well," Malachi murmurs. "This should be interesting."

Frankie takes a breath and walks toward Charles, who's practically glowing with happiness. They hug, and I watch her shoulders relax slightly.

Then Mom descends.

I can see the exact moment Frankie's walls go up. The way her grip tightens on that purse. How her smile becomes a little too bright.

Mom's probably calculating seating charts and wondering if Frankie's dress is appropriate for a Hamptons garden party.

Then Frankie opens her mouth.

"I'm sorry, I brought one more guest with me who wasn't on the invite list. I hope you don't mind."

Mom's face goes white. She's mentally rearranging place cards and checking the caterer's head count.

"It's really best if you don't bother saying hello," Frankie continues, her eyes dancing with mischief. "Don't acknowledge and don't engage. In fact, I'm hoping he won't be here long."

What the hell is she talking about?

Then she bursts into laughter. "I'm kidding! The uninvited guest is the pimple on my chin."

I nearly choke on my whiskey.

Mom sags with relief while Dad actually chuckles from across the patio.

No one has ever talked to my mother like that. *Ever.* Mom thrives on formality and social hierarchies. She lives for people kissing her ass.

And somehow, Frankie just charmed them both in under thirty seconds.

"Your sense of humor is lost on them," I say when she eventually makes her way over.

She turns, and for a split second her mask slips. I see the hurt flash across her face. The way her knuckles go white again around that purse.

Then her armor slides back into place.

"Hayes." Her voice could cut glass. "You look . . . well."

"So do you."

Understatement of the century. She looks like everything I've been missing without knowing it. Like the answer to a question I didn't know I was asking.

We stand there, staring at each other while the party swirls around us. Weeks' worth of things to say, and neither of us knows where to start.

"How's the new job?" I ask finally.

"Fine. Boring. Everything I thought I wanted." She pauses. "How's . . . everything?"

"Fine. Boring. Everything I thought I wanted."

A smile almost crosses her face. Almost.

"Hayes!" Mom appears with Victoria in tow. "Victoria is here, isn't that great?"

Perfect timing.

Victoria extends a manicured hand. "Nice to see you again."

I shake her hand briefly, my attention still on Frankie.

"Victoria was just telling me about a trip she took to Provence," Mom continues. "Isn't that where you were recently?" she says to Frankie.

"Yes, with Charles—we were near Nice and went on toward Marseille," Frankie says, nodding.

"How lovely," Victoria says. "There's this darling little vineyard near Aix-en-Provence that makes the most divine rosé."

I watch Frankie's face carefully. She's being polite, but I can see the irritation brewing behind her eyes.

"Excuse me," Frankie says. "Speaking of Charles, I should find him. Make sure he's not overdoing it."

She walks away without looking back.

"Such a sweet girl," Mom says once she's gone. "Though I'm not sure she quite fits in with our crowd."

"She doesn't," I say.

Mom's smile falters.

I spend the next hour being the dutiful son. I chat with relatives, laugh at old jokes, pretend to care about Victoria's opinions on modern art.

But I'm tracking Frankie the whole time.

She's working the crowd like she was born to it. Making senators' wives laugh. Charming my father with stories I can't hear but wish I could. She fits in without trying to fit in, which is more than I can say for most people here.

"She's quite the character," Victoria says, following my gaze to where Frankie's talking to Congressman Bradley's wife.

"Yeah. She is."

"I mean, that joke about the pimple? So . . . unexpected."

Unexpected. Like it's a bad thing.

"She's honest," I say.

"Oh, I'm sure she's very nice. It's just . . . well, she's not quite what one expects at these sorts of gatherings."

Something hot and protective flares in my chest. "What exactly do you expect?"

Victoria blinks. "I just meant—"

"Because Frankie's the most genuine person here. She actually gives a shit about people instead of just pretending to for social points."

"Hayes." Victoria looks hurt. "I was just making conversation."

I run a hand through my hair. "That was . . . sorry."

But I'm not sorry. I'm pissed. At Victoria for her casual dismissal. At my mother for her social hierarchies. At myself for caring so much about what happens to a woman who probably hates me.

The fireworks start at sunset. Everyone gathers on the lawn, and I lose sight of Frankie in the crowd.

Victoria moves closer, her hand finding my arm. "This is magical."

The sky explodes in gold and red and blue. Reflected in the pool, in the windows of the house, in Victoria's perfectly painted features.

All I can think about is watching fireworks with Frankie somewhere quiet. Her head on my shoulder, making jokes about the shapes they make in the sky. She's changed, or maybe I have. I can't explain it, but Frankie has shifted from the annoying assistant to the person who matters most in the world.

"Hayes?" Victoria's looking at me expectantly.

"Sorry, what?"

"I asked if you wanted to—"

Shouting erupts behind us. A crash.

I turn and see Charles on the ground, Frankie kneeling beside him.

Everything else disappears.

I push through the crowd, Victoria forgotten, my heart hammering against my ribs.

"Call an ambulance," Frankie says without looking up. Her hands are on Charles's chest, checking his pulse.

"What happened?" I drop down beside them.

"He just . . . collapsed. One second he was laughing, the next . . ." Her voice cracks.

Charles's eyes flutter open. "I'm fine," he whispers. "Just tired."

"You're not fine," Frankie says firmly. "You're going to the hospital."

The paramedics arrive within minutes. Professional. Efficient. And terrifying.

As they load Charles onto a stretcher, he grabs my hand with fingers that feel too fragile.

"Take care of her," he says quietly.

I look at Frankie, who's climbing into the ambulance without hesitation.

"I'm coming with you."

She doesn't argue.

As the ambulance pulls away, I catch a glimpse of Victoria standing on the lawn, looking confused and abandoned.

I don't give a shit.

Right now, the only thing that matters is the woman sitting across from me, holding Charles's hand and whispering reassurances we both know she doesn't believe.

And the crushing realization that I might be about to lose them both.

Chapter Thirty-Five

The Last Goodbye

Frankie

Charles looks so small in the hospital bed, buried under white blankets that seem to swallow him whole.

The sterile smell of disinfectant clings to the room, and there's an incessant beeping from a variety of monitors.

Hayes sits in the chair across from me, still wearing his dress shirt from the party. He's got grass stains on his knees from when he dropped down beside Charles on the lawn, and his hair is a mess from running his hands through it.

We haven't spoken in three hours.

"The doctor should have results soon," he says suddenly.

I nod without looking at him. My eyes are fixed on Charles's face, searching for any sign that he's still in there. Still fighting.

"Frankie."

Hayes's voice is softer now. Careful.

I finally meet his eyes. They're bloodshot and worried, and for a second I forget that I'm supposed to hate him.

"He's going to be okay." The words taste like ash. "He has to be."

Hayes doesn't answer. We both know better than to make promises we can't keep.

Dr. Patel appears in the doorway, her expression grave. I've learned to read people's faces over the years. This isn't the look they wear when delivering good news.

"Mr. Winthrop's condition has deteriorated," she says without preamble. "The tests show significant cardiac damage. We're doing everything we can to keep him comfortable."

Comfortable. That's doctor-speak for dying.

"How long?" Hayes asks.

"It's difficult to say. Hours, maybe days."

Hours.

The word hits me like a physical blow. I grip the arms of my chair to keep from falling over.

"I can have someone from hospice come in and speak to you about next steps."

"Can we . . . can we stay with him?"

Dr. Patel nods. "Of course."

She leaves us alone with the beeping and the awful fluorescent lights and the man who changed both our lives.

Charles stirs, his eyes fluttering open.

"Hey, Charlie." My voice cracks on his name.

He turns his head toward me, smiling that same gentle smile he's been giving me since the day we met.

"There's my girl."

I reach for his hand. His fingers are cold and fragile, like bird bones.

"How are you feeling?"

"Like I got hit by a truck." He chuckles, then winces. "But I've been worse."

Liar. He's never been worse than this.

Hayes moves closer to the bed. "The doctor says—"

"I know what the doctor says." Charles's voice is weak but firm. "I'm not an idiot."

We sit in silence for a moment. The weight of unspoken words fills the room like smoke.

"I need to tell you both something." Charles struggles to sit up higher, and Hayes immediately adjusts his pillows. "The trips you went on, the places we were able to visit before—it all meant so much to me, you know?"

My throat closes up. "Charles—"

"Let me finish." He squeezes my hand. "I spent fifty years alone after Betsey died. Fifty years convincing myself I was fine. That I didn't need anyone."

His gaze moves between Hayes and me.

"Then this crazy girl shows up in my nephew's office, arguing about God knows what. Forces chocolate muffins on me and changes my Wi-Fi password to something ridiculous. And suddenly I wasn't alone anymore."

Tears streak down my cheeks. I don't bother wiping them away.

"You gave me the best summer of my life, Frankie. You made me remember what it felt like to laugh. To live."

"Don't talk like this is goodbye."

"It is goodbye, sweetheart. And that's okay."

"No, it's not okay." My voice breaks completely. "You're supposed to get better. We're supposed to go to Spain. You promised me liverwurst in Barcelona."

Charles laughs, which turns into a cough that makes my heart stop.

"I promise you'll still go to Spain. Both of you."

Hayes shakes his head. "Charles—"

"You two are the best thing I ever did. Even if I had to trick you into it."

"Trick us?" Hayes frowns.

"You think I hired Frankie just to travel with me?" Charles's eyes twinkle despite everything. "I hired her for you, you idiot."

My brain stutters. "What?"

"From the moment you stormed out of that interview, I knew. You were exactly what he needed. Someone to call him on his bullshit. Someone real."

I stare at Charles, then at Hayes, who looks just as stunned as I feel. But Charles isn't done.

He draws another slow breath. "Don't waste time being scared. Life's too short for that shit."

Hayes chokes out a laugh. "Did you just say *shit*?"

"I'm dying. I can say whatever I want."

We sit with him through the night. Taking turns holding his hand. Sharing memories of *Wordle* games and Scrabble matches and the way he'd fall asleep watching *Jeopardy!* every night at seven thirty.

Hayes tells stories about childhood tennis matches and college graduation. How Charles never missed a single important moment.

"I love you both," Charles whispers just before dawn. "Live the life you want. Not the one you think you should have."

Those are his last words.

The beeping stops at 6:17 a.m.

I dissolve.

There's no other word for it. I just . . . fall apart. Like someone cut the strings holding me together and I collapsed into a pile of broken pieces.

Hayes's arms come around me, and I don't have the strength to push him away. I sob into his chest while he holds me, his own tears falling into my hair.

"I can't do this," I whisper against his shirt.

"I know. I know."

But Charles is already gone. The man who made me laugh and taught me about stocks and the simple art of not giving a crap. Who taught me that family isn't just blood. Who showed me what it felt like to matter to someone.

Gone.

"Frankie." Hayes tilts my chin up, forcing me to meet his eyes. "We'll get through this."

Will we?

After making a couple of phone calls to set the arrangements in motion, Hayes drives me back home. Well, *home* is relative. Since I'm currently in between places, he drops me off at Tessa's.

"The funeral will be Tuesday," he says, eyes full of grief.

I nod and exit the car.

I spend the rest of the night staring at the ceiling, thinking about Charles. About Hayes. About the fact that in less than four days, I'll have to say goodbye to the best man I've ever known.

And I'll have to figure out what the hell I'm supposed to do with the rest of my life.

Chapter Thirty-Six

Liverwurst and Love

Hayes

The funeral was everything Charles would have hated.

Too many flowers. Too many people giving speeches about his "philanthropic legacy" and "commitment to excellence." My mother orchestrated the whole thing like a goddamn Broadway production.

Frankie sat in the front row, staring straight ahead while senators and CEOs took turns at the podium. She looked like she might shatter if someone breathed on her wrong.

When it was her turn to speak, she walked to the microphone in this simple black dress that made her look impossibly small.

"Charles Winthrop was the best man I ever knew," she said, her voice steady despite the tears streaming down her cheeks. "He taught me that family isn't about blood. It's about showing up. Every single day."

She paused, gripping the podium.

"He showed up for all of us. Even when we didn't deserve it. Especially when we didn't deserve it."

Her eyes found mine across the packed church.

"He'd want us to keep showing up for each other."

That was it. Thirty seconds that said more about Charles than hours of formal eulogies.

Now we're back at his apartment—my apartment, I guess, since everything's mine now. The will reading was yesterday. He left me the business, the properties, more money than I'll ever know what to do with.

And he left Frankie five million dollars.

She hasn't touched the check.

"You should eat something." I set a plate of Chinese takeout in front of her.

She's been camped out on Charles's couch for three days, still wearing yesterday's clothes. Her hair's in a messy bun that looks like she twisted it up and forgot about it.

"Not hungry."

"You haven't eaten since the service."

"I had coffee."

"Coffee's not food."

She finally looks at me. Her eyes are red rimmed and hollow. "Why are you still here?"

Good question. I should be back at work, dealing with the dozen crises that piled up while I was playing grief counselor. Instead I'm here, watching Frankie fall apart in slow motion.

"Where else would I be?"

"I don't know. Your penthouse. Your office. Somewhere that isn't watching me have a mental breakdown."

I sit down across from her, pushing the take-out container closer. "Charles asked me to take care of you."

"That's not your job."

"Maybe I want it to be."

The words slip out before I can stop them. Frankie's eyes widen slightly.

"Hayes—"

"I have an idea." I stand up before she can finish whatever she was going to say. "But you're going to hate it."

"What is it?"

"Let's order liverwurst. We'll have dinner together in his memory. We can even play Scrabble."

A short laugh bursts from her lips. The first real sound she's made in days.

"You're right. I do hate that idea." She wipes her eyes. "But let's do it."

Two hours later, we're sitting at Charles's dining table with a spread that would make him proud. Liverwurst and onions from the German place downtown. Terrible red wine that tastes like it came from a box. Scrabble board between us like a peace treaty.

"He would have loved this," Frankie says, cutting into her sausage.

"He would have beaten us both at Scrabble."

"Remember that time in Montana when he got 'quixotic' on a triple word score?"

"And then acted like it was no big deal." I shake my head. "Smug bastard."

Frankie actually smiles. Small, but real.

We eat in comfortable silence. The kind Charles and I used to share during those late-night phone calls about nothing and everything.

"I still can't believe he's gone," she says eventually.

"Yeah."

"I keep expecting him to walk in and complain about us eating on his good china."

I glance at the plates we grabbed from his kitchen. She's right—these probably cost more than most people's cars.

"He'd be more upset about the wine."

"This wine is perfectly fine."

"Frankie. This wine tastes like someone dissolved cardboard in grape juice."

"You're such a snob."

"I'm discerning."

"Same thing."

We're bickering. Like we used to. Before everything got complicated and I messed it all up.

After dinner, I clear the table while she sets up the Scrabble board. Her fingers shake slightly as she arranges the letter tiles.

"You okay?"

"Fine." She doesn't look at me. "Just . . . this was our thing, you know? Mine and Charles's. Playing games, talking about nothing. Now it's just . . ."

"Different."

"Empty."

I want to tell her it doesn't have to be empty. That we could fill the silence with our own words, our own games. But that's not what she needs right now.

"What was your first word with him?" I ask instead.

"'Muffin.' I got fourteen points, and he acted like I'd just discovered fire." She traces the edge of a tile. "He bragged about you constantly, you know. Your tennis matches, your business deals. How smart you were."

My throat tightens. "He talked about you too. I know you were the daughter he never had."

Frankie's face crumples. For a second I think she's going to start crying again. Instead, she picks up seven tiles and studies them like they hold the secrets of the universe.

"'Wizard,'" she says, placing the letters down. "Double word score. Twenty-eight points."

"Show-off."

I study my own tiles. Nothing good. A bunch of consonants and a single *E*.

"'Hex,'" I manage. "Eleven points."

"Pathetic."

"I'm out of practice."

"Charles would have destroyed you."

"Charles cheated."

"He did not!"

"He absolutely did. I caught him looking up words on his phone."

Frankie gasps in mock horror. "You take that back."

"Never."

She throws a tile at me. It bounces off my chest and clatters to the floor.

"Charles Winthrop was a saint."

"Charles Winthrop was a competitive old bastard who hated losing."

"Don't speak ill of the dead."

"I'm speaking truth to the dead."

Another tile flies in my direction. This one I catch.

"You're terrible at this," I tell her.

"At what?"

"Throwing things. Your aim is shit."

"I wasn't actually trying to hit you."

"Good thing. You'd miss."

She picks up another tile, weighing it in her palm. "Want to test that theory?"

"Bring it."

She throws the tile. I duck, laughing as it sails over my head.

"Told you."

"Shut up."

But she's laughing too. Actually laughing, for the first time since Charles collapsed.

We play three more games. I win two, she wins one, and we both agree Charles would have kicked our asses.

"I should go," I say around midnight.

Frankie's curled up in Charles's chair, looking smaller than ever in his oversize cardigan. She found it in his closet and hasn't taken it off since.

"You don't have to."

"You need sleep."

"I won't sleep anyway."

I know the feeling. I haven't slept properly in weeks.

"Want me to stay?"

The question hangs between us. Not romantic. Not sexual. Just . . . present.

"Yeah," she whispers. "I think I do."

Chapter Thirty-Seven

New Beginnings

Frankie

"Mrs. Goldstein, I understand your concerns about the Mediterranean cruise, but I promise you—the railings are perfectly safe."

I'm sitting in my tiny office above a bagel shop in Hoboken, talking an eighty-year-old woman off the ledge about handrail height regulations while simultaneously trying to ignore the smell of everything seasoning wafting up through the floorboards.

Two months ago, I was sleeping on Tessa's couch and entering data about toilet paper purchases. Now I'm the proud owner of Golden Adventures, a luxury travel company for seniors who want to see the world without breaking a hip.

It's not exactly what I planned, but turns out Charles's money came with a purpose. Who knew?

"And what about the food?" Mrs. Goldstein continues. "My Harold has very specific dietary needs."

"We work with the cruise line to accommodate all dietary restrictions. Harold's low-sodium, gluten-free requirements will be handled by the executive chef personally."

"Executive chef? How fancy."

I grin. "Very fancy. Think of it as *Downton Abbey*, but on water. With better Wi-Fi."

She laughs, and I know I've got her.

After we hang up, I lean back in my office chair and stare at the vision board Tessa forced me to make. Pictures of exotic destinations. Happy elderly couples holding hands on beaches. A photo of Charles and me in Provence that makes my chest ache every time I look at it.

My phone buzzes. It's an email from another potential client.

> Dear Golden Adventures,
>
> My wife and I are interested in your "Romance in Rome" package for our 50th anniversary. We're both in our seventies and want to recreate our honeymoon—only now we have bad knees and a better budget.
>
> Please advise.
>
> Best, Richard Allen

I'm typing a response when I hear footsteps on the stairs. Heavy. Deliberate. Definitely not Mrs. Kowalski from the bagel shop coming up to complain about my music again.

The door opens.

My fingers freeze over the keyboard.

Hayes Winters stands in my doorway of my tiny office, wearing a charcoal gray suit that probably cost more than my monthly rent. His hair's shorter than I remember, and there's something different about his face. Less rigid. Like someone loosened a screw I didn't know was there.

"Hi."

The word comes out smaller than I intended. My heart's doing this stupid hummingbird thing against my ribs.

"Hello, Francesca." He steps inside, closing the door behind him. "Nice place."

I glance around my shoebox office with its mismatched furniture and motivational posters. "It's not much, but—"

"I wasn't being sarcastic."

Our eyes meet. Hold.

God, I've missed looking at him.

"What are you doing here?"

"I heard about your business. Golden Adventures." He moves closer, and I catch a whiff of his cologne. The same one he wore on the yacht. The one that still makes my brain short-circuit. "Congratulations."

"How did you hear about it?"

"Charles left me his subscription to *Travel + Leisure*. There was an article."

Travel + Leisure wrote about me? Holy shit.

"Small piece," Hayes continues, like he can read my thoughts. "But they called you 'innovative' and 'compassionate.' Said you were revolutionizing senior travel."

Heat creeps up my neck. "It's just . . . I wanted to do something that mattered. Something Charles would have been proud of."

"He would have been."

The certainty in his voice makes my throat tight.

Hayes glances at my vision board, his gaze lingering on the photo of Charles and me. "You look happy in that picture."

"I was."

"And now?"

The question hangs between us like a loaded gun.

"Now I'm . . ." I gesture vaguely at my office. "Building something. Moving forward."

"Good. That's good."

We stand there, staring at each other. Two months of missing him crashes over me all at once. The way we bantered. How he'd frown when he was concentrating. The sound of his laugh when I caught him off guard.

How he held me when Charles died.

"Frankie—"

My desk phone rings, shattering the moment.

"I should . . ." I reach for it, grateful for the interruption.

"Golden Adventures, this is Frankie."

"Ms. Anderson? This is Patricia Gallagher. I'm calling about your 'Tuscan Dreams' package."

Patricia Gallagher. As in, Gallagher Textiles? As in, billionaire widow who could fund my entire company with her jewelry budget?

I meet Hayes's eyes and mouth *important call.*

He nods and settles into the chair across from my desk. Not leaving. Just . . . waiting.

"Mrs. Gallagher, how can I help you?"

"Well, I'm planning a trip for twelve of my closest friends. We're all in our seventies, and we want to celebrate my late husband's birthday in style. He always loved Italy."

Twelve wealthy widows. In Tuscany. My brain starts calculating commission rates.

"That sounds wonderful. When were you thinking?"

"October. We'd require private villas, reservations at MICHELIN-starred restaurants, personal sommeliers, but we'd want to make sure we were getting a deal."

I'm trying to focus on her requirements, but Hayes is sitting three feet away, watching me work. His presence fills my tiny office until there's barely room for anything else.

"Absolutely. We can arrange private cooking classes with renowned chefs, wine tastings at family-owned vineyards . . ."

Hayes's mouth quirks up at the corner. He's impressed.

"And transportation?" she asks.

"Private luxury coaches with experienced drivers who know the region intimately."

"And the pricing?"

"I'm confident we can work within whatever budget you had in mind."

"Perfect. When can we meet?"

"I'm free tomorrow afternoon—"

"Actually," Hayes interrupts, "tomorrow's not good."

I blink at him. Mrs. Gallagher's still talking, but all I can hear is the blood rushing in my ears.

Did he just . . . ?

"Mrs. Gallagher, could I call you back in one hour to confirm our meeting time?"

After I hang up, I slowly turn to face Hayes.

"Did you just interrupt my phone call?"

"You can't meet with her tomorrow."

"Why not?"

"Because you're having dinner with me."

The words hit me like a slap. Not a request. A statement.

"Excuse me?"

Hayes stands up, moving around my desk until he's close enough that I have to tilt my head back to meet his eyes.

"I said you're having dinner with me tomorrow night."

"That's incredibly presumptuous."

"Is it wrong?"

My mouth opens. Closes. No words come out.

Because the truth is, if Hayes Winters asked me to dinner tomorrow night—or any night—I'd probably say yes. Even though he broke my heart. Even though he ran away when things got real.

Even though I'm terrified of letting him close enough to hurt me again.

"Why?" I manage.

"Because I've spent two months missing you. Because I've been going to therapy and learning how to not be a complete emotional disaster. Because I'm tired of pretending I don't think about you every single day."

My heart stops.

"And because," he continues, leaning closer, "I'm pretty sure you've been missing me too."

He's right. God help me, he's so right it hurts.

"One dinner," I hear myself say.

"One dinner."

"Not a date."

His smile is pure sin. "Definitely not a date."

He turns to leave, then pauses at the door.

"Wear something nice. But not too nice. And Frankie?"

"Yeah?"

"Cancel your afternoon meeting. You're going to be busy tomorrow."

Then he's gone, leaving me alone with the smell of bagels and the terrifying realization that Hayes Winters just steamrolled his way back into my life.

And I'm not even mad about it.

Shit.

Chapter Thirty-Eight

The Perfect Date

Hayes

My tie's crooked. I've retied it four times, and it's *still* crooked.

"You look like you're about to throw up," Maddie observes from my bed, where she's sprawled out with her Nintendo Switch.

"I'm fine."

"Uh-huh." She doesn't look up from her game. "Is this about the girl?"

I pause, my hands still on the tie. "What girl?"

"The one you've been moping about for like, forever. Frankie, right?"

How does an eight-year-old know about my love life?

"I haven't been moping."

"You totally have. Dad said you've been weird since Uncle Charles died."

My chest tightens. Even Maddie noticed.

"And now you're wearing your fancy tie and that cologne that makes you smell like a magazine."

I glance down at my outfit. Navy button-down, dark jeans, my favorite sport coat. Dressy but not overdone. The cologne she's talking about is the same one I wore in France.

"It's just dinner."

"With the girl."

"With Francesca, yes."

Maddie finally looks up, grinning like she knows something I don't. "Are you nervous?"

"Why would I be nervous?"

"Because you like her."

When did my baby sister become a relationship expert?

"It's complicated."

"How?"

I sit on the edge of the bed, giving up on the tie. "We used to . . . We worked together. Sort of. And then Uncle Charles died, and things got messy."

Maddie sets down her Switch, suddenly serious. "I miss Uncle Charles."

"Me, too, kid."

"He was funny. Remember when he taught me that card trick?"

I smile despite myself. "You mean when he let you win at poker and told you it was magic?"

"That wasn't magic?"

"Definitely not magic."

Maddie processes this betrayal for a moment. "I still liked it."

"He would have liked that you liked it."

We sit in comfortable silence. Maddie picks at the comforter while I stare at my reflection in the mirror across the room.

"Hayes?"

"Yeah?"

"If Uncle Charles liked Frankie, she must be pretty cool."

My throat gets tight. "Yeah. She is."

"So why are you scared?"

The question lands like a punch. Because that's exactly what I am. Terrified.

"What if I mess it up again?"

"Then you'll say sorry and try harder."

Eight years old and already wiser than me.

"What if she doesn't want to try again?"

Maddie shrugs. "Then at least you'll know."

Simple. Direct. Logical.

Why can't I think like an eight-year-old?

My phone buzzes. It's a text from Malachi.

Malachi: Good luck tonight. Try not to completely screw this up. Again.

Helpful, as always.

I stand up and check my reflection one more time. The tie's still crooked, so I decide to remove it. Maybe that's not the worst thing. Maybe perfect isn't what Frankie needs from me.

"Wish me luck," I tell Maddie.

"You don't need luck. You just need to not be stupid."

"Gee, thanks."

"You're welcome." She's already back to her game. "Oh, and Hayes?"

"What?"

"Bring her candy. Girls like candy."

An hour later, I'm standing outside Frankie's apartment building with a bag from Dottie's Candy Bar and my heart hammering against my ribs.

This is insane. I've negotiated billion-dollar deals without breaking a sweat. I've given presentations to boards of directors who could destroy my career with a phone call.

But the thought of Frankie opening her door makes my palms sweat.

I press the buzzer for apartment 4B.

"Hello?" Her voice crackles through the intercom.

"It's me."

"Hayes?"

"Were you expecting someone else?"

A pause. "I'll be right down."

Five minutes later, the lobby door opens and my brain short-circuits.

She's wearing jeans that hug her curves and a soft green sweater that makes her eyes look like sea glass. Her hair's down, curling around her shoulders, and she's got on just enough makeup to make her lips look like they're begging to be kissed.

"Hi."

"Hi, yourself."

We stare at each other for a beat too long.

"You look . . ." I clear my throat. "Good. You look good."

"Thanks. You clean up pretty well yourself."

She's nervous. I can tell by the way her fingers toy with the strap of her purse, twisting it in slow, anxious loops.

Good. I'm not the only one affected here.

"This is for you." I hand her the candy bag.

Her eyebrows lift. "Candy?"

"My sister said girls like candy."

"Your sister's eight."

"Your point?"

Frankie opens the bag and peers inside. Her face lights up like it's Christmas morning.

"Holy shit, Swedish Fish?"

"Among other things."

"I haven't had Swedish Fish in forever." She pulls out the package and hugs it to her chest. "This is better than flowers."

"That's what I was hoping for."

She looks up at me, and for a second her walls drop completely. I see the girl who used to eat gas station snacks and name Wi-Fi networks after terrible puns.

"So," she says, closing the bag carefully. "Where are we going?"

"It's a surprise."

"I hate surprises."

"No, you don't."

"How would you know?"

"Because you spent months traveling with Charles, never knowing where you'd wake up. And you loved every minute of it."

She opens her mouth to argue, then closes it. Point to me.

My car's waiting at the curb. A black Tesla, because I didn't want to hire a driver tonight. I wanted her all to myself without anyone eavesdropping.

"Nice ride," she says as I open her door.

"Thanks."

I programmed the GPS this morning, double-checked the route, called ahead to confirm reservations. I have everything planned down to the minute.

Except for the traffic jam on the FDR that adds forty minutes to our drive.

"Where exactly are we going?" Frankie asks as we crawl through Midtown.

"Patience."

"That's not an answer."

"It's the only answer you're getting."

She huffs and opens her Swedish Fish, popping one in her mouth. The smell fills the car—artificial cherry and childhood memories.

"Want one?"

"I'm good."

"More for me."

We inch forward another few feet. At this rate, we'll miss our reservation entirely.

"You're stressed," Frankie observes.

"I'm fine."

"Your jaw's doing that ticcing thing."

I consciously relax my face. "What ticcing thing?"

"The thing where you clench your teeth when you're trying not to lose your shit."

She knows me too well.

"Traffic happens. It's fine."

"Hayes."

I glance over at her. She's studying me with those sharp green eyes that see everything.

"It's okay if this isn't perfect."

"It should be perfect."

"Says who?"

"Says me." The words come out harder than I intended. "I messed up before. I ran away like a coward and hurt you. The least I can do is plan one decent evening."

Frankie goes quiet. We crawl forward another block.

"You know what I remember about our time in France?" she says finally.

"What?"

"The mistakes. The times things went wrong and we figured it out together." She shifts in her seat to face me. "Like when you couldn't work the washing machine. Or when I got seasick and you gave me motion sickness pills."

"Those weren't exactly romantic moments."

"Maybe not. But they were real."

The GPS announces we've arrived at our destination. I look around, confused. We're in front of a random office building in Midtown.

"Recalculating route," the GPS chirps helpfully.

Frankie starts laughing.

"This isn't funny."

"It's a little funny."

"I had everything planned."

"Plans change."

I pull over and grab my phone, frantically searching for the restaurant's actual address. Frankie reaches over and gently takes the phone from my hands.

"Hayes."

"What?"

"Where did you want to take me?"

"There's this place in Brooklyn. They make gourmet versions of junk food. Mac and cheese burgers, truffle fries, milkshakes with cereal mixed in."

Her eyes widen. "Seriously?"

"I thought . . . I wanted to take you somewhere that felt like you. Not some stuffy place with tiny portions and wines with names we can't pronounce."

"You researched junk food restaurants."

"I may have done some research, yes."

She's staring at me like I just told her I built her a rocket ship.

"That's the most romantic thing anyone's ever done for me."

"Taking you to eat overpriced burgers?"

"No." She leans over and kisses my cheek. Soft. Quick. "Listening."

My skin burns where her lips touched.

"So," she says, settling back in her seat. "Brooklyn?"

"Brooklyn."

I restart the GPS, and this time it actually knows where it's going.

Twenty minutes later, we're sitting in a tiny restaurant called Elevated Comfort, sharing a plate of mac and cheese spring rolls and trying not to stare at each other.

"This is incredible," Frankie says around a bite of what might be the best thing I've ever tasted.

"Worth the detour?"

"Absolutely."

The restaurant's packed and loud, nothing like the places I usually take women. But watching Frankie light up over deep-fried comfort food makes me realize I've been doing everything wrong for years.

"Can I ask you something?" she says.

"Shoot."

"Why now? Why tonight?"

I set down my fork. "Because I've been miserable without you."

"That's not a reason to date someone."

"It's not the only reason."

"What are the other reasons?"

Of course she's not making this easy.

"Because you make me laugh. Because you called my mother on her bullshit at that party and somehow made her like you anyway. Because you held Charles's hand when he was dying and didn't let him go alone."

Her eyes get suspiciously bright.

"Because," I continue, "I spent two months trying to forget you and failing spectacularly. Because every woman I meet is boring compared to you. Because I'm tired of pretending I don't want you."

"Well that's . . . inconvenient."

I laugh despite myself. "Inconvenient?"

"Well, it is. I just got my life back together. I have a business to run, goals to achieve. I can't afford to get distracted by some emotionally unavailable billionaire with commitment issues."

"What if I'm not emotionally unavailable anymore?"

"Are you?"

"I'm here, aren't I?"

She considers this, twirling pasta around her fork. "What about the commitment issues?"

"Working on those too."

"How?"

"Therapy. Lots of therapy. Turns out growing up with parents who treated marriage like a blood sport left me with some baggage."

"Shocking."

"I know, right?" I lean forward. "I also learned that running away when things get scary is a defense mechanism I developed to protect myself from getting hurt."

"And?"

"And I'm done running."

Frankie sets down her fork. "Hayes."

"I'm serious, Frankie. I want this. I want to see where this could go."

"What if it doesn't work?"

"What if it does?"

We stare at each other across the small table. The restaurant noise fades into background buzz.

"I missed you too," she whispers finally.

"Yeah?"

"Yeah. I missed your terrible morning hair and the way you drink coffee like it personally offended you. I missed arguing with you about stupid things."

"My hair isn't terrible."

"It's pretty terrible."

"Anything else you missed?"

Her cheeks flush pink. "Maybe a few things."

The air between us shifts. Charges. Like right before lightning strikes.

"Frankie."

"What?"

"Can I take you home?"

She meets my eyes. "Which home?"

"Mine."

The single word carries enough heat to melt steel.

"Yeah," she breathes. "You can take me home."

I signal for the check with probably more urgency than necessary.

This time, traffic can go fuck itself.

Chapter Thirty-Nine

The Perfect Date

Frankie

His penthouse is exactly what I expected and nothing like I imagined.

Yes, there's the floor-to-ceiling windows overlooking Central Park. Yes, there's art on the walls that probably cost more than most people's houses. But there are also throw pillows that don't match, a stack of books on the coffee table, and—is that a friendship bracelet on his kitchen counter?

"Maddie made that," Hayes says, following my gaze. "She insists I display it prominently."

"It's very . . . colorful."

"That's one word for it."

We're standing in his living room like two teenagers whose parents just left for the weekend. The energy between us is so charged I'm surprised we haven't started a fire.

"Can I get you something to drink? Wine? Water? I think I have—"

"Hayes."

He stops mid-sentence.

"Come here."

He moves toward me slowly, like he's afraid I might bolt. Smart man.

When he's close enough that I can smell his cologne, I reach up and fix his crooked collar.

"This has been driving me crazy all night."

"Sorry."

"Don't be sorry." I smooth the silk against his chest. "I like that you're not perfect."

"I'm far from perfect."

"Good. Perfect is boring."

Our eyes meet. The air between us thickens.

"You do something to me that I can't explain," he says quietly.

Before I can respond, his hands are in my hair and his mouth is on mine.

The kiss is soft at first. Tentative. Like he's asking permission.

I give it to him by pressing closer, fisting my hands in his shirt.

That's when he really kisses me. Deep and desperate, like he's been drowning and I'm oxygen.

My back hits the wall. When did we move? His body cages me in, solid and warm and perfect.

Then my brain kicks in.

Shit. Shit shit shit.

I break the kiss, pressing my palms against his chest.

"Wait."

Hayes steps back immediately, his breathing ragged. "What's wrong?"

"I can't . . . we can't . . ."

"Frankie." His voice is gentle. Patient. "Talk to me."

The words tumble out before I can stop them. "You're going to realize that I'm too much for you. That I'm too messy and emotional, and you're going to come to your senses and leave."

Hayes blinks. "Am I?"

"You are. And I'm terrified it's going to break my heart."

Again.

He pauses, takes a slow breath. There's a little crease between his sculpted eyebrows, like he's working through a complex equation.

"The truth is, I love how deeply you feel your emotions. Growing up, everyone pretended all the time. No one was real, not ever. I love that you're never going to fake it, and I like that I don't have to pretend around you."

It's the sweetest thing anyone's ever said to me. For a moment, I'm speechless.

"Frankie?" He places his palm on my cheek, turning my face up toward his so he can meet my eyes. His gaze is filled with so many questions and a torrent of emotion. "I think I love you."

Holy shit.

That's it. That's my entire brain right now. Just those two words on repeat like a broken record.

Holy shit holy shit holy shit.

He loves me. Hayes Winters—emotional fortress, billionaire, man who probably has his feelings organized in a color-coded spreadsheet—just said he thinks he *loves* me.

My heart's doing this weird hummingbird thing where it's beating so fast I'm pretty sure I'm about to pass out. Or throw up. Or both.

Don't cry. Do not cry. Crying is not sexy.

But God, the way he's looking at me right now. Like I'm something precious instead of the disaster human who stress-ate an entire sleeve of saltines yesterday. Like I matter.

This is happening. This is actually happening.

And the terrifying part? I love him too. Have loved him for months, probably since that day on the yacht when he helped me while I was seasick. Maybe even before that, when he was being an ass (one of the many times) but I could see something real underneath all that expensive armor.

Say something, you idiot.

But what do you say when the person you thought you'd lost forever just handed you their heart? When everything you've been too scared to want is suddenly right there, waiting for you to be brave enough to take it?

Don't mess this up, Frankie.

A weird little laugh escapes me. Seeing Hayes so distraught, so full of emotion, is mind bending. Gone is the stoic, perfectly controlled suit I once thought he was.

"Thank God, because I know I love you."

"Frankie," he breathes against my mouth. "Say it again."

"I love you," I whisper against the brush of his lips. "Hayes?"

"Hmm?" His lips hover over mine.

"Take me to bed."

He's never been good at taking orders, yet he wastes no time fulfilling my command. He lifts me from my feet, sweeping me up into a kiss while simultaneously walking toward the bedroom.

We bump into a wall. My giggle breaks our kiss, but only for a second. Every bit of intensity that I've come to know Hayes for is funneled into this moment.

I'm deposited onto his bed, and all my giggles and nerves disappear.

There's never been anything quite as perfect as this.

In his presence, gone are any feelings of inadequacy. Gone is the voice in my head that says I'm not enough, not right, not worthy of someone like him.

There's only Hayes, looking at me like I'm everything he's ever wanted.

"You sure about this?" he asks, his voice rough.

"I've never been more sure of anything."

He smiles then—the real one, not the polished version he shows the world. "Good. Because I'm done letting you go."

My sweater hits the floor. Then his shirt. Somewhere between my breathless laugh and the way he whispers my name, I realize this is what I've been missing my entire life.

Not just sex. Connection.

Not just desire. Home.

"I love you," he tells me against my skin.

"I love you too," I breathe back.

And then he's kissing me again, and I'm lost.

Completely, utterly lost.

And for the first time in my life, I don't want to be found.

Chapter Forty

Morning After Everything

Hayes

I wake up to the smell of bacon and the sound of Frankie singing off-key in my kitchen.

For a second, I think I'm dreaming. Then I remember last night—her taste, her laugh, the way she said my name like a prayer—and my chest does this stupid expanding thing that makes it hard to breathe.

She's here. In my kitchen. Making breakfast.

I grab a pair of sweatpants and pad barefoot toward the noise. The perfect chaos that only she can bring.

Frankie's standing at my stove, wearing nothing but my dress shirt from last night and a pair of my socks that go up to her knees. Her hair's a disaster—sticking up in twelve different directions—and she's using my expensive spatula to flip bacon while humming what sounds like a Top 40 song I don't recognize.

She looks perfect.

"Morning," I say, leaning against the doorframe.

She turns, and her face lights up. "Oh good, you're not dead. I was starting to worry I'd killed you with my feminine wiles."

"Feminine wiles?"

"That's what my mom used to call it when women got what they wanted from men. Though I'm pretty sure she was being sarcastic."

"Did you get what you wanted?" I give her a sly look.

Her gaze dips lower, across my chest and down my torso. The way she's looking at me—like I'm her personal buffet and she's starving—makes my blood run hot.

"Maybe," she says, her voice dropping to that husky register that does things to me. "Though I think I might need a repeat performance. You know. Just to be sure."

"Is that so?"

She steps closer, close enough that I can smell my soap on her skin. "Mm-hmm. Quality control is very important in my line of work."

"And what line of work is that again?"

"Professional temptress, apparently." Her fingers trail down my chest, and I have to bite back a groan. "Though I'm still learning the ropes."

"You're a fast learner."

"I had a very thorough teacher."

Damn. The way she says *thorough* should be illegal.

Because that's exactly what last night was. We spent hours together tangled in my sheets, learning exactly what the other liked.

I reach for her, but she dances away with a laugh, spatula still in hand.

"Uh-uh. Breakfast first. I didn't slave over a hot stove just to watch it get cold."

"I can think of better ways to work up an appetite."

"I'm sure you can." She waves the spatula at me like a weapon. "But I'm not letting you distract me with your . . . your . . ." She gestures vaguely at my entire existence.

"My what?"

"Your stupid perfect chest and your bedroom hair and that thing you do with your mouth."

"What thing?"

"You know what thing."

I absolutely do know what thing. But watching her get flustered is too entertaining to stop.

"I'm afraid you'll have to be more specific."

Her cheeks flush pink. "The smirking thing. Where you look all smug and satisfied like you know exactly what you're doing to me."

"Don't I?"

"That's not the point."

"What is the point?"

"The point is breakfast. Food. Sustenance." She turns back to the stove with more force than necessary. "Some of us need actual nutrition to function."

I move behind her again, caging her against the counter.

"Hayes." Her voice is breathless.

"What?"

"You're doing it again."

"Doing what?"

"The thing."

"Still not specific enough."

She turns in my arms, and the look she gives me could melt steel.

I move closer, wrapping my arms around her waist and tugging her close. She fits against me like she was made for it.

"What are you making?"

"Breakfast. Obviously." She touches her lips to mine—just a quick kiss. "Hope you don't mind I raided your kitchen. Though honestly, your food situation is tragic. Who keeps seventeen types of mustard but no decent coffee creamer?"

"I don't drink coffee with creamer."

"Of course you don't. You take it black like some kind of sociopath."

"I am not a sociopath."

"Jury's still out."

I press a kiss to her neck, tasting salt and the faint sweetness of her perfume. "What's the verdict on breakfast?"

"Well, I found bacon, eggs, and some fancy bread that was probably baked by someone with the word *artisan* in their title."

"Perfect."

She turns in my arms, studying my face. "You're different in the morning."

"Different how?"

"Softer. Less . . ." She waves the spatula vaguely. "Intimidating corporate overlord. More like a regular human who might actually eat carbs."

"I eat carbs."

"When?"

I pause. When do I eat carbs? My trainer has me on this ridiculous protein-heavy diet that makes everything taste like cardboard.

"Exactly." Frankie grins. "When's the last time you had pancakes? Or a doughnut? Or literally any food that brings joy instead of optimized nutrition?"

"I don't really—"

"That's what I thought." She turns back to the stove. "We're fixing that. Starting now."

The bacon sizzles. She's cracked eggs into a bowl and is whisking them with the kind of violent enthusiasm that makes me slightly concerned for their molecular structure.

"When did you learn to cook?"

"I decided it was time." She gives me a shy smile.

"Can I help?"

"Can you make coffee without it tasting like motor oil?"

"I think so."

"Then yes. Coffee duty is yours."

I move to my espresso machine—a Italian monstrosity that cost more than most people's cars—and start the familiar ritual.

"Geez," Frankie mutters, watching me. "Even your coffee routine is intimidating. Do you have a special certification for that thing?"

"It's not that complicated."

"It has more buttons than my washing machine."

I glance over at her. She's pouring the eggs into the pan with one hand while flipping bacon with the other. Multitasking like she's been doing this her whole life.

I'm impressed.

The espresso machine hisses. Steam rises from the milk frother.

"Have you learned to use a washing machine yet?" she asks over one shoulder.

"My parents didn't exactly encourage domestic skills."

"Too busy teaching you how to crush your enemies and acquire wealth?"

She's joking, but she's not wrong.

"Something like that."

Frankie plates the eggs and bacon, then turns to face me. Her expression's gone soft.

"Hey. I wasn't making fun of you."

"I know."

"It's just . . . different worlds, you know? Sometimes I forget how different until moments like this."

I hand her a perfect cappuccino. She takes a sip, and her eyes roll back.

"Okay, maybe the fancy coffee machine is worth it."

We sit at my kitchen island—something I've never done before. I usually eat standing up, checking emails, already mentally at the office.

This is . . . nice.

"So," Frankie says around a bite of bacon, "what's the plan for today?"

"Plan?"

"Yeah. It's Saturday. Normal people have weekend plans."

I don't have weekend plans. I have conference calls and reports to review and—

"What do you usually do on Saturdays?" I ask.

"Depends. Sometimes I hang out with Tessa. Sometimes I catch up on laundry, clean my apartment. Exciting stuff." She takes another sip of coffee. "What about you?"

"Work."

"Work work? Or rich-people work?"

"What's the difference?"

"Rich-people work is like, checking your stock portfolio and complaining about your yacht captain. Real work is actual work."

I consider this. "Probably rich-people work."

"Thought so." She grins. "Well, today you're doing normal-people Saturday."

"Which involves?"

"I don't know yet. We'll figure it out."

The idea of a day without a schedule makes my palms sweat. "I should probably—"

"Nope." Frankie reaches over and plucks my phone from the counter. "No phones. No work. Just us and whatever random shit we feel like doing."

"Frankie—"

"When's the last time you had a day off? And I mean a real day off, not a working vacation where you answer emails by the pool."

I can't remember. Literally cannot recall the last time I went twenty-four hours without checking email.

"Exactly." She tucks my phone into the pocket of my shirt. "So today, we're going to be aggressively normal."

"What does that mean?"

"I have no idea. But it's going to be fun."

Three hours later, we're in Central Park and I'm learning that *aggressively normal* involves a lot of activities I've never considered.

Like feeding ducks.

"This is ridiculous," I say, watching Frankie throw breadcrumbs at a particularly feisty mallard.

"It's not ridiculous. It's therapeutic." She hands me a piece of bread. "Throw it."

"I'm not throwing bread at ducks."

"Why not?"

"Because I'm a grown man."

"So? Grown men can't enjoy simple pleasures?"

The mallard waddles closer, eyeing me expectantly.

"He's judging me."

"He's hungry. Throw the bread, Hayes."

I toss the bread half heartedly. It lands about two feet away. The duck gives me what I swear is a look of disappointment before waddling over to retrieve it.

"See? That wasn't so hard."

"This is insane."

"This is living." Frankie bumps my shoulder. "When's the last time you did something pointless just because it made you happy?"

I don't answer because I can't. Everything I do has a purpose. Every decision calculated for maximum efficiency.

"That's what I thought."

We walk toward the playground. There are families everywhere—kids on swings, parents looking exhausted and happy. The kind of chaos I usually avoid.

"Man, I love watching kids," Frankie says, settling onto a bench. "They have no filter. No shame. Just pure, unprocessed emotion."

I watch a little girl throw herself down a slide with complete abandon, shrieking with joy.

"Terrifying."

"Why?"

"All that . . . feeling. What if she gets hurt?"

"Then she'll cry for thirty seconds and go down the slide again." Frankie looks at me. "That's how you learn. Trial and error. Not everything can be controlled."

The words hit harder than they should.

"I know that."

"Do you?"

I turn to study her face. She's watching the playground, but I can feel her attention on me.

"What's that supposed to mean?"

"Nothing. Just . . . you like your ducks in a row. Your plans planned. Your outcomes predictable."

"That's called being responsible."

"Sometimes. Sometimes it's called being scared."

"I'm not scared."

She finally looks at me. "No?"

"No."

"Then why did you run in France?"

The question hits like a slap. We've been dancing around this all morning—the careful politeness of people pretending the past doesn't matter.

"That was different."

"How?"

"I was . . ." Damn it. "I was terrified."

"Of what?"

"Of you. Of how you made me feel. Of fucking it up."

Frankie nods like this makes perfect sense. "And now?"

"Now I'm still terrified. But I'm more scared of losing you again."

She reaches over and takes my hand. Her fingers are small and warm and somehow steady in a way that makes my chest tight.

"I'm scared too."

"Yeah?"

"Terrified. You're everything I thought I didn't want. Rich, complicated, emotionally unavailable—"

"I'm not emotionally unavailable. Not anymore. Not with you."

The look she gives me is so sweet and soft, I want to drag her straight back to my bedroom. Instead, I stand up, pulling her with me. "Come on."

"Where are we going?"

"Ice cream."

"Ice cream?"

"You said normal-people Saturday. Normal people eat ice cream in the park, right?"

Her smile could power the city. "They do."

"Then that's what we're doing."

An hour later, we're sharing a cone of chocolate chip cookie dough—her choice, obviously—and arguing about whether *Die Hard* is a Christmas movie.

"It takes place at Christmas," she insists.

"That doesn't make it a Christmas movie."

"It absolutely does. Christmas is part of the plot."

"Christmas is the setting. That's different."

"You're wrong."

"I'm never wrong."

"Oh my God." She stares at me. "You actually believe that."

"I have an excellent track record."

"Everyone's wrong sometimes, Hayes. It's part of being human."

"I don't like being wrong."

"Nobody does. But it happens anyway."

I consider this while she takes another bite of ice cream. A drop of chocolate lands on her chin.

"You've got . . ." I gesture at my own face.

"What?"

Instead of telling her, I lean over and kiss the chocolate away. She tastes sweet and cold and perfect.

"Better?"

"Much."

We finish the ice cream and walk aimlessly through the park. No destination. No timeline. Just wandering.

It should make me anxious. Instead, I feel . . . calm.

We've stopped in front of a fountain. Kids are making wishes and throwing pennies while their parents watch indulgently.

"What would you wish for?" Frankie asks.

"I don't make wishes."

"Humor me."

I think about it. Really think about it.

"More days like this," I say finally. "More mornings in the kitchen. More pointless conversations about Christmas movies."

"With me?"

"With you."

She smiles and digs a penny out of her purse. "Then wish for it."

"That's not how wishes work."

"How do you know? Have you ever made one?"

I take the penny. It's warm from her hand.

"This is ridiculous."

"Good. You need more ridiculousness in your life."

I close my eyes and make a wish I've never let myself want.

The penny hits the water with a small splash.

"What did you wish for?" Frankie asks.

"Can't tell you. It won't come true."

"That's superstitious nonsense."

"Maybe. But I'm not taking any chances."

We walk home as the sun starts to set. My penthouse feels different when we return—warmer somehow. Less like a museum and more like a place where people actually live.

After we've worn each other out—more than once—Frankie curls against my side, quiet and warm. "I should probably head back to Tessa's," she says, but she doesn't make any move toward her clothes.

"Should you?"

"Yeah. I mean, we haven't really talked about . . . this. What it means."

I sit on the edge of the bed and pull her down beside me. "What do you want it to mean?"

"I don't know. I'm not good at this stuff."

"What stuff?"

"Relationships. Feelings. Not completely fucking up a good thing."

I laugh. "Neither am I." I lean over and kiss her forehead. "We'll figure it out."

"Will we?"

"Yeah. We will."

She curls into my side, her head on my chest. "Hayes?"

"Mmm?"

"I'm glad you made a wish."

"Me too."

"Even if it was ridiculous?"

"Especially because it was ridiculous."

She falls asleep in my arms while I stare at the ceiling and think about how everything in my life just shifted on its axis.

For once, I'm not scared of the uncertainty.

I'm excited by it.

Epilogue

New Adventures

Frankie
Six Months Later

"You named the Wi-Fi 'PrettyFlyForAWiFi' again." Hayes shakes his head, staring at his laptop screen. "We're on a yacht in the Greek islands. Couldn't you have gone with something more . . . sophisticated?"

"Like what? 'YachtRockOnly'? 'BillionaireBoysClub'?" I'm sprawled across the sun lounger in a bikini that cost more than my old monthly clothing budget, but whatever. Golden Adventures is officially killing it, and I can afford nice things now.

"Those are actually better than your usual choices."

"Excuse me, but my Wi-Fi names are art. Remember 'MartinRouterKing'? 'TheLANBeforeTime'? Those were comedy gold."

Hayes closes his laptop and moves to the lounger next to mine. Six months of being together, and he still looks at me like I'm some fascinating puzzle he can't quite solve.

"You're ridiculous."

"You love my ridiculousness."

"I do."

The simple admission still does things to my chest. Even after all this time.

We're anchored off Santorini, taking a break from the Golden Adventures Mediterranean tour I'm personally leading. Twelve couples in their seventies, all having the time of their lives exploring Greek islands without worrying about mobility issues or dietary restrictions.

Hayes invested in the company three months ago. Not because I needed the money—Charles's inheritance took care of that—but because watching me build something from nothing apparently does things to his possessive streak.

Case in point: Yesterday, when Dimitri, our very attractive Greek tour guide, spent too much time explaining Byzantine history to me.

"He's just being thorough," I told Hayes when he appeared at my elbow like a gorgeous, territorial shadow.

"He's being thorough with his eyeballs on your ass."

"My ass is covered by a very respectable sundress."

"Doesn't matter," he muttered. Then he kissed me in front of the entire tour group, marking his territory like some kind of billionaire caveman.

Our clients loved it. Mrs. Martinez actually clapped.

Now we're having a rare afternoon alone while the group explores Oia. Hayes is reading some architecture magazine—he's been taking classes, slowly figuring out what he actually wants instead of what he's supposed to want.

"Mrs. Patterson cornered me this morning," I tell him.

"What did she want?"

"To know when we're getting married."

Hayes goes very still. "What did you tell her?"

"That it's none of her business."

"And?"

"And that if she keeps asking personal questions, I'll book her the worst cabin on the next cruise."

He laughs, but there's something careful in his expression. We haven't talked about marriage. Haven't talked about the future beyond next month's tour schedule.

It's not that I don't want those things. It's that I'm still getting used to having them be possible.

"What if . . ." Hayes sets down his magazine. "What if we did?"

"Did what?"

"Got married."

I nearly choke on my iced coffee. "Are you proposing?"

"I'm asking a hypothetical question."

"That's a terrible hypothetical proposal."

"It's not a proposal. It's market research."

"Market research?"

"I'm gauging interest levels."

I stare at him and try not to laugh. "You're treating marriage like a business venture?"

"Everything's a business venture if you think about it strategically enough."

"Oh my God. You're serious."

"I'm always serious."

"That's the problem."

Hayes shifts on his lounger, suddenly looking less like a confident billionaire and more like a guy who's trying not to panic.

"Forget I said anything."

"No." I sit up, swinging my legs over the side of my chair. "You don't get to bring up marriage and then retreat into corporate speak."

Hayes runs a hand through his hair. Six months together, and he still does this when he's nervous—tries to fix things that aren't broken.

"I'm not retreating. I meant . . ." He takes a breath. "I meant I love you. I meant I want to spend my life with you. I meant the idea of you not being mine officially makes me want to buy this entire fucking island just to prove a point."

There it is. The possessive streak that should probably annoy me but instead makes my stomach do flips.

"Yours officially?"

"Poor word choice."

"Was it?"

"Yes. No. Maybe." He stands up, starts pacing the deck. "I don't know how to do this."

"Do what?"

"Be vulnerable without a safety net. Ask for things I want instead of things that make sense."

I watch him pace, this beautiful, complicated man who's learned to crack jokes and eat carbs and let me see him fall apart.

"What do you want, Hayes?"

He stops pacing. Looks at me like I'm holding the answer to every question he's ever had.

"You. Forever. In every way that matters."

My heart does that hummingbird thing it's been doing since the first time he kissed me.

"That's all you had to say."

"Is it a yes?"

"It's an 'ask me properly and find out.'"

Hayes grins—the real one, not the polished version he shows investors. "I can work with that."

Three hours later, I'm getting ready for dinner when my phone buzzes with a text from Hayes.

Hayes: Meet me on the upper deck. Wear the blue dress.

I find the blue dress—the one he bought me in Paris, the one that makes me feel like a movie star—and head upstairs.

The upper deck is transformed. String lights everywhere, candles, a table set for two overlooking the sunset. It's like something out of a romance novel.

Hayes stands by the railing in a navy suit, holding a small velvet box.

"Oh, shit."

"That's not the reaction I was hoping for."

"I mean . . . oh, wow. Good wow. Not bad wow."

"Better."

He's nervous. I can tell because his tie's perfectly straight—he only obsesses over details when he's freaking out internally.

"Francesca."

"Yeah?"

"Last year you walked into my uncle's life and changed everything. You made him laugh again. You made him remember what it felt like to live instead of just exist."

My throat gets tight.

"But what you did to me was even bigger. You made me remember what it felt like to want something. Really want it, not just accept what was expected."

"Hayes . . ."

"I'm not finished." He drops to one knee, and my brain short-circuits. "You make me want to be better. Not perfect—you've made it very clear you have no use for perfect—but better. Real. Present."

He opens the box. The ring is gorgeous—vintage, unique, nothing like the massive rocks other billionaires probably buy their girlfriends.

"It was my great-grandmother's. Charles left it to me with very specific instructions about who should wear it."

Of course he did. Bossy old bastard.

"Francesca Anderson, will you marry me and continue to call me on my bullshit for the rest of our lives?"

I stare at him. At the ring. At the way he's looking at me like I hold his entire future in my hands.

Which, I guess I do.

"Can I negotiate the terms?"

"What?"

"I want to keep my business. I want to travel. I want kids who eat junk food and make terrible jokes. There's no way in hell I'm going to be one of those gluten-free, dairy-free, fun-free weirdos. I want a life that's messy and real and nothing like the one you grew up in."

Hayes's smile could power the entire Greek electrical grid.

"Deal."

"And I want to start a foundation. For seniors who can't afford to travel but deserve adventures."

"Done."

"And I want you to stop pretending you don't want things just because they might make you happy."

His eyebrows lift. "Meaning?"

"Meaning if you want to do something other than manage money for the rest of your life, do it. Charles left you enough fuck-you money to tell your family to shove their expectations."

"Anything else?"

I pretend to think about it. "Yeah. One more thing."

"What?"

"I want you to promise me that when we fight—not if, when—you won't run. You'll stay and figure it out with me."

His expression goes soft. Vulnerable in a way that still catches me off guard.

"That's all I want too."

"Good. Then yes."

"Yes what?"

"Yes, I'll marry you, you beautiful disaster."

He slides the ring onto my finger and kisses me while the sun sets over the Aegean Sea. It tastes like promises and possibilities and the kind of love that sneaks up on you when you're not looking.

When we break apart, I notice my phone lighting up between us—a new notification blinks at the top. "Did you change the Wi-Fi password for this?"

Hayes grins. "Check your phone."

I pull up the network list. There's a new one: "WillYouMarryMe?"

"The password is 'PrettyFlyForAWife.'"

I burst out laughing. "That's terrible."

"I thought you'd appreciate the callback."

"I do. I really do."

Hayes
Six Months Later

Our wedding is everything Frankie wanted and nothing my mother planned.

We're back in Provence, in the same lavender fields where we had our first real date. Tessa's the maid of honor, Maddie's the flower girl, and Malachi's my best man, despite threatening to tell embarrassing stories in his speech.

Mom spent three months trying to convince us to have the ceremony at the estate. "Think of the photos, darling. The networking opportunities."

Frankie shut that down fast. "We're getting married, not hosting a corporate retreat."

Now Mom's sitting in the front row, wearing lavender and trying to pretend she's not crying. Dad's beside her, looking genuinely happy for the first time in years.

But the chair that matters most is empty. Charles should be here, probably making inappropriate jokes and trying to spike the punch.

Instead, we have his picture on a small table next to the officiant, surrounded by the kind of tacky flowers he would have loved.

Frankie appears at the end of the makeshift aisle, and my brain stops working.

Her dress is simple, elegant, nothing like the princess gowns Mom tried to push. Her hair's down, the way I like it, and she's carrying wildflowers she picked this morning.

She looks perfect. More than perfect.

She looks like home.

My home.

My forever.

The ceremony's short—neither of us wanted a production. But when the officiant asks if I take Francesca to be my wife, my voice cracks on the "I do."

"You okay?" she whispers.

"Never better."

When it's her turn, she doesn't just say "I do." She says, "I do, but I'm keeping my name professionally, and if you ever run away from me again, I'll hunt you down and make you regret it."

The crowd laughs. And me? I fall a little more in love.

We kiss while lavender petals fall around us like confetti, and I think about wishes made in Central Park fountains. About how sometimes the best things happen when you stop trying to control everything.

The reception's held at a local vineyard. Nothing fancy, just good food and wine and the people we actually want to celebrate with.

During dinner, Frankie stands up to make a speech.

"So, I'm not good at this stuff," she starts, and immediately gets a laugh. "But I wanted to say something about love and second chances and the man who taught us both what those things really mean."

She raises her glass toward Charles's picture.

"Charles Winthrop was a pain in the ass. He meddled in our lives, manipulated us into spending time together, and probably planned this whole thing from the moment I walked into that coffee shop."

More laughter.

"But he also showed us that family isn't about blood or money or meeting expectations. It's about showing up—every day—for the people who matter."

Her voice gets thick.

"Hayes and I wouldn't be here without him. So this first dance isn't just for us—it's for Charles, who believed in love stories even when the people in them were too stupid to see what was right in front of them."

The band starts playing—some jazz standard that Charles used to hum while doing crosswords.

I pull Frankie into my arms, and we dance on grass under string lights, surrounded by people who love us.

"Any regrets?" I ask.

"About what?"

"Marrying an emotionally constipated billionaire with control issues?"

"Former control issues," she corrects. "And no regrets. You?"

"Just one."

She looks worried. "What?"

"I should have kissed you that first day in my office."

"I would have slapped you."

"Probably."

"Definitely."

"It would have been worth it."

We dance until the band stops playing and the guests start heading back to their hotels. Maddie fell asleep in Dad's lap hours ago, and even Malachi's given up trying to scandalize the elderly relatives.

Finally, it's just us and the vineyard owner's cat, who's been eyeing the leftover salmon all evening.

"So," Frankie says, leaning against me. "What now?"

"Now we go on our honeymoon."

"Which is where, exactly? You've been very secretive about it."

I grin. "It's a surprise."

"I told you I hate surprises."

"You'll like this one."

"How do you know?"

"Because we're going back to the yacht. Just us this time. No tour groups, no schedules, no one to impress."

Her face lights up. "Really?"

"Really. I figured we could recreate our first trip. Except this time, when I kiss you, I'm not running away."

"Good plan."

"I thought so."

We walk back to our hotel room—the same one where Charles stayed during his last visit to Provence. It feels right, somehow. Like he's still with us, still orchestrating our happiness even from beyond the grave.

The room's been decorated with rose petals and champagne, courtesy of Tessa's romantic streak.

"Very subtle," Frankie says, eyeing the heart-shaped arrangement on the bed.

"I may have mentioned to Tessa that subtlety isn't always necessary."

"Smart man."

She kicks off her shoes and pulls the pins from her hair, shaking it loose around her shoulders. It shouldn't still undo me the way it does, but it does—every time.

"Come here, wife."

"I like the sound of that."

"Which part?"

"All of it."

I pull her close, kissing her slowly, thoroughly, like we have all the time in the world.

Which we do.

Outside, the lavender fields stretch toward the horizon, purple and endless under the star-filled sky. Somewhere in the distance, I swear I can hear Charles laughing.

The old bastard was right. The best adventures aren't the ones you plan. They find you when you're brave enough to say yes. They're in the chaos of a woman who drives you crazy and makes you feel alive.

Love like that doesn't ask permission. It just barges in. And Frankie? She kicked down the door—with liverwurst, terrible Wi-Fi puns, zero apologies, and a smile that wrecked me completely.

And me? I'm not going anywhere. Not now. Not ever. I'm all in.

Acknowledgments

I am deeply grateful to the many people who helped bring this book to life.

To my agent, Jane Dystel, whose professionalism, wisdom, and unwavering support have guided me for over a decade—thank you for believing not just in this book, but in me. Lauren Abramo, your enthusiasm and tireless advocacy for my work with publishers and coagents around the world have meant more than I can express. I feel incredibly lucky to have such a brilliant team in my corner.

To Maria Gomez at Montlake, thank you for your dedication and care. To my editor, Krista Stroever, your guidance has shaped this book in ways I'll always be grateful for.

To my dear friends who love loudly, pray fiercely, and never do anything halfway—you inspire me every day. Thank you for showing me the beauty of female friendships filled with so much generosity and encouragement.

To my guys! Thank you for making me a boy mom—the best role on the planet! I love watching you grow and do all the things, even as I silently beg time to slow down.

To John, I'm endlessly thankful to walk through life with you by my side. Thank you for believing in me and constantly lifting me up and putting my feet back on the path when I wobble.

To my readers, who have blessed me with a career I never imagined possible—thank you. Every email, every comment, every review matters. You've made this wild, unexpected ride unforgettable.

And finally, to my King, Jesus—thank you for so many answered prayers and for holding me steady through it all.

About the Author

Kendall Ryan is a *New York Times*, *Wall Street Journal*, and *USA Today* bestselling author of contemporary romance novels, including *A Beginner's Guide to Forever*, *Playing for Keeps*, *The Boyfriend Effect*, *The Rival*, and many others. Her books have been translated into several languages, selling millions of copies worldwide, and her work has been featured in publications like *USA Today*, *Newsweek*, *Cosmopolitan*, and *InTouch Weekly*. Kendall lives in Texas with her husband and two sons. Visit www.kendallryanbooks.com to learn more.